DARKNESS

BAND OF BELIEVERS, BOOK 4

JAMIE LEE GREY

Copyright © 2018 by Jamie Lee Grey

Cover design by Hannah Linder Designs.

✾ Created with Vellum

CONTENTS

To my brothers,
And to Amy and Chi Chi,
My sisters in love.

1

———

"Are we gonna have dinner tonight?" Danny turned his little brown face up toward Jacob's, his dark eyes filled with a sad mix of hope and grief that shouldn't be seen in a child so young.

"Yes, you'll have dinner." Jacob wasn't certain whether he himself would eat, but the boy would.

Danny slipped his hand into Jacob's as they walked toward Heidi's neighborhood.

"I'm hungry now."

The child's hand felt bony and cold. His face was thinner than a month ago. He'd been losing weight, when he needed to be gaining it.

Without thinking, Jacob pulled a small boiled potato from his pocket.

"Here." He handed it to the boy.

Danny bit into the potato, eating it like an apple as they turned onto Heidi's street.

A cool wind signaled the approaching autumn as Jacob turned to look at Willow's Wilderness. The Christians up there must be in a scramble to prepare for winter. They'd need to be getting firewood, and harvesting as much food and wild game as possible.

It'd be a lean winter, for sure. The wildfires had no doubt destroyed much of the wildlife, as well as most of the habitat. And the forests were still burning, destroying and smoking up the whole region.

Soon, the fall rains would come and tamp down the fires. Winter would put them totally out. But devastation would remain where they'd chewed through the forest, and it'd take decades to restore it all.

Decades? Jacob frowned. Was there that much time left?

Not according to his adoptive parents. As Christians, they'd been convinced that the end of the world was imminent.

And Jacob was beginning to think they were right. Maybe.

A trio of teenage boys approached. All three stared at Danny. And his half-eaten potato.

Idiot! Jacob cursed his stupidity. What had possessed him to give Danny a morsel of food in broad daylight? In public!

Instinctively, he rested his right hand on his Glock, and pulled Danny closer with his left hand.

"Heads up!" He hissed.

Danny looked up and dropped his potato when he saw the teens, one of whom swung a baseball bat as he swaggered toward them. Danny bent to pick up the vegetable.

"Leave it there," Jacob ordered, gripping the child's hand firmly.

He stared at the teens, who alternately watched his gun hand and glanced at the potato. He didn't want to kill anybody, but these kids were starving and desperate. If they forced a confrontation, he'd have to make it lethal.

"We are going to cross the street," Jacob announced as he pulled his Glock from his holster. "If any of you follow us, I'll shoot you."

Gripping Danny's hand tightly, he stared at the ravenous teenagers. Not taking his eyes off them, he turned Danny into the street and began to cross it.

The moment after he stepped away from the fallen food, the teens moved in like hyenas in a mad scramble for the half-eaten potato.

Jacob hustled Danny across the street, then holstered his handgun and scooped up the kid. While the teens were distracted with their fight over the morsel, Jacob turned, sprinted around the corner, and raced into the alley that ran behind Heidi's house.

They were only two blocks away. At the end of the first block, Jacob slowed and glanced back. No one was following, as far as he could tell.

He hurried to Heidi's back yard and set Danny down. Pushing the gate open, he softly announced his arrival – hoping it was loud enough that she'd hear, but the local hoodlums wouldn't.

He closed the gate and rushed Danny to the back door.

Heidi answered it as soon as he knocked.

"You should put a padlock on your alley gate," he said, pushing Danny inside. "Who knows who might come through there."

"Why'd you come that way?" She smoothed her short black dress. Other than ruby red lipstick, she didn't appear to be wearing any makeup. Her blue eyes looked dull and tired.

"Ran into some trouble."

"What kind of trouble?" Marcus came from the living room and stood in the kitchen entryway. "Do I need to bash some heads?"

"Hungry teenagers." Jacob handed his remaining potato to Danny. "Here's your dinner. Why don't you go play upstairs?"

Marcus stared accusingly at Jacob. "Hungry? How'd they know you had food?"

"I gave Danny a little potato."

The police captain's face turned red. "You did WHAT? Are you crazy, or just plain stupid?"

Jacob let him fume a moment before he answered.

"I had my mind on something else."

"Like what? A woman?" Marcus smirked.

Jacob's gaze shot toward Heidi. Averting her eyes, she put a dirty glass in the sink and brushed past him, disappearing down the hall.

"It doesn't matter. It won't happen again."

"It better not. You could get killed! You could get us all killed!" Marcus crossed his arms.

Unlike the rest of Ponderosa's population, Marcus didn't seem to be losing any weight. And Heidi's slim figure looked exactly the same as it did a month ago. They were eating just fine. Meanwhile, many residents were starving, like the feral teenagers down the street. And others were headed that way, like Jacob and Danny.

Which reminded Jacob... he needed to talk to Marcus about his pay.

Marcus unfolded his arms and sauntered back to the living room. Jacob followed.

"We need to re-negotiate my salary," Jacob said. "I'm losing weight, and so is Danny."

"You and the rest of the country," Marcus growled. "Nobody's getting fat around here!"

"It's getting more dangerous out at the farm," Jacob persisted. "I can't keep working for wages that are going to leave us starving this winter."

"So. You want to quit and starve now?"

"We need more calories. Look at the kid, he's getting skinnier every day!"

"He looks fine." Marcus dropped into the recliner and stared at the carpet. "But speaking of Danny, we need to get him chipped."

"What?" Jacob couldn't believe his ears. "What on earth for?"

"It's the law. All students have to be chipped before the first day of school."

"There is no school. You think teachers are gonna show up and not get paid? Besides, there are no functional chip readers, since the EMP fried everything."

"All I know is, next week is September, and the teachers better show up."

Jacob shook his head in disbelief.

"They won't. Plus, Danny is only four. Nobody has to be chipped until they turn six."

Marcus turned his dark eyes toward Jacob.

"Age six, or when they start school. Danny will be in kindergarten." He raised his hand as if to ward off Jacob's protest. "We've got the supplies at the station. Bring him down tomorrow, and we'll get it done. Then you won't have to worry about it later."

Jacob stared at Marcus. This was craziness. Who cared if anyone had the ID chip anymore? They didn't work. And they wouldn't, until everything was fixed from the EMP.

"I don't understand why you're even bringing this up." Jacob took a deep breath. "It has nothing to do with anything. There's literally no point in chipping anyone. The stupid things are useless!"

"Because it's the LAW!" Marcus thundered. He rose angrily from his chair and moved toward Jacob. "Besides, if it doesn't matter, why NOT get it done?"

He eyeballed Jacob suspiciously. "Unless you're opposed to the chip? Maybe you don't have the I.D. yourself?"

He reached for Jacob's right hand, but Jacob sidestepped.

"Don't be ridiculous!" He shoved his hands in his pockets.

WILLOW ARCHER TOOK a break from filleting the trout. She stretched and yawned. August had been a hot, hard month, and she was looking forward to September, which would bring cooler temperatures and maybe some rain.

She was sick of breathing smoke.

On the bench in front of her lay three more trout for dinner. The rest were to be smoked and put away in the cache for this winter.

Raven's uncle Tony had promised to teach them how to properly smoke the fish so the meat would remain edible. He'd already done a lot – teaching the group about better hunting techniques and how to make jerky. He'd also helped them build the cache, a miniature log cabin perched on four tall poles designed to keep food away from bears and other marauders.

Across the clearing, she watched Matt and Josh chopping logs into firewood. With axes, it was a slow, tedious process.

Raven, Mom, Deborah and Jaci worked in the garden with the teen girls, weeding and harvesting. Nights were getting colder now, and soon they'd have a hard freeze. The short growing season was one of Montana's big survival obstacles.

Well, that and the winter, obviously. And the constant struggle for food.

She glanced at Maria, playing with Gilligan and a couple of pine cones. Everyone made sure the adorable toddler ate well, even when the rest of the group went to bed hungry. Since Candy died, Maria had been adopted by everybody. And Willow still hadn't revealed the fact they were half-sisters. How would Mom take it? It could be devastating.

She turned her attention back to the fish. Soon, Alan and Clark would return from the new family's cabin, where Uncle Tony was helping them work on the roof. If they couldn't find, fabricate, or scavenge a stove, they'd have to build a fireplace before winter. Other than that, it was almost habitable now.

A sharp bark from Gilligan turned her attention to where he was looking – the far side of the clearing.

A rider on a big bay horse stepped out of the forest, and the man waved his hat until Willow raised her arm in a welcoming wave.

John Anderson was coming to see them!

He wouldn't make the trip over here unless he had a reason. She hoped it was good news. Or at least not bad news.

The last time she'd seen John was the week after Mom arrived. Willow's group had volunteered to help John and Jeannie move all the gear that had survived the fire in their old mine/root cellar to their new place down the road. In return, the Andersons had given them two breeding pairs of rabbits, which now resided in their little shed-turned-barn.

John rode up to her. His gelding tossed his head and snorted at Gilligan.

"Hi," Willow said, watching John's face for any indication of concern or worry. She saw none.

"Hey, there." John dismounted and patted the bay's neck. "How are you guys doing?"

"Okay, I guess." Willow's friends began to gather around them. "Just getting ready for winter. How about you?"

"The same." He shook hands with the group. "That's why I'm here, actually."

He fixed her with a gaze.

"I've got two chainsaws, with extra chains and tools to sharpen them, but no gas or oil."

Wow, that was a bummer. Getting wood in for the winter was a huge project, and having a functional chainsaw would reduce the work and time by ninety percent, probably. She frowned slightly.

"I'm sorry we can't help. We don't have any oil or gas, either."

"I didn't expect you would, but I still think you can help." John glanced around the group. "I believe there are several vacant homes down the road from my place, and if we could take a team to scavenge, I'd share whatever we collect, plus give one chainsaw to you."

Josh grinned.

"Yes!" He looked at Matt, who exchanged a fist-bump with him.

"We're in!" Matt agreed.

"Not so fast." Willow narrowed her eyes at her brother. "That will be real dangerous. Someone might be home in what you think is a vacant house. Or squatters might have moved in. Or you could meet trouble on the road. Any of those situations could result in a shoot-out."

John nodded.

"That's why we need a team, instead of just me and my three. More eyes and ears, for one thing."

"And more guns, if something goes wrong," Willow added. She shook her head. "I'd hate to lose anyone over a chainsaw. We have axes. We'll get by."

"You're not the one chopping," Josh argued.

"And I'm not saying prayers at your funeral," she shot back. She focused a meaningful look at their mother. "Some help, please?"

Laura sighed as she looked from her son to her daughter.

"I can see both sides. Who knows? You might actually come

across some good gear, or even food, in one of those houses." Lines crossed her forehead as she frowned. "Or, you might get shot. I'd be inclined to vote no."

"Thanks, I think," Willow said, rolling her eyes. She turned to John. "Obviously, our group will need to discuss this and pray about it."

"No problem. I expected as much." He shooed a deer fly from the bay's flank. "You all sort this out and let me know. You know where to find us."

"Sounds good," Willow said.

"If you're in, why don't you come by early tomorrow morning? If I don't see you, I'll know you chose not to participate."

He shook her hand, swung into the saddle, and tipped his hat to the group before trotting back the way he'd arrived.

2

—————

As dusk fell, Jacob walked through the gate and hurried up the driveway to the farmhouse. His shift didn't actually begin for another hour, but he preferred to do most of his traveling during daylight hours now. It was easier to see who was around, and what they were up to – like those hungry teens in town. He'd hate to meet them in the dark and not see them coming.

So, as the days grew shorter, he had started arriving for work earlier. He didn't get paid anything extra, but he couldn't put a price on safety.

It was like that ballistic vest Marcus had given him. There was no way Jacob could've bought anything like that in this new evil world, and it might save his life someday. In fact, he was wearing it now, as he always did when he was awake. Over his t-shirt and under a lightweight cotton shirt.

He scowled as he picked up the farmer's rifle and started making his rounds of the property.

Marcus was a conundrum.

On the one hand, Marcus had given Jacob a place to stay, a job, and the ballistic vest that he'd obviously pilfered from the

Ponderosa Police Department, where he worked. On the other hand, he was only paying starvation wages for work that was getting more dangerous by the week.

And now he wanted to chip Danny.

Why?

It truly made no sense. The chip readers weren't functional. Plus, Danny was only four years old. But Marcus had gotten livid about it.

Worse, he now suspected that Jacob didn't have the chip. It'd taken some impressive blustering to get away from Marcus without revealing the truth this afternoon.

Jacob stopped and kicked a fallen branch out of his path.

Truth was, he didn't have the chip. He'd managed to bluff his way through the first few months when it was mandatory. He'd spent a lot of time camping in the wilderness, away from nosy neighbors and suspicious officials.

Then the EMP hit, and nobody asked about it anymore. For one, everyone assumed everybody else already had it, and for two, the chips became irrelevant anyway. The scanners didn't work. So what if your banking and medical information was connected to your chip? You weren't going to do any banking, or buy anything with money, or get treated at any hospital. Banks, stores and medical facilities were all closed indefinitely.

Those factors had all worked in Jacob's favor this summer in Ponderosa.

He reached the southwest corner of the farm and began walking north along the western boundary. A yellow jacket buzzed his face, and he swatted at it. Stupid bees!

His thoughts turned to his adoptive parents. They were the real reason he'd held off on getting the I.D. chip. They'd been convinced it was the Mark of the Beast mentioned in the Bible, and that anyone who got it would be damned to hell.

Jacob wasn't fully convinced of that, but he could see eerie correlations between biblical prophecy and current events. What if they were right?

A bee landed on his arm. He brushed it off.

If they were right, he had more problems. There was the problem of his soul. The problem of Jesus. Of heaven and hell.

What if he couldn't rely on his Jewishness to pave his way into eternity?

Reaching the northwest corner of the farm, he stopped and looked back. Deep shadows draped the farmhouse and the barn. Night was falling fast.

He needed to quit thinking about esoteric stuff, and focus on today's problem. Marcus. And Danny.

His gaze shifted toward the mountains southeast of town.

Willow's Wilderness.

Maybe he should go back. And take Danny with him.

Things in town were getting too dangerous. And things with Marcus were getting too weird. Perhaps Jacob could go work for the Andersons. Guard duty, wood cutting or water hauling or whatever.

It could earn his keep, and Danny's. Besides, John and Jeannie liked the kid. Jeannie had obviously wanted to keep him.

They'd probably be happy to have Jacob and Danny there. Plus, they had that nice, off-grid house and all the food and gear necessary to ride out the apocalypse. They'd spent decades preparing for it.

He yawned and stretched, then started walking again.

Why had he stayed in town so long, anyway? He should leave. And soon.

Maybe tomorrow.

POLICE CAPTAIN MARCUS LARAMIE rolled out of bed and walked

to the outhouse he'd built behind Heidi's garden shed. A new spider web gleamed in the early rays of the sun. He brushed it out of his way as he entered the little shack. Inside, a lidded coffee can held a roll of toilet paper to keep it dry and keep bugs out of it.

Heidi went through TP like crazy. Maybe all women did. He'd never noticed.

Now he noticed, though, because they only had one more roll.

After that, they were out.

And where could they ever get more?

It ticked him off as much as when they had run out of coffee. No coffee was bad, but no TP was uncivilized. What was he supposed to use? Leaves? They'd be buried under three feet of snow pretty soon.

When he went back into the house, Heidi was getting dressed.

"We're almost out of toilet paper," he growled.

"I'm hardly using any!" Blue eyes glared and red lips pouted. "Like four squares!"

"Pretty soon you'll be using zero squares."

"Can't you find more? What happened to all that was in the grocery store? You guys confiscated it."

"It's been doled out." He picked up his shoulder holster. "That's why we've had some for months. Your neighbors probably ran out in July."

She ran her fingers through her thick blonde hair. Then, turning to him, she smiled.

"You can find some more, right?" She approached and laid her hand on his chest. "You're good at providing."

"It doesn't grow on trees, Heidi!" His tone was harsher than he'd intended. And actually, it did grow on trees.

She pulled away.

"I'm quite aware of that." She slid her feet into sandals.

"I'll see what I can do." He pulled her to him and planted a kiss on her lips. "I'm headed to the station. Remind Jacob, when he gets here, to bring Danny by for his I.D. chip."

When he arrived at the station, two officers were standing guard outside the front door. Usually there was only one.

"What's up?" Marcus asked.

"Getting threats." Officer Lannigan rubbed the dark stubble on his jaw. "The local yokels seem to think we've got too much food stored here."

"They're wrong about that." Marcus turned his key in the door. "We're practically out."

"I know that, and you know it, but they don't know it," Lannigan said.

"In a month, we'll all be in the same boat." He pushed the door open.

"Except you've got that little side business with the farmers," Officer Thompson said.

"And I still need more team members, if either of you has the notion to earn extra grub." He looked from Lannigan to Thompson.

"We're thinking about it," Thompson said. "Might have to, once we run out of food here."

AS THE SUN crested the mountains and flooded the farm with golden light, Jacob made up his mind. He and Danny would be leaving Ponderosa.

Today, before he had another hassle with Marcus.

He knocked on the farmhouse door at the end of his shift.

Chad Litton opened the door a few seconds later, handgun

in hand. He glanced from Jacob to the porch, and around to the barn.

"Everything okay?"

"It's fine. But I wanted to let you know that this is my last shift. I'll be moving on."

A frown creased the farmer's face. "I'm sorry to hear that. You've done good work. Is there anything I can do to change your mind?"

"Afraid not." Jacob handed Chad's rifle to him. "Thanks, though."

The farmer brushed some dust off his overalls.

"You're leaving town? Or got a better job?"

"I'm leaving. Looking for greener pastures, as they say."

"I see." He fixed Jacob with a sad stare. "Hope you find it. Is Marcus sending someone new tonight?"

"I'm not sure. You should talk to him." Jacob took a step back. He didn't want to tell the farmer he had no intention of seeing Marcus before he left. He planned to leave a message with Heidi.

Chad thrust out his hand, and Jacob shook it.

"Real sorry to see you go."

"Thanks. It was good working here."

As he turned and started down the porch steps, Jacob felt a burden lift from his shoulders. Things were getting dangerous in town, and the danger was spreading to the farms as the harvest was coming in. He was glad to take Danny and get out.

Now, if he could just avoid running into Marcus and having a confrontation. The last thing he needed was a fight about the I.D. chip. Or for Marcus to discover that he really didn't have one.

HEARING RUSTLING, Willow forced her eyes open. The cabin was already bright. The sun was up. She'd slept in.

Rubbing her eyes, she rolled over. Raven, frying eggs on the wood stove, turned and grinned at her.

"Mornin', Sleepyhead!" She dusted the eggs with salt and pepper. "Everybody else is up and at 'em."

Willow mumbled a response and sat up.

"They want to go scavenging with John," Raven continued.

"Huh." Willow slid down from her bunk and reached for her boots.

"So?" Raven persisted. "Did you pray about it? What do you think?"

"I prayed." She shoved her left foot into a boot and laced it. "I got a 'Yes' and a 'No' on going. I must have my wires crossed."

"Our God isn't a god of confusion." Raven turned the eggs.

"I know." Willow laced her other boot and stood up. "Did you pray about it?"

"Of course I did." She sounded hurt.

"And?"

"And I think we should do it."

Over breakfast, Willow spoke to the rest of the group, except Uncle Tony, who was out hunting. Her mom was still ambivalent, but everyone else was on board for the expedition.

"Alright, we need volunteers to stay here and hold down the fort. And the new fort," she added, glancing at the new family. "Mom has to stay, since her foot isn't fully healed yet. Who else?"

Deborah volunteered. And Jaci informed her daughters they'd be staying home with her and their grandmother. Beth and Delia immediately protested, but Jaci was firm, and Willow was sure she saw relief in their faces, as well as disappointment.

"I'd like to have at least one guy stay behind, too," Willow said. "Just in case."

Alan and Clark exchanged a glance.

Matt crossed his arms, and Josh copied his friend's posture.

"I'll stay," Alan finally said. "This time."

Deborah linked her arm through her husband's and smiled, her blue eyes twinkling as the sun highlighted her grey hair.

"Okay, then." Willow glanced around the group. "It looks like Clark will be going with Matt, Josh, Raven and me."

"And me!" Maria squeaked.

"No, not you, Pumpkin!" Willow lofted the little girl into the air. "You get to stay here!"

"I 'anna go!"

Willow swung her around. "Don't you want to play with Delia?"

"Yeah!" The child stretched her arms to the teenager, who happily took her.

"Maybe you can help Delia and Beth milk the goats."

Maria grinned and wrapped her fingers in Delia's long black curls.

"Alright, then. Everybody pack extra ammo and water, but otherwise, leave your backpacks empty," Willow said. "Hope-fully we'll bring them back full."

Soon, the group was on the trail to the Andersons' new home. It wasn't long before they left the part of the forest that the fires hadn't consumed, and began trekking through ash. The sun warmed the blackened landscape.

Willow stepped over a charcoaled log. Her boots were covered in soot and ash. The greyish black misery dusted the hems of her jeans.

The boys plunged ahead with Clark, raising little plumes of soot with each step. Gilligan trotted beside them, the ash coming several inches up his legs.

She glanced at Raven.

"We should have left Gilligan at the cabin."

"Maybe. But he hates being left behind." Raven pushed her thick black braid over her shoulder.

"Well, good thing you don't have a white dog." Willow laughed. "I mean, seriously! How would you ever get him clean?"

Gilligan's white feet had turned charcoal, but the rest of his coat was primarily black and didn't show any soot.

"He's just got his night camo on," Raven said. "You know, like those men in black from a couple months ago."

Willow shuddered. "Don't remind me. That was awful."

"Well, they're all gone, if what Jacob told the Andersons was true."

"One can only hope."

"I wonder how he's doing."

"Jacob?" Willow stopped and cocked her head as she gazed at her friend. She shrugged and began walking again. "Who cares?"

"He was a friend. Kind of." Raven picked up her pace.

"Until he wasn't."

"I don't think it's that simple. He chased that ninja guy miles back to town."

"According to him. Actually, that's second hand, from the Andersons. And he never came back. What kind of friend is that?" Willow grabbed Raven's elbow to slow her down. "You have to admit that's weird."

"Maybe a little," she conceded. "But they said he had a job, and he was taking care of that orphan...."

"Whatever. I don't know what's true and what's not, when it comes to that guy. Anyway, I wouldn't trust him. If we ever see him again, which we probably won't."

Willow and Raven picked up their pace to catch up with the guys as they crested the ridge behind the Andersons' former retreat. From there, they walked down the hill to the Forest

Service road, and followed it down to the home the Andersons had settled in after the fire.

"This is so bizarre," Josh said. "Thousands of acres of burned forest, and then walk around a hill and the trees over here are just fine."

"It's sad," Raven said, kicking a pinecone down the road.

As they walked in the Andersons' driveway, Willow called out a greeting to announce their arrival. John and Jeannie promptly came out the door, followed by their friends Mike and Julie.

A big smile lit John's face. "I'm surprised you came."

"We're running a little late," Willow said. "Why don't you fill us in on your plan?"

"Sure." John patted Gilligan. "It's not very strategic or anything, but Mike and I have been scouting a little, and we're pretty certain one of the houses down the road is vacant. There are some others we're less sure about."

"Then we will go to the vacant house," Clark said in his deep accent. "How far is it?"

"About a mile and a half. I've got my gelding saddled up so we can tie a load on him, but I want to leave the mare here." John exchanged a look with Jeannie. "Just in case anything happens."

"We all brought backpacks, too, so we can pack stuff." Matt's blond hair blazed in the sunlight. It was long overdue for a cut.

"If you're ready, we can head out, then." John looked at Willow.

She nodded. "Let's pray before we go. Clark?"

The group formed a circle and joined hands, and Clark led the group in a brief prayer for protection and blessing. When he finished, Willow felt more optimistic about the day's undertaking.

"I've asked Mike to stay here and guard the house with Jeannie," John said. "Julie volunteered to come with us."

"Sounds good." Willow took a sip from her water bottle. "Lead on, then. I guess everyone knows to keep as quiet as possible as we head down the road."

John led his big bay gelding to the front of the group, and everyone fell in single file behind him, with Clark bringing up the rear. Other than the sound of footsteps and birds singing, the trek was quiet.

Willow constantly scanned the forest and the road ahead for any signs of trouble. It was out there; she could feel it. But hopefully, they would avoid those problems today.

They quietly passed one driveway, then another. The homes were set far enough back in the trees that she couldn't see them. Just before they reached the entrance of the third driveway, John stopped his horse and turned so he could see everyone.

He pointed in the driveway, and they nodded that they understood.

This was the place.

Willow's jaw clenched and her mouth dried. She glanced at Raven, who offered a weak smile. As the group moved forward, Willow signaled for Josh and Clark to station themselves in the trees at the entrance of the driveway.

"To keep a lookout," she whispered.

Clark nodded and Josh frowned, but she glared at him, and he took his post across from Clark. She took a deep breath and followed the others in the driveway.

As they approached the house, Willow's lungs constricted. She watched for any movement in the windows or around the sides of the two-story, cedar-sided home. As the others held back, John handed his horse's reins to Raven, then walked straight up to the door and knocked.

He waited, then knocked again. After another pause and a

third knock with no response, he turned back to the group and shrugged, then gave a thumb's up signal. Apparently, no one was home.

He moved to the front window, cupped his hands and peered through the glass. Then he walked back and tried the door knob. It didn't give.

"It's locked," he said quietly.

"Let's try the back door." Willow led the way around the house.

Upon rounding the corner, it became evident that someone had already broken into this place. The door had a half window, and the pane nearest the knob was broken out.

Willow froze as the rest of the group came up behind her.

"It's been vandalized," she whispered. "Somebody might be in there."

3

W illow's heart thumped in her ears. She reached for her Smith & Wesson M&P and held it at low ready.

"I'll go first." John moved forward. "You guys cover me."

He stepped up on the porch and tried the door knob. It turned. With his handgun in his right hand, he pushed the door open with his left.

The hinges creaked as the door swung open.

Willow held her breath. She forced herself to glance around, checking the surrounding area for threats, instead of just staring at John and the back door.

John stepped inside. Matt moved in behind him. Julie and Willow hung back with Raven, watching the windows and the perimeter of the yard. Behind her, the gelding snorted, and Willow flinched.

The horse flung his head into the air and snorted again, while Raven tried to quiet him with calm words and a hand on his neck.

Meanwhile, John and Matt had disappeared into the house.

Seconds crept by as Willow's heart hammered against her ribs. Finally, John appeared in the doorway.

"All clear. Nobody's here." He came out and took his horse's reins from Raven. "I'm gonna tie this guy to a tree."

Willow sucked in a deep breath and let it out slow. She stepped into the house and waited a moment for her eyes to adjust to the dim light.

The place was a wreck.

It looked like a tornado had blown through. Whoever had vandalized it had taken everything valuable to them, and left everything else turned over and scattered across the floor. They'd even taken the art off the walls, maybe looking for a hidden wall safe.

Standing in the living room, she saw the kitchen off to her right, and headed that way.

It had been ransacked. Still, there might be something useful.

Any food that had been there was gone, but she found spices and a box of salt. That precious substance would be critical for survival. She put it in her backpack, along with the spices. She heard Julie and Raven enter the house and walk down the hallway.

The looters had apparently been looking for valuables and food, because they'd left basic housewares.

Willow and her friends needed those things. She wrapped sharp kitchen knives and steak knives in a couple of kitchen towels, and slid them in her pack. In a cupboard, she found coffee filters and a sieve, which she took to pre-filter ash and debris out of their water supply.

John and Matt came into the kitchen.

"You guys find anything?" She picked up a half-empty bottle of dish soap.

"Not much," John said. "Some blankets and warm clothes that might fit somebody."

"And a couple pairs of boots," Matt added. "Raven's going through the bathrooms with Julie."

"We're going to check the outbuildings." John headed toward the door. "I really need some oil and gas."

"That's what we came for." Willow found a box of strike-anywhere matches in the back of a drawer and held them up with a smile. "Score!"

"Nice!" Matt gave her a fist-bump before he left.

Not finding anything else helpful in the kitchen, Willow wandered around the house. The entire building was a looted mess, but it obviously had been nice until recently. The rooms were filled with quality furniture, the windows still sparkled, and the clothing the looters had strewn across the bedroom floors was not from Wal-Mart.

Then she noticed the bed pillows.

Big, fluffy white pillows filled with down!

She grabbed two and hugged them.

For months, she'd been without a proper pillow. Oh, how she would love to rest her head on these! It might be silly, but she was taking them. And extra pillowcases, too.

Raven walked into the room and smiled. "Pillows! Nice!"

"These are heaven. They're down!" Willow tossed one to her. "We should take them."

"No kidding." Willow headed toward the hallway. "I want to find some garbage bags to put them in. To keep them clean."

"Good plan. I'll check the other bedrooms. Only two of us have pillows now, so it'd be great to take as many as we can."

"It's kind of ridiculous, I know," Willow said.

"A good night's sleep is not ridiculous. It's necessary."

In a few minutes, they'd found eight pillows and bagged them in black lawn and leaf bags.

"We can tie them to the outside of our packs." Willow tried to squish out the extra air to make the pillows more compact.

"And reuse the garbage bags for ponchos or something later."

"If we get nothing else, this will make the trip totally worth-while." Willow strapped a pillow to her pack.

Julie joined them as they walked outside and found the guys in the woodshed.

"Any gas or oil?" Willow asked.

"One two-gallon can about half full of gas, and two quarts of oil," John answered. "It's not much."

"But better than nothing, right?"

John shrugged. "We need a lot more."

"We did find an axe, a splitting maul, and two hatchets, though," Matt said. "All in good shape, and sharp."

"That's great!"

A familiar low whistle sounded from the end of the driveway.

"That's Josh!" Willow's stomach knotted. "Something's going on out there!"

JACOB HUSTLED past the police station and rushed toward Heidi's neighborhood. If he picked up Danny and hurried back to Raven's house, he could get packed up and out of town by noon. It'd be another exhausting day with no sleep, but if he was going to avoid Marcus, he needed to move quickly.

Danny was playing in the fenced front yard as Jacob approached the house. His jet-black hair flopped over his brown face as he plowed a toy tractor into a rock.

"Get your stuff together, kiddo."

The boy jumped to his feet and raced toward Jacob, launching himself at Jacob's legs, which he wrapped in a hug.

Jacob patted the kid's back.

"I'm going to get our grub," he said. "Pack up your things, okay?"

Danny nodded.

"Bring your toys, too."

"I keep some here," Danny said. "For next time."

"Well, this time, we're taking them all with us. Hurry up!" Jacob strode up the steps to the front door, knocked once, and opened it. "Heidi?"

"In the kitchen," she called back.

He followed the sound of her voice. "Hey."

"Hey yourself." She gave him a big smile and handed him a brown paper bag. "I just packed up your wages. More potatoes, sorry."

"It's fine." He accepted the wrinkled bag they'd been re-using for a few weeks. It felt light. "Is Marcus around?"

"Nope. He went to work." She wiped her hands on a towel. "And he said to remind you to bring Danny in for his I.D. chip this morning."

"So... look... would you give him a message?"

She stared at him with suspicion in her blue eyes. "Why? You'll see him before I will."

"Would you tell him he'll need someone new to guard the Litton farm? I'm moving on."

"Why?" She frowned, then put a delicate hand on his arm. "If it's about pay, I'm sure Marcus –"

"It's not just that. It's getting dangerous. Besides my run-in with that looter, I know of three other guards who've been shot at. It's not worth it."

"What are you going to do? Are you leaving?" Now her big eyes grew watery. "What about Danny?"

"He's going with me. I know a family that wants to take him in."

"But –" Her lip quivered. "But what will you do?"

"I've got some plans. I'm headed south." He didn't want to tell her too much. The less anyone knew, the better.

"You should stop at the station and say goodbye to Marcus."

"If I have time." He had no plans to do that, which was why he was having this conversation with Heidi instead. He stepped back from her, and called out for the kid.

"Danny? You ready to go?"

Little footsteps thudded down the stairs. A moment later, the boy raced into the kitchen, his tiny backpack bulging with his toys.

"Ready!" He thrust his hand into Jacob's.

"Alright, then." Jacob gave Heidi a solemn nod. "Take care."

"You, too." She knelt and embraced Danny, then stood and fixed her gaze on Jacob. "If it doesn't work out, you're always welcome here."

"Thanks." He led the child toward the door, and didn't look back.

WILLOW MOTIONED for her friends to move out of the clearing around the house, and get into the forest.

"Hurry!" She whispered, grabbing her pack and rushing toward the trees.

John, Matt, Julie and Raven moved quickly. John's gelding snorted again, but otherwise they were pretty quiet. Gilligan ran to follow them from the back porch of the deserted house.

Once in the cover of the forest, Willow stopped and waited for the others to gather around.

"Clark and Josh must have seen something," she said. "Josh only whistles like that when it's important."

"It sounded like a bird," Julie whispered.

"It wasn't," Willow assured her. "You all wait here, and I'll go take a look and report back."

"I'm going with you," Raven said.

"Fine, but leave Gilligan here. We can't risk him barking or growling."

Raven nodded and turned to the dog. "Gilligan! Stay!"

The border collie let out a low whimper and lay down in front of Matt.

"Let's move!" Willow started through the underbrush, trying to be silent as she rushed to get to the Forest Service road.

It only took a moment to reach a vantage point on a knoll where she could see through the tree branches to the road and the entrance of the driveway.

Her brother and Clark were nowhere to be seen.

She scanned the trees and brush.

Where were they? Well hidden, or gone?

Her heart thudded.

Movement on the main road caught her eye. She squatted to see better between the branches.

A tall, lanky man was walking up the road.

He wore dusty black pants, a brown shirt, and a dark green baseball cap. He moved slowly, a rifle in his hands, scanning the forest as he walked.

Willow sank to the ground and in her peripheral vision, saw Raven doing the same.

The man paused. His head turned toward her.

She stopped breathing.

Had he heard something? Surely he couldn't see her through the foliage.

After another long moment, he moved toward the entrance of the driveway. But instead of walking in, he stopped there.

Could he see Josh? Or Clark?

What was he waiting for?

Time slowed as Willow reached for her handgun. Slowly, she drew it from her holster. Keeping her finger off the trigger, she leveled the sights at the man's chest.

If she had to shoot, she couldn't afford to miss. She didn't know how close to the stranger Clark or Josh might be. Failing to hit the stranger could mean hitting her brother.

She took a breath and let it out.

The man turned and looked down the road. Then, he raised his arm and beckoned.

After a moment, a figure emerged from the trees in the far side of the curve below the driveway. Then a second, and a third.

As they approached the man, Willow sized them up. Two men, and a woman. All were skinny. All were armed with hunting rifles, and all were carrying backpacks. They hurried toward the driveway where the first man remained, waiting for them.

Willow looked over her shoulder at Raven, who stared back, wide-eyed.

"Go! Warn the others," Willow whispered. "Take them out through the forest!"

Raven nodded, and rose to her feet.

A moment later, she was gone without a sound.

Willow touched her tongue to her dry lips as she watched the group below. Their voices were quiet and muffled. She couldn't make out a word they said.

Soon, the first man started in the driveway alone, leaving the other three members of his group at the entrance of the driveway.

While she still couldn't see her brother or Clark, they

were probably close enough to hear everything the strangers said. If Josh moved or sneezed, they'd find him instantly.

For a moment, Willow considered making her presence known and leading the newcomers away from her brother and her group. But it seemed better to simply wait out the strangers, and then her group would be able to sneak away without them ever knowing she and her friends were here.

She prayed her brother and Clark would be hidden in silence by their angels.

And then she waited.

Minutes ticked by. Finally, the first man returned to the end of the driveway where his friends stood silently in the shade of the cedars.

More muffled conversation was followed by the entire group walking in the driveway toward the house.

When they'd disappeared from view, Willow rose and crept toward the driveway. Her eyes scanned the trees and brush.

Where was Josh?

She crouched in tall bracken ferns near the road.

And then she saw Josh's boot, not six feet away. And then his other boot, and his legs. He was lying prostrate under the fern cover.

"Josh!" She hissed.

"Willow?" He whispered, turning slightly.

"You okay? Where's Clark?"

"He's on the other side. I'm fine."

Slowly, Willow rose to her feet. The strangers hadn't returned.

"Let's get him and get out of here!" She moved silently to the middle of the driveway and whispered, "Clark?"

"I am here." He rose from behind a moss-covered log.

"Let's go!" She led the way across the Forest Service road and into the woods. After they'd walked east for a minute, she stopped.

"Did you hear them? What did they say?"

"They were arguing about the house," Josh said. "About going there or not."

"Do you think they lived there?"

He shook his head. "Couldn't tell, but don't think so."

"Clark?" She gazed at his dark features.

"They did not say a lot, but I do not think they live there. I think maybe they are squatters." He ran a hand over his jaw. "Or perhaps they are looters."

"How did you know they were coming before that first guy came up the road?"

Clark motioned toward the Forest Service road. "I had scouted down so I could see around the next bend. They were walking together at first, then three of them went into the forest, and I came back and told Josh what I had seen."

"That's when I whistled for you," Josh added.

"Good thing I was outside and heard it." Willow pushed a wisp of hair away from her eyes. "Just before that, I was in the house. Probably wouldn't have heard it there."

"The Lord or His angels guided you outside." Clark smiled.

"Yes, I guess so." Willow adjusted her pack. "Let's get on back to the Andersons' place. I sent the others through the forest."

"That should be fun, with a horse," Josh said. "Did you guys find anything good?"

"Pillows!" Willow smiled. "And some salt and kitchen stuff for Clark's family."

"That is wonderful. Thank you." Clark gave a nod in her direction.

"What about chainsaw gas?" Josh asked.

"A little oil, a little gas, and some hand tools."

"Better than nothing." Josh swatted at a fly.

"Right." Willow turned and led the way through the woods toward John's home. She made a point of staying close enough to the Forest Service road that she could see it from time to time. Eventually she saw the Andersons' driveway, and walked down to it.

Hoof prints in the dusty road indicated the others had already arrived.

"They made good time," Willow said, mostly to herself.

Matt was waiting on the front porch as they walked in the driveway. He bounded down and pummeled Josh's shoulder playfully.

"What took you so long? Raven was starting to worry about you guys!"

"You sure it was Raven doing the worrying?" Josh looked around pointedly. "I only see you waiting around for us."

He gave Matt a playful push.

Willow covered her grin as she headed inside. John and the others had gathered in the living room. Jeannie was making a list of the items they'd gathered from the vacant house.

"This is just in case the real owners ever come home," she explained. "We'll return whatever we haven't used up, and try to reimburse what we consumed."

"So it's more like borrowing than looting?" Raven asked.

Jeannie winced. "It's not looting if the owners are dead or never return."

Willow rattled off a list of what she'd found in the kitchen, plus the pillows. Julie added that she'd picked up three sweaters, four decorative candles and two books – one on foraging, and one on herbal remedies. That, plus the blankets, clothes, hand tools and small containers of gas and oil that Matt and John found, rounded out the list.

"Not bad," Jeannie said.

John sighed and leaned back in his chair. "Not what we were hoping for, though."

"We all returned safely," Clark said. "Thank the Lord for that."

"You're right." A small smile brightened John's face. He looked around at the others. "Let's get these things divided up, so you all can get home before dark."

JACOB FINISHED PACKING his belongings into his backpack at Raven's house, then gathered all of Danny's clothing and bedding into a garbage bag. With his firearms, his protective vest, his winter coat and boots, and Danny's stuff, it was a heavy and unwieldy load.

He'd look like a loaded mule walking down the road. If there were any incidents, his response time would be deadly slow.

Still, he needed all this stuff, just for basic survival. What could he leave behind? His tent? Nope. Cooking kit? Nope. Ammunition? Double nope.

His pack had to weigh sixty pounds. Good thing the kid was old enough to walk.

He trudged downstairs and found Danny in the living room. He'd emptied his little pack. All the toys were scattered across the rug. He launched a plastic airplane, complete with take-off sound effects.

"Time to go!" Jacob walked to the door. "Pack up!"

"Can we eat? I'm hungry." The kid's dark eyes watched him carefully.

At the mention of food, Jacob's own stomach rumbled.

"If you can get all your toys packed in thirty seconds, I'll see what we've got to eat."

The kid scrambled. Jacob shrugged off his pack and set

down his rifle and the plastic bag with Danny's clothes. He found the paper bag Heidi had given him, and opened it.

Inside, there were two large potatoes. And she'd already boiled them.

Jacob pulled his out his pocket knife and cut one potato in half.

"Done!" Danny yelled triumphantly, and ran to Jacob.

They each ate their half in silence.

"Is there any more?" Danny asked when he finished.

"Sorry, kid. Not until dinner." He mussed the boy's straight black hair. It looked like Heidi had washed it. "Get your pack on."

Jacob gathered his things and adjusted his pack straps, then opened the door and let the kid out first. He glanced back. It had been a good place to stay for the summer.

"Thanks, Raven," he said softly. Then he turned his eyes toward Willow's Wilderness. Hopefully, things were better up there than they were down here.

He followed Danny to the street and turned west. Soon, they reached the highway that ran through town, and they started south.

They hadn't walked a block when he saw a figure hurrying toward them.

And if he wasn't mistaken, it was Marcus.

4

Jacob shaded his eyes from the afternoon sun. The approaching man was still several blocks away. Had he seen them? Maybe not.

"Danny!" Jacob hissed. "Come here."

The child, a few yards ahead, slowed and looked back. Jacob caught up with him, grabbed his elbow, and steered him into the nearest yard, pushing him behind some lilac bushes.

The boy yelped.

"Shhhh!" Jacob crouched beside him. "Quiet!"

The man hurried along the far side of the street, and when he was within two blocks, Jacob was positive. It was Marcus.

Long, swift strides indicated he was on a mission.

Danny saw him, too. He turned questioning brown eyes to Jacob.

"It's just Marcus," he said, standing up.

"Shhh!" Jacob pulled the child down beside him and put his hand over the kid's mouth.

Danny squirmed.

"Hide and seek!" Jacob whispered into the boy's ear. "Marcus is looking for us, and we have to hide until he finds us."

The child stilled, peering between the lilac leaves as Marcus continued on his path. He was on their block now, but at least he was on the other side of the road.

What if he turned and looked in this yard?

The lilac bushes weren't the best cover. Marcus would probably see them. But there was no time to move somewhere better. He'd definitely notice movement in his periphery.

What would Marcus do if he saw them hiding in the bushes?

What could Jacob say? It'd be hard to bluff his way out of that! Maybe he'd say the kid had to take a leak.

Jacob looked over his shoulder. Had anyone inside the house noticed them yet? Lacy curtains hung over the windows, so Jacob couldn't see inside.

His gaze shot back to Marcus, whose pace had slowed. Had he noticed something?

Marcus glanced around, like he'd heard something odd.

He stopped.

So did Jacob's breathing.

Seconds ticked by like hours.

Finally, Marcus started walking. Away from them now.

Danny wiggled, but Jacob kept a firm hand on him.

"Shhh. Stay still," he whispered.

Marcus reached the end of the block and crossed the intersection.

Jacob glanced around. He saw a lacy curtain fall into place in the front window. Someone was home, and had spotted them. It was time to get out of here.

But he couldn't walk up the highway until he was sure Marcus was long gone. They'd have to use a side street or an alley.

He reached for Danny's hand.

"We have to go."

Danny pulled back. "But he hasn't found us yet!"

"Come on." His tone left no room for argument. Jacob gripped the kid's hand and hustled him through the side yard, and back to the alley.

From there, they hurried out to a street that ran parallel to the highway. Jacob kept looking over his shoulder, but saw no one. They could follow the side street until it reached the south end of town, then return to the highway.

He hurried as fast as he thought Danny could go. The little guy's stride was so short. And he'd tire easily.

Jacob pressed on, anxious to get out of town and away from Marcus. The man had been on a mission. Was it to find Jacob? Why?

Maybe the farmer had come into the station to talk to Marcus, and told him Jacob was leaving. Marcus would want to catch Jacob and Danny before they left town. No doubt to berate Jacob and grill him about where he was going, and to get Danny chipped.

As Jacob approached the end of the street, he heard a shout behind him.

A quiet curse flew from his lips as he turned around.

"Your kid dropped this!" A tall old man yelled, holding up Danny's teddy bear.

Danny pulled away from Jacob's grip and raced back to the man, his backpack bumping against his body as he ran. The top of the pack was unzipped, and the plastic airplane bounced, then flew out.

"Thanks!" Jacob waved to the guy, who nodded.

Danny took his bear, then came back, picking up his plane as he passed it.

"You gotta keep your pack zipped, buddy." Jacob took the toys from Danny and put them in the kid's pack, then zipped it closed.

Turning toward the highway, he sighed. Kids!

THE SUN HAD SET, and a cool breeze blew across the mountain-side as Willow and her team trudged home. Rain clouds formed in the west and quickly bore down on them. The sky grew dark. It didn't look like a big storm, but it was moving fast.

They couldn't outrun it. They were going to get wet before they got to the cabin.

She was glad they'd packed the pillows in garbage bags. At least they wouldn't get soaked.

The group was less than thirty minutes from home when the sky broke loose. There were no trees to take cover under, because the fires had destroyed this part of the forest. Her team was caught out in the open and pelted with huge raindrops, then sheets of blowing rain, then stinging rain, then a deluge.

Ten minutes later, it stopped as suddenly as it had begun.

Everyone was thoroughly soaked.

"Well, that's one way to get a shower," Matt groused, pushing dripping blond hair away from his eyes.

Goosebumps stood out on Raven's arms as she slicked water off her face.

Willow wiped her eyes with her fingers. The air temperature had dropped dramatically as the sun went down, and it dropped again during the storm.

She shivered as darkness closed in. They should have brought more flashlights. She'd thought they'd be home much earlier than this.

"Let's pick up the pace." She stepped over a charred log. "We're almost home."

As the wind blew, she rubbed her arms. She couldn't wait to get back to the cabin to warm up and dry off.

A mournful howl rose and fell as dusk deepened into darkness. A second howl joined in, then a third.

The wolves didn't sound terribly close, but it was hard to tell where they were. Willow walked faster.

More voices joined the creepy chorus, filling the night with their plaintive calls.

Finally, the cabin came into view, and Willow forced herself not to break into a run to the door.

MARCUS LARAMIE WOKE EARLY the next morning. Between worry and anger, he'd had a bad night – Jacob had left town with the kid, and Marcus hadn't found anyone to fill in for Jacob at the Litton farm.

On top of that, he was running out of food and toilet paper. Without one, he wouldn't need the other, but he'd only survive comfortably if he had both.

At five o'clock, he gave up on sleep, since he wasn't getting any.

He rolled out of bed, got dressed, and headed to the police station. Maybe he could poke around in the city's supply closets and find a few rolls of toilet paper. A brisk breeze cut through his shirt. The sun wasn't up yet, but the sky had lightened enough that he could make out the smoky haze of the forest fires.

He'd be glad to see some cool autumn rains. They'd knock down the fires and blow away the smoke. Soon after that, winter would be on them.

And Marcus wasn't ready for winter.

Sure, he was getting some vegetables from the farmers in exchange for his security guards, but how long would that last? Only as long as his guys stayed on the job and didn't get killed.

He clenched his jaw as he thought of Jacob. Taking off like that. Not even bothering to say goodbye. Ingrate!

As he turned the corner to the street the police station and city hall were on, he stopped dead in his tracks. From two blocks away, he could tell something was wrong.

Way wrong.

The front door was propped open, and no one was standing guard.

Yesterday, Lannigan and Thompson said there'd been threats from angry citizens. Had someone made good on those?

Marcus pulled his service weapon from his holster and moved away from the middle of the sidewalk, toward the cover of the adjacent buildings.

What should he do? He couldn't call for backup, or radio for help.

Suddenly, he heard shouts, followed by shots.

His men were in trouble!

He took a few steps forward, then stopped as several guys ran out of the police station, their arms full of boxes and bags. Some looked like teenagers.

Thompson was on their heels.

Marcus broke into a sprint.

Two of the looters turned and fired at Thompson, who returned two shots. Then he fell.

A half-dozen more looters came out of the building, pushing Lannigan ahead of them.

Marcus stopped, sliding into the cover of a doorway. There were at least nine bad guys. How could he take on that many armed looters? Plus, there could be dozens more inside.

Thompson wasn't moving. Lannigan was held hostage.

Were there any more officers at the station?

Probably not. The police force had dwindled as their food storage ran low, and most of the guys were only there during the day now. Things got too feral after dark, especially since they couldn't radio for backup.

At night, the low guys on the totem pole got assigned to guard the building. Or, truthfully, to guard the remaining food the police had commandeered from the grocery store after the EMP.

A shot rang out, and Lannigan stumbled, then dropped.

They'd shot him in the back! A young guy stepped up, handgun aimed at Lannigan.

Marcus fired a wild shot at the teenager.

It missed, but it got their attention. Several turned his way, while others took off running with their loot. The teen ran.

Marcus fired at him again.

And missed again.

The gunshots brought more looters out of the building. About a half dozen. How many had there been?

How many were still inside?

He aimed carefully at the tallest one. The guy flinched, fell, then scrambled to his feet and ran. The others ran, too.

After waiting a moment to see if anyone else would come out of the building, Marcus began moving forward, making his way from the cover of the doorway to an abandoned truck, then to a telephone pole, then darting into another recessed doorway.

Lannigan wasn't moving. Neither was Thompson.

The looters were, though. As the sun came up, they scattered in all directions, like cockroaches.

Finally, Marcus took the last cover he could find – a decorative concrete extension on the front of Ponderosa City Hall – and paused there.

He was about sixty feet from Lannigan, and maybe eighty from Thompson. No motion from either one. No one came out of the building.

There was no way to know if anyone was still inside. Good or bad.

The looters outside had run off.

Keeping his head up and his handgun ready, he took a deep breath and sprinted to Lannigan. Blood formed a huge pool from an exit wound just below his ballistic vest. His eyes were vacant and glazed, and Marcus knew he was gone, but he felt for a pulse anyway.

He stared at the open doorway as his fingers pressed Lannigan's neck.

Nothing.

He ran to Thompson. One bullet had torn his neck open, and the other had ripped through his jaw. He'd probably been dead by the time he hit the ground.

Marcus cursed.

He dashed for the nearest cover – a concrete pillar at the front of the station.

Now what? Entering the building alone, when he didn't know how many bad guys might be in there, was foolish. Leaving the building to get help also left the building open to new looters who might show up.

He curled his fist and smashed it into the concrete pillar. Then he yelped and cursed again.

5

M arcus needed help. And since he couldn't call his guys, he'd have to go find them. The police chief lived clear across town, and he'd essentially quit immediately after the EMP, leaving Marcus in charge.

He'd start with the officers who lived closest. That'd be Dalton Carlson and Soren Stein.

He hated the idea of leaving the fallen officers out in the parking lot, but what could he do?

Knock on doors, that's what. Compel assistance.

Looking around, he saw several people tentatively approaching the station. No doubt they'd been drawn out of their warm beds by the sounds of gunfire.

He strode up to the nearest guy. A tall, skinny dude with greying black hair and an overgrown beard, the man eyed him apprehensively as Marcus approached.

"I need you to stay here with these downed officers until I get back." Marcus used his authority voice that allowed for no questions. "Find somebody to go get sheets to cover them with. Got it?"

The man nodded slowly.

"I'll be back." Marcus clamped his hand on the guy's shoulder, and looked him square in the eye. The guy gave him another slow nod.

Marcus took off toward Carlson's house.

Dalton Carlson was the youngest officer on the force. He'd just joined in February, and still looked like a teenager, although his ID stated he was twenty-four. He lived in a studio apartment three blocks from the station.

Marcus took the steps to the second-floor bachelor pad two at a time. He pounded on the door.

"Carlson!" He shouted. "Open up!"

He heard movement inside.

"Who's there?" A young voice demanded.

"It's Marcus! Get dressed and get out here!"

In less than thirty seconds, the door opened and Carlson appeared, pulling a t-shirt over his head. His pants were belted, but his feet were still bare.

"What's going on?" His brown eyes were wide, his black hair all bed-headed.

"The station was attacked. They killed Lannigan and Thompson."

Carlson flinched at the news. His jaw dropped open, but no words came out.

"Get your gear on, and get over there! I'm going to get Stein."

The rookie stared at him, transfixed. He didn't move or speak.

"Are you deaf? Get moving!" Marcus grabbed the kid's shoulder, turned him around, and pushed him back inside. "I want you there in five minutes, got it?"

"Okay," he finally squeaked. "I'll be there."

"Good!" Marcus yanked Carlson's door shut, glared at the neighbors who'd come out of the next apartment to see what all the commotion was about, and hurried down the stairs.

Now to get Stein.

Soren Stein had been with the department for six years. He was a tough guy, always ready for anything. He was divorced – three times, that Marcus knew about. Obviously not easy to live with, and there were hushed rumors of tempers and violence, but who knew if there was any truth to that. Small towns were always rumor mills.

One thing Marcus knew, he could count on Stein in a pinch. He was fearless like a pit bull. Maybe he was a brawler, too, or a bully, but as long as he behaved in uniform – well, what an officer did outside of work wasn't Marcus's concern.

Stein was coming out his front door as Marcus jogged up the sidewalk.

"I heard shots," Stein said. "What happened?"

"The station was attacked. Lannigan and Thompson are dead." Marcus stopped to catch his breath. "I sent Carlson over. I don't know if anybody is in the building."

Stein loaded a magazine in his Glock.

"Let's go see."

From the look in his ice-blue eyes, he didn't even need the gun. He'd be happy to take out those murdering, looting thugs with his bare hands.

WILLOW WOKE up with a crick in her neck. In spite of the fluffy new pillow, she'd managed to tweak something in her spine and pinch a nerve. Every time she turned her head left, she felt a stabbing pain.

She rubbed her neck as she climbed down from her bunk and told her mom about it.

"It means you're an adult." Mom put her warm hands on

Willow's shoulders and massaged gently. "You're starting to get aches and pains."

"Lovely." Willow brushed the knots out of her auburn hair and noticed spit ends. "If anyone has decent scissors, we could all use haircuts."

"I saw a pair around here somewhere."

Mom had always cut Willow and Josh's hair. Now it looked like she'd be the hairdresser for the whole group.

Raven fired up the woodstove and whisked some sourdough batter.

"We'll be having hotcakes this morning." She put the cast iron pan on the stove. "What are your plans for today?"

Willow rolled her aching neck.

"The Collins family is almost finished with their cabin. I think if we all pitch in, we can get it done today. Except the fireplace."

Mom laced up her boots. "They won't have a woodstove?"

"Unfortunately, no." Willow pulled her hair into a ponytail. "They weren't able to scavenge one, and we don't have the tools or knowledge to fabricate one ourselves."

"It's too bad." Raven poured pancake batter into the hot skillet. "But it's a little cabin, and they should be able to keep it warm with a fireplace."

"They'll go through a lot more wood," Mom said. "Fireplaces are so inefficient."

"True." Willow stretched. "But what can you do?"

Raven began flipping the pancakes. "Call everyone for breakfast!"

After everyone was dished up, Josh blessed the food. Willow's mouth watered at the tangy sour aroma. They didn't have butter or extra honey to put on the pancakes, but they smelled delicious.

And tasted it, too! Willow's eyes closed as she savored the first bite.

She sat in front of the cabin, the sun warming her head and face, the fresh air filling her nostrils with the scent of swaying pines.

Wait, fresh air? Her eyes flew open. What about the wildfire smoke?

It was all but gone. She could see it in the distance, but here at home, last night's storm had cleared the air. Overhead, the sky was nearly blue.

She smiled. Life was good.

"So, how about those wolves last night?" Uncle Tony's question destroyed her reverie.

Willow glanced at him. He forked a bite of pancake into his mouth. A real mountain man, his watery blue eyes studied her from under bushy grey eyebrows.

"Creepy," she said. "How many do you think there were?"

He swallowed. "Hard to say for sure. I've seen their tracks, though. At least ten in one pack that I came across."

"Should we be concerned?" Raven asked.

"You should be concerned about everything." Tony set down his fork and scratched his grizzled beard. "Keep a close eye on your livestock."

Willow's gaze moved to the chicken pen, where one of the hens clucked at her young chicks, calling them to a prized morsel of bug or beetle. Beyond them, the three goats were staked out a safe distance from the garden. In the barn, the rabbits were expected to produce many babies.

They couldn't afford to lose any of their animals. The hens were laying enough eggs for breakfast every morning. The goats provided milk. The rabbits would eventually become stew meat. In dire straits, the chickens and goats could be slaughtered, too.

She hoped it wouldn't come to that this winter. They needed

as many live animals as possible, if they were going to continue living in the wilderness. Eating them would be tantamount to killing the goose that laid the golden egg.

But if it came to that or starvation, well....

Gilligan trotted over and sat in front of Raven, begging for a morsel of her breakfast. She left a sliver of pancake on her plate, and slipped it to him as she stood up.

"Well, hopefully those wolves will just move on," she said.

Her uncle finished his last bite. "Not gonna hold my breath."

After breakfast, everyone headed up to the new cabin.

Josh and Matt used a crosscut saw to cut a cedar tree trunk into 36" lengths. Uncle Tony had taught Alan and Clark how to use a mallet and froe to make shingles, and Clark worked steadily to split shingles out of the rounds the boys had cut. Beth and Delia handed the shingles up to their grandfather Alan, who carefully placed and secured each row on the roof.

Inside, Deborah and Jaci fastened clear plastic into the first window frame, while Tony built a frame for the second window.

Willow and Raven entered with a load of rocks for the eventual fireplace.

"Someday, it'd be nice to have glass windows, but for now, plastic will do," Jaci said.

"It lets in plenty of light," her mom agreed.

"It makes it easier for the bears to get in," Tony groused.

"What? You think bears will try to get in?" Jaci's hazel eyes widened.

Willow grinned. The windows were very small. No way a bear could get through there. Unless it was a baby bear.

"Bears'll try anything." Uncle Tony winked. "Just be ready with your rifle, though, and you'll be having a feast. Bear steak, bear stew, bear heart –"

"WHAT?" Jaci stared at him. "You eat the heart?"

"Of course! Why waste it?" He grinned. "I've heard polar

bear liver is toxic, so if you catch any polar bears, don't eat the liver."

He chuckled to himself and turned back to his project.

Raven rolled her eyes and shook her head.

Willow dropped her load of rocks at the rear of the cabin, where the fireplace was to be built. Above her, Alan pounded away on the roof. She glanced around, admiring the family's work.

It was small, about sixteen feet by twenty, but it'd be snug once it was chinked and the roof was finished. The floor was bare earth. It'd be neat if they could scavenge a couple of big rugs to put down there.

Still, it should serve the Wilcox and Collins family well this winter. And they'd be out of their tents, and not have to worry about bears. Who would be hibernating soon, anyway.

She smiled as she walked out into the sunshine. That ole Tony. He was such a troublemaker!

JACOB BRUSHED the hay off his jacket and stood up. He and the kid had slept in an old barn. They hadn't gotten far yesterday afternoon – only about two miles south of town.

Danny didn't have any stamina for long treks. He was constantly hot, tired, hungry or had to go to the bathroom.

At this rate, it'd be winter before they ever got to Willow's Wilderness.

If they got there at all.

They were out of food. Jacob had divided their last boiled potato for dinner. By the time they hit the sack, both of them were hungry again.

He had no idea what they'd eat for the rest of their journey. It was possible they wouldn't find any food between here and the Andersons' retreat. The thought spurred him to get moving. The sooner they got to their destination, the sooner they'd have a real meal.

He sure didn't want that to be sometime next week.

Bending down, he gently shook Danny's shoulder.

"Wake up, buddy! Time to go."

Danny yawned and turned over, never opening his eyes.

"Come on!" Jacob shook him again.

The boy frowned and wiped his face with his shirt sleeve. Slowly, the big brown eyes appeared. He fixed them on Jacob.

"Breakfast?" His tone was filled with hope.

"Am I a miracle worker?"

The boy looked at him quizzically.

"No." Jacob fastened his ballistic vest. "No breakfast."

Danny contorted his little face and slumped back in the hay. "I'm hungry!"

"Get used to it. Everyone's hungry."

The child stared at him like he was from another planet. Finally, he got up. He fidgeted with the top of his jeans.

"I have to go."

"Go out behind the barn." Jacob shook out the kid's bedding. "And make it quick!"

6

D anny hustled outside.
Jacob rolled up the bedding and packed it. By the time he finished getting his gear together, the kid was back. With an apple.

"Hey! Where'd you get that?"

"Out there." Danny pointed behind the barn and took another bite.

Jacob stepped outside and hurried around the corner of the old building. A couple of ancient apple trees clung to life. It didn't look like they'd ever been pruned, watered or fertilized. At least, not in the last decade.

Still, each tree had at least a dozen apples low enough to reach without a ladder. And some were ripe. Or ripe enough.

He looked around. There were no homes nearby. He'd made sure of that last night, before he decided to crash here.

The trees were on someone's property, so someone owned them. But it didn't look like anyone realized they were here. They couldn't be seen from the road. And they were totally neglected.

Well, he'd be having an apple for breakfast. And more for
lunch and dinner.

Carrying them would be a problem, but he'd make room.
Too bad he couldn't turn them into apple pie. Now, that'd be
delicious!

He picked the best-looking, ripest apples. They probably all
had worms, but who cared? More protein, right? They filled the
wrinkled brown paper bag that used to hold his potato
allowance from Marcus.

At the thought of that guy, Jacob frowned and looked over
his shoulder. What would Marcus do, if he saw them again?
He'd have a conniption fit if he discovered Jacob didn't have
the chip.

It was time to get moving. They were still too close to town.
Too close to Marcus.

THE FINAL SHINGLE was fastened before dinner. Willow watched
as Alan and Clark climbed down from the roof of the new cabin.
Deborah and Jaci embraced their husbands, big grins all
around.

Spirits ran high as the project came to completion.

"It looks nice," Raven said. "We should celebrate!"

"Yes," Willow agreed. "But how?"

"Champaign," Mom joked.

"Hot dogs and s'mores," Beth said, running her fingers
through her long black curls and watching Josh from the corner
of her eye.

"How about a fish fry?" Uncle Tony walked over with a string
of trout on a stick.

"Now, that, we can do!" Raven took the fish with a grin. "Hey,
everybody, we're having a party!"

Clark built a small fire in the rock fire ring they'd fashioned outside the new cabin, and as the sun set, everyone ate until they were full. Gilligan cleaned up the entrails and scraps. The bones were tossed into the fire.

Willow leaned back against a log, watching the sky turn shades of pink and lavender. Maria came over and snuggled against her, and Willow wrapped an arm around the little girl. Her half sister. She kissed the child's head and sighed.

"What're you thinking?" Mom asked, eyeing her with the toddler.

"Oh." Willow gulped. "Nothing."

She hated lying to anyone, ever – but lying to her mom was the worst. On the other hand, how could she tell her the truth?

That Dad had cheated on her, and this little one was the result of his infidelity. It'd crush her. Mom had trusted Dad. Never doubted him.

Willow couldn't think of a way to break the truth to her without destroying Mom's image of Dad.

But the cover-up was eating away at Willow. She berated herself for not being able to tell Mom. For not being able to tell Josh that he had another sister. She despised Dad and Candy, although they were both dead now, for putting her in this situation. For putting everyone in it.

As the sky darkened, she watched the first star come out. Then the second.

In the distance, a lone wolf howled. Soon, it was echoed by another.

Willow stood up and hefted her little sister.

"It's getting dark." She rested the child on her hip. "Let's go home."

As her group started down the darkened path to their old cabin, the wolves' cries filled the forest and lifted the hair on the back of Willow's neck.

MARCUS TOSSED AND TURNED, his dreams filled with gunfire and bloodied friends and deep black graves. As dirt was shoveled over him, he woke up hollering. Catching his breath, he stared wildly around.

Heidi was gone, her side of the bed rumpled. Dawn brightened her bedroom window. The light brought some relief.

Daylight felt good after a night like that.

He dragged himself out of bed and got dressed. After a trip to the outhouse in the backyard, he returned and found Heidi in the kitchen.

"You sounded like you had PTSD last night." She handed him a cup of water.

"Maybe I do." He slowly downed the entire contents of the glass. "I've certainly earned it."

"We're out of toilet paper."

He cursed. At God, at the world, at the situation.

Heidi cringed and drew back.

"What're we going to do?" She asked after he finished his tirade.

"I don't know, Heidi! Find some old newspaper and crumple it up!"

She threw her mug in the sink and stormed back to the bedroom, evidently not too pleased with his answer.

He wasn't pleased with it, either, but hey – how could he be expected to have all the right answers?

She could have been a lot more understanding, knowing he'd lost two friends and co-workers yesterday!

He sank into a chair at the table, and rested his face in his hands. Thompson and Lannigan deserved a lot better – they didn't deserve to be gunned down at the police station by looters and thugs!

Ponderosa had never been a place for those kinds of criminals. It'd been a quiet little town. Sure, it had its occasional bar brawls, domestic violence and theft, but it'd never been considered dangerous. Until this year.

After the EMP, people had started going nuts. Doing stuff they'd never have done in normal situations.

It was like civility was a thin veneer, stripped off in the first big crisis, revealing the vile undercurrent of humanity.

Marcus was sick of it.

And after yesterday, maybe a little scared by it, too.

Since the looters had stolen all the remaining food stored at the station, he didn't bother posting guards there last night. There was no reason to go to work today, either. He wasn't gonna get paid. Why get shot for free?

Yesterday afternoon, he'd enlisted a crew of local residents to dig graves in the city park behind the police station, because he'd had no way to transport his men's bodies clear across town and up the hill to the cemetery. Later, he'd brought over the only pastor remaining in town to do the funeral for Lannigan and Thompson.

Then he, Carlson and Stein had shoveled in the dirt.

Marcus wiped his face with his sleeve.

Was he gonna go out like that?

He stood up. Not if he could help it.

A thunderous banging sounded at the front door. He reached for his handgun. Putting it on was a habit in the morning, like putting on his socks. He moved into the living room.

Heidi came down the hall.

"Wait!" he whispered, as the pounding started up again. She froze.

"Who's there?" Marcus yelled.

"Stein and Carlson." It was Stein's deep, gravelly voice. "Hurry up!"

Marcus went to the door, unlocked it, and opened it.

The rookie slid past him into the house, fear written on his face. Stein stood where he was, hot anger in his cool blue eyes.

"We've got trouble," he said.

"C'mon in." Marcus stepped out of the way. "What's going on?"

Soren moved into the house with sure strides, all business.

"We were both working our farms last night, and –"

"And somebody shot at us!" Carlson's young voice reached a high pitch. "They hit my hat!"

The rookie threw his baseball hat to Marcus. Sure enough, there was a hole right through the bill. He turned it over in his hands.

"Maybe they don't like the Yankees?"

"I could've been killed!" Carlson grabbed his hat back. "It's not funny!"

"No, it's not. But you are!"

Stein cleared his throat. "I was shot at, too."

"Did you return fire?"

"You bet I did!" He squared his shoulders. "But the point is, it's not worth dying for. There's gotta be a safer way to rustle up some grub."

"Sit down, guys." Marcus waved them toward the couch. "Heidi, would you bring them something to drink?"

She'd been watching, wide-eyed, from the corner of the room. Might as well give her something to do.

Slowly, she turned and went into the kitchen.

Marcus sank into the easy chair. Jacob had left his farm post yesterday, and now Carlson and Stein were quitting, too. That was three farmers who wouldn't be paying him anymore, until he could find new guards.

As much as he hated to admit it, no one would want the job.

Unless they were already starving, in which case they'd probably rob the farmers instead of guarding them.

So, police work was already out of the question. It couldn't pay. And the farm guard enterprise was about over, too. Marcus only had one other guy stationed at a farm – and he'd probably bail when he learned about the other three's experiences.

His plans were all falling apart.

How was he gonna eat this winter, if he wasn't going to get food from the farms or the police station?

Heidi returned with two glasses of water, and handed them to the guys. Stein thanked her, then turned his gaze to Marcus, but the rookie stared at Heidi until she left the room.

"Dalton!" Marcus thundered.

The rookie's eyes shifted his way.

"She's taken."

"I know." His face blazed red, and he took a gulp of water.

Soren laughed and slapped the kid's back, spilling water in his lap. "Can't blame him for wishing!"

"I was not," Carlson sputtered, brushing water from his pants.

Stein and Marcus shared a look and guffawed. Carlson's face grew even redder, if that was possible. He stood up.

"We just came over to give you our notice. We're done at the farms." He set his empty glass on the table and started for the door.

"Whoa, now, hold on." Marcus waved him back toward the sofa. "Sit down a minute, and let's have a conversation."

The rookie stopped where he stood. "What's there to talk about? We're done."

"Fine." Marcus sat back in his chair. "But unless you're just planning to starve this winter, maybe you'll want to sit down and talk. Come up with a new game plan."

Slowly, Carlson made his way back to the sofa.

"I haven't mentioned this yet, but we've got another problem, too," Stein said. "Some neighbors have been hassling me about having food. They know we're officers, they know we took the grocery store's inventory, and they think we've got it squirrelled away in our kitchens or something."

"Yeah," Carlson piped up. "I'm getting that, too."

"It's just a matter of time –"

"I know." Marcus held up his hand. "I've been hearing mutterings around here, too."

"They're gonna come after us some night, like they came at the police station," Stein said. "Maybe we should leave town."

"And go where, exactly?" Marcus asked. "It's not like the next town is any better off."

"Right, but maybe the rural areas –"

"We ARE rural!" Marcus scowled.

"I mean, the rest of the county. The farms, vacant homes..." Stein studied Marcus, as if looking for some indication that he was on board. "If we're done being cops."

"So now we'll be robbers?" Marcus glanced from Stein to Carlson. Neither seemed shocked or offended by his question. "What, are you kidding? We've always been the good guys."

7

"Look, all I'm saying is, maybe we can scrounge for a living," Stein said. "I'm not talking about forming an armed gang or anything."

"But we would be armed," Marcus said.

"Obviously!" Stein snorted. "The point is, maybe we can find a place out of town, where neighbors won't hassle us because we're the cops who stole the grocery store food –"

"We didn't steal it!" Carlson objected.

"Right! We took it fair and square," Stein laughed. "Whatever. We can find a spot to settle while things in town cool off, and we can scavenge and scrounge for what we need."

Marcus blew a heavy breath out through his mouth. This situation stank, and he hated it. But Stein's idea wasn't necessarily a bad one.

"There'd be safety in numbers," Stein continued. "If there's four or five of us –"

"There's only three of us," Carlson pointed out.

"I was thinking of Peter McGinniss, or Josh Miller–"

"McGinniss is out. No way." Marcus couldn't stand the guy.

"Okay, Miller, then." Stein folded his arms. "That's four. Like

I said, safety in numbers. They might try to pick us off individually at the farms, or even at our homes. But with four of us in one place?" He shook his head. "Not likely."

"Or at least we could fight back," Carlson said. "We'd have half a chance."

"Unlike our brothers yesterday." Stein leaned forward and fixed his gaze on Marcus. "So? What do you think?"

Marcus tightened his jaw. He didn't love the idea. But, he also didn't love the idea of staying here with nothing to eat. In his peripheral vision, he saw Heidi sidle into the room.

What about her?

She could be a pain, but she could also be a pleasure.

If he left her behind, she'd have no food. Until she attached herself to the next available provider. And he had no doubts she'd do just that, as quickly as possible.

He'd miss her company, though. Maybe he could take her with him. He glanced her way.

She was stunning in a short red summer dress that matched her lipstick, her blonde curls falling around her shoulders. Oh, man!

Take her, or leave her?

JACOB ROLLED out of the tent and bee-lined for the outhouse. He and Danny had eaten too many of those almost-ripe apples, and they were paying for it. Maybe it was fortunate that they'd only walked four miles yesterday.

By mid-afternoon, their stomachs had been churning, and they'd come to the old county park with the creaky wooden outhouse. Miraculously, there was a partial roll of toilet paper.

If he were traveling alone, he was confident he could make it to the Andersons' retreat by nightfall. But with the kid –

well, it was unlikely. They were looking at probably a
two-day walk.

He washed his hands and face in a little creek that mean-
dered through the park, then turned toward Willow's
Wilderness.

A glorious morning was underway, the blue sky filled with
puffy white clouds. Much of the smoke had cleared out over the
past day or two. The nights were cooler than they had been even
two weeks ago. The days were slightly cooler, too, which made
for good walking.

He let Danny sleep in until the sun was high enough to
warm up the tent.

They didn't have anything for breakfast, so it would be a
hungry day. Actually, they still had some apples, but he didn't
want any, and he doubted Danny would, either. He entered the
tent and tugged at the kid's foot.

"Sleepyhead! Wake up!"

Danny flopped over, half-opened one eye, and closed
it again.

"Come on! Day's a-wasting."

Danny opened the other eye, just a slit. "Breakfast?"

"Are you kidding? How can you be hungry already?" He
jostled the kid's leg. "Get up, it's time to go."

He knew the kid was hungry. They both were. But they'd
both have to deal with it until they got to the Andersons' place.
The sooner, the better.

"Happy September!" Mom's cheery greeting at breakfast
surprised Willow.

"Is it? September already?"

"I think so." She stabbed at her eggs. "Close enough."

"You can feel it in the air," Raven said. "It's cooler. Crisper."

"It's gonna get downright nippy," Uncle Tony said. "Before you know it, it'll be snowing!"

"Ugh. I hope not!" Willow glanced around. The leaves hadn't even begun turning yet. The idea of snow was... terrible. She dreaded winter, with its cold, its ice, and its long, dark nights. The thought made her shiver.

"Speaking of snow, we need more meat," Tony said. "I'm gonna go out hunting this evening, and maybe the boys can go out tomorrow morning."

"I'm sure they'd love that. They're sick of chopping firewood."

Tony's grizzled eyebrows lifted just a little. "I thought John was going to send over a chainsaw after you all went scavenging with him."

"Yes, and he did. But there's so little gas and oil for it, we're saving that for disasters or emergencies." Willow rose and took her plate inside, then put a pot of water on the stove to heat for dishwashing.

Raven brought a bucket of water from the creek, and set it on the table. Outside, Gilligan barked and whined.

A minute later, the water in the bucket rippled, like it'd just been set down.

"Hey, check that out!" Willow pointed at the water. "It's alive!"

"Or it's an earthquake. Let's get outside!"

They hurried out the door, but didn't notice anything unusual except Gilligan whining and panting.

"What's the matter with him?" Willow asked.

Raven patted his shoulder. "Animals can sense earthquakes. I think we did just have a small one, even though we didn't feel it."

Her uncle walked over to them.

"Or we had a big one, far away," he suggested.

"I can live with that," Willow said.

She went back inside to wash the breakfast dishes. The morning flew by, with hauling water for the animals, the garden, and the laundry. Everyone pitched in to scrub clothing, wring it out, and hang it up to dry in the afternoon sunshine.

By late afternoon, Willow's arms, legs and back were all sore. She sat down in the shade of the north side of the cabin, and soon found her eyelids growing heavy. Sprawling out on the grass, she let the breeze carry her to sleep.

When she awoke, the air had cooled considerably. The sky grew dark. Especially off to the west. She sat up.

That was one wicked-looking storm blowing in! A huge wall of dark grey clouds approached, blocking out the sun.

The laundry! She jumped to her feet. It was all going to get soaked!

She ran toward the clothes line, and found Mom there with Raven, pulling half-dried jeans off the line. Willow took an armload and rushed for the cabin.

The wind picked up, blowing her hair around her head, and shaking tree branches.

"Where are the guys?" She yelled over the growing ruckus.

"Putting the animals in the barn," Raven hollered.

Moments later, her group had gathered in the cabin, minus the new family, who were most likely waiting out the storm at their new home. Matt was the last to come inside.

"It's not rain," he said.

His ominous announcement sent a chill down Willow's spine. She exchanged a glance with Raven, and they both rushed for the door.

Outside, a few fine grey flakes floated from the darkened sky.

"Oh, no!" Raven grimaced.

"Another ash storm!" Willow let a grimy flake fall on her hand.

Maria ran past her legs. Willow lunged after her.

"No, you don't!" She scooped up the child. "You can't be out in this!"

The girl clung to her as they all retreated inside the cabin.

"Now what?" Josh asked.

"Now we wait," Willow answered. "And pray this blows over."

WITH STEIN AND CARLSON, Marcus was nearly to Josh Miller's house south of town when the ash storm arrived. They hurried to get to the front door and under the covered porch.

Marcus banged on the door.

"Josh! It's Marcus!" He yelled over the growling wind.

After a moment, Stein pounded on the door. "Miller! Open up!"

Thudding footsteps indicated Miller was hurrying down stairs. Moments later, the door opened.

"Get in here! Are you guys crazy?" The young officer's red hair sported a fresh cut.

Inside, the men shed their backpacks. Miller looked quizzically at the gear.

"You going somewhere?" His eyes turned to Marcus. "What's going on?"

"For now, we're going to stay here." Marcus stretched his arms. "If that's okay with you and Melanie."

"Of course! You can't go anywhere else for a while. There's a volcano going off!" He turned and yelled, "Mel? We got company!"

Moments later, his slender young wife came down the hall. Her green eyes widened on seeing the three visitors. She reached up and touched her light brown hair, smoothing it into place.

"Hi. Um, come on in." She smiled shyly, then glanced at her husband. "Why don't you take them to the living room? I'll – I'll bring something to drink."

She turned and disappeared back the way she'd come.

Miller led the officers into his living room, cluttered with building blocks and dolls and stuffed animals. Two children jumped up as the men entered.

"I guess you all know my daughter, Lily, and my son, Andrew."

"Sure!" Marcus smiled at the kids. "You two sure are getting big!"

Lily grinned and hid her face behind her doll.

"How old are they now?" Stein asked.

"Lily's five, and Andy is three."

Melanie came in with water glasses on a tray. Miller cleared off the coffee table so she could set it down.

"Sorry about the mess," she said, scooping up teddy bears and depositing them in a toy box in the corner. "We weren't expecting visitors."

"Babe, why don't you take the kids upstairs so we can talk?" Miller asked.

"Sure." Melanie grabbed Andy's hand and ordered Lily to come with her. After some minor protests, they were gone.

Marcus's thoughts turned to Heidi. He'd decided to leave her in town, but he'd only told her he'd be gone a few days. That wasn't fair to her, since he really wasn't planning to return anytime soon, but it worked to his advantage because it left his options open. Or he hoped so, anyway. If this scheme didn't pan out, he might want to go back to her.

"Please. Sit." Miller motioned to the furniture. "Now, what's going on?"

Marcus and the guys told him about the events of the past two days, and how they'd decided to quit police work and farm security patrols. Miller looked stunned to hear about the murderous attack at the station, but less surprised about the farm shootings.

"So, now what?" He looked from Marcus to the others. "I mean, you're welcome to hang out here for a while, but I don't have anything to feed you."

"No worries," Marcus said. "We don't want to impose. We'll take care of our own needs. And we were hoping you'd join us."

"Meaning what?" Miller rubbed his short red beard.

"Meaning, go with us on scavenging runs."

"And share the stuff we get," Stein added.

"Your place is perfect," Carlson said. "You're three miles south of town, so it's unlikely the city residents will walk out here looking for us."

"It's a good base of operations," Marcus pointed out. "From here, we can scavenge further south and stay away from the town folks."

Miller rose and looked out the window. After a moment, he turned back to the officers.

"I'll need to talk it over with Melanie." He sighed. "But I don't see a lot of other options. We're low on everything, too. And we've got kids to feed."

"Good man!" Marcus went to stand beside him. He clamped his hand on Miller's shoulder. "You can convince her to get on board."

He glanced out the window. The ash storm had turned daylight to dusk. Grey flakes were building up on the vehicles, lawn and trees. He frowned. What was going on? It was like the planet had gone haywire.

JACOB SET up his tent as quickly as he could, then dusted ash out of Danny's hair and off his clothes before he sent the kid inside. He dusted off his gear and tossed it in, too, then he shook ash out of his clothing before entering the flimsy shelter and zipping the entrance closed.

Man! Nothing ever went right anymore!

"I'm hungry." Danny pouted, crossed his arms and stared at him, his little nose still lightly dusted with pale grey ash. There was no food, and Danny had to know it.

It took all of Jacob's self-control to not snap at the kid. Instead, he said nothing. He rolled out his sleeping bag, flopped down on it, and closed his eyes.

It wasn't bedtime, and he wasn't particularly tired, but there was nothing else to do. Besides, that way he didn't have to entertain the kid or answer his questions or explain – again – why there was no food to eat.

Actually, there were still a couple of nearly-ripe apples, but he wasn't ready to assault his stomach, or Danny's, with those.

He huffed out a sigh.

They were stuck here until the ash settled. And then they'd have to finish their hike in it. How far did they have left to go?

Being rather new to the area, he wasn't familiar with all the landmarks on the highway, but he estimated they were within one or two miles of John and Jeannie's turn-off. From there, it was another three or four miles – all uphill.

Even with Danny's slow pace, they'd do that hike in one day, ash or no ash. There was no way Jacob was waiting longer for a real meal. The kid needed one, too. Or actually, months' worth of real food, to regain the weight he'd lost over the summer when he should have been growing.

If only he'd sent Danny with the Andersons weeks ago, when they left Ponderosa!

It hadn't helped the kid any to stay in town. He would have been better off at the cushy mountain retreat the Andersons had set up.

But now, Jacob was making that right.

Or he would, as soon as this stupid ash stopped falling on them.

8

As the ash drifted silently onto the tent, Jacob watched daylight fade into complete darkness. His eyes felt dry and gritty, but he didn't dare wipe at them.

Particles of volcanic ash in his eyes or on his fingers could get ground into his eyeballs like sandpaper, turning them red and possibly damaging his vision. So, he repeatedly yawned, trying to conjure up tears that might provide rinsing relief.

Beside him, Danny had fallen into a fitful sleep. The kid rarely rested quietly. He tossed, turned, mumbled, and occasionally kicked.

What could he be dreaming about?

Jacob could only remember one dream from his childhood. He'd probably been about Danny's age, or a little older. It was not long after his parents died and he got adopted.

He'd dreamed he was standing at the entrance of a great, shining city, and when the gate was opened, he saw his grandfather inside. He tried to run to Grandfather, but a very tall man, dazzlingly white, blocked his path.

"Not yet, Jacob." The man's kind voice rolled like thunder.

"You still have much to accomplish. In due time, you will return."

Then he'd woken up, but as he did, he was sure he saw a bright light fading from his bedroom, and he heard the tall man's voice echoing against his walls.

That had jarred Jacob enough that he'd never forgotten that one dream.

But it seemed like Danny had crazy dreams every time he slept.

Jacob yawned again, closed his eyes, and tried to ignore the hunger gnawing at his stomach. Eventually, he dozed off. Sometime during the night, the temperature dropped quite a bit. Danny scooted closer and curled up against Jacob's side.

Finally, dim grey light found its way into the tent. Jacob reached up and flicked the tent wall with his fingers. A thin covering of ash slid off, letting more light inside.

He sat up, pulled on his boots and ballistic vest, and quietly unzipped the door flap.

Outside, a grey world waited in silence. Nothing moved. No breeze, no birds, no nothing.

On the bright side, there was no more ash falling, either. And it looked like they'd only gotten about an inch this time.

That was good. It wouldn't be too hard to walk in that. Of course, their footprints would be obvious on the road, but who cared?

It wasn't like anyone was looking for a man and a boy.

By this evening, he and Danny would be at the Andersons' retreat, enjoying a feast, taking hot showers, using flush toilets and sleeping in clean, laundered sheets!

He couldn't wait!

"Danny!" He jostled the kid repeatedly. "Wake up!"

After some prodding, the kid got with the program. Jacob

rolled and packed their gear, and in less than twenty minutes, they were on their way.

They passed several houses and a shade-tree mechanic's garage, but no one was outdoors. It was like the entire grey world had hibernated.

After about an hour, they came to a road that Jacob felt sure was the one that led to the Andersons' place. He recalled it being on the east side of the highway, joining it at right angles, with a left-hand curve just up the hill. This road looked exactly like that.

He turned back to check on Danny's progress. The kid trailed him by about thirty feet.

"This is it, kiddo!" He was surprised by the enthusiasm in his own voice. "Only a few miles up this road, and we'll eat until we pop!"

Danny picked up his pace and soon was walking alongside Jacob.

"Is that it?" he asked as they approached the first driveway. The home was modern, without any outbuildings on the property.

"Nope. It's a ways further." Jacob hated to tell him they'd probably be walking most of the day. "It's up there, in the mountains."

He pointed ahead at the ash-covered forest.

"I'm hungry," Danny reminded him.

"So am I. But we're going to take care of that. Just as soon as possible."

As the morning wore on, the ash didn't slow him down, but Danny's pace did. The little guy just wasn't up to all this walking.

And Jacob couldn't carry him. He was burdened down with his pack, which grew heavier with each step, and his guns and the garbage bag filled with Danny's bedding and clothes.

They trudged on through the ash at a snail's pace. The road grew steeper as it climbed into the mountains.

Danny's steps grew shorter. And slower.

The sky remained grey through the morning and afternoon. It didn't dump any more ash, but it also didn't turn blue.

It was almost like there was a high, ashy grey overcast. And maybe it wasn't clouds. Maybe it was actually ash. Jacob studied it, but couldn't be sure.

WILLOW STARED out the window at the vast grey expanse. Except to care for the animals, nobody left the cabin that morning. Uncle Tony saved the day when he arrived with a deck of cards.

"It's for Solitaire, usually," he explained. "But we can play Rummy or War or Go Fish."

Willow only knew how to play Go Fish. But the cards were a good distraction. Soon, the cabin was filled with shrieks and laughter.

She glanced at her mom and smiled. It'd been a long time since they'd had this much fun.

Uncle Tony taught them a new game every hour, which they took turns playing until everyone had the hang of it. Turned out, Josh was very good at War.

In the afternoon, Willow and Raven got their hair trimmed, but Josh refused.

"I like it like this," he said, shaking his curly brown mop.

"You like it?" Matt goaded. "Or Beth does?"

"I don't see you lining up to get a cut," Josh returned. "And we all know Delia *loves* your golden mane!"

"It's unruly, Josh," Willow pointed out. "At least get a trim."

But he refused, and Willow glanced at Mom, who just shrugged.

"He's old enough to decide about his own hair," she said, putting the scissors away.

The cabin door banged open, and Delia and Beth stood in the doorway.

"Well, speak of the devils," Raven whispered, winking at Willow.

The girls came inside, and Matt and Josh began teaching them War. Willow watched them from her bunk, listening to their banter and laughter. They were having a fun time in a sad world.

Would they have time to grow up? Beth had just turned 13, and Delia was almost 15. Matt would soon be 16, and Josh would be 15 next month. Would they all survive to their next birthdays? She lay back, resting her head on her wonderful new pillow, and stared at the loft boards above her head.

It wasn't guaranteed. Willow had turned 18 this summer, and she held no illusions about the certainty of her 19th birthday.

First, they'd have to survive the winter. Hopefully that was possible. For sure, it'd be a huge struggle.

She turned so she could look out the window.

Grey grass. Grey trees. Grey sky.

She flung herself on her side and pulled her pillow over her head. Nothing was easy out here, but why did it always have to keep getting harder?

MARCUS STOOD on Josh Miller's porch and stared at the ash-covered driveway and trees. Josh had told them he couldn't feed them, and it was true. His cupboards were bare. There was nothing to eat in the house.

On the south side of the home, a garden languished under

the volcano's dust. Ashy potato plants and carrot tops poked up from the earth.

But Marcus wouldn't impose on Josh for those tender morsels. The guy had little kids to feed.

And besides, Marcus had said he and his men would provide for themselves, and he meant to do just that.

He returned inside and closed the door quietly. The Millers didn't have a proper guest room, so Marcus and his guys had crashed on the living room floor. And he'd encouraged them to get lots of sleep.

Stepping into the living room, though, he found Stein and Carlson awake and huddled in conversation with Miller.

He strode over to them.

"Night's best," Stein was saying. "It's too easy for someone to shoot us with a rifle from a distance during daylight hours."

"Making plans?" Marcus asked. "Why didn't someone call me in to join you?"

"We're just discussing ideas," rookie Carlson said. "About the best time to go scavenging."

"I don't want to be away from my family at night," Miller said. "They're pretty vulnerable here. Anybody could come up to the house – "

"Melanie knows how to shoot. I've seen her at the range," Marcus said. "Impressive, actually."

"But the kids – " Miller shook his head. "I don't like it."

"No matter when we scavenge – day or night – someone could come when we're away." Stein glanced from Marcus to Miller. "It's not like anyone's family is ever perfectly safe."

"But Mel would be awake during the daytime. She could see them outside. Night is dangerous for my family." He looked to Marcus for help. "Right?"

Marcus sighed and sat down on the sofa beside Stein.

They couldn't afford to lose Miller's support. They were

staying in his house, for crying out loud! Maybe they could find a compromise.

"Okay, how about this." Marcus turned to Miller. "We can try this once, maybe, and see how it goes. Carlson, Stein and I will go out at night. You'll stay home with your kids. You'll patrol around here during the day to protect us while we sleep. And you'll share your garden veggies – "

"No way!" Miller objected, but Marcus held up his hand.

"I'm not finished! In return, we'll share what we find with you and your family. The garden, the scavenging – it'll all go into one pot for everybody."

"But there'll only be three of us out there," Stein objected. "We need four, at least, to be on the safe side."

"Maybe Melanie can come with us," Marcus suggested.

"WHAT?" Miller rose to his feet. "No. No way!"

"Just as a lookout," Marcus said. "Not actually in harm's way."

"No!" Miller shook his head. "That's not happening."

Marcus scowled and exchanged a look with Stein. This wasn't going well. He turned to Miller and threw up his hands.

"Fine! What do you suggest?"

"I don't know." He scratched his chin. "I'm willing to go with you during the daytime. I'm willing to let you all stay here for a while. You gotta meet me halfway."

Marcus scowled. No, they didn't have to. But if they didn't, things would get ugly. He stared at Miller.

"Here's what's gonna happen. Me, Carlson and Stein are going out tonight as soon as it gets dark. In the morning, we can sort out how things will happen going forward." He looked at his men. "Agreed?"

Carlson nodded.

Stein glowered. "Just this one time."

"Okay." Miller didn't look happy, but he'd won this round.

"Good. Everybody get your gear in order." Marcus glanced out the window. "It'll be dark soon, and we'll head out."

JACOB'S STOMACH cried with hunger as he carried his gear up the road. Behind him, Danny's footsteps were dragging. The kid was a trooper – he'd walked all day – but he was slow, and it seemed like they had to stop every fifteen minutes to adjust a pack or tie a shoe or filter water or find a bush.

He'd never realized how much work kids could be. And this was just one! Some crazy parents had four or more!

Danny was a nice kid, for sure, but Jacob would be relieved to see Jeannie's sweet face. That little grandma would be so thrilled to see the boy. And she'd take him off Jacob's hands.

Hopefully less than an hour from now.

Daylight was fading, but Jacob was beginning to recognize landmarks on the road. Eventually, they came to the driveway of the home where the men in black had taken residence and prisoners. He'd never forget that place, for sure!

His dramatic escape, his return with Willow's group to break Matt out, the ensuing gunfight and then his night-long chase of one of the black-clad ninjas clear to Ponderosa. No, it'd be a very long time before he forgot that house!

He paused at the entrance to the driveway and considered going in and crashing there for the night. It was nearly dark.

But they were so close to the Andersons' retreat. He could be there soon, even if he had to drag Danny by his shirt collar.

Besides, what if someone had moved into that house? A lot of weeks had passed since they'd driven out the men in black, and it was pretty likely somebody had taken refuge there by now.

So he pressed on as darkness fell.

Finally, he came to the curve in the road just below the Anderson property. And, in the remaining moments of dusk, he stared at the devastation ahead of him.

A wildfire had roared through here, destroying everything in its path. The Andersons were gone. Their home was destroyed, its location marked only by its masonry chimney.

The barn, gone.

The animals, gone.

Everything. Gone.

9

J acob stared into the gathering darkness.

Now what?

The Andersons were gone, their retreat destroyed. There would be no delicious feast tonight. No comfortable bed to crash into afterwards.

In the distance, a wolf howled.

Danny shoved a cold hand into Jacob's. His little stomach gurgled. The kid had to eat.

First things first, though – where were they going to spend the night? Maybe they could walk back down to one of the homes they'd passed earlier. Knock on the door, ask to sleep in the woodshed or barn. Surely the owners wouldn't turn away a guy with a kid.

But no – that was too dangerous. It was dark out now. He was likely to get shot before the homeowners even noticed a boy was with him.

He'd need to set up the tent somewhere. And since he couldn't see anything, he'd need to get his headlamp out and use it.

Since the world went crazy, he'd been avoiding using the headlamp because he might never be able to replace the batteries. But this qualified as an emergency, almost. He'd just use it for a few minutes.

Pulling off his pack, he set it in the ash and felt around in the pockets until he found the headlamp.

The wolf howled again. Or maybe a different one. It sounded closer. He'd definitely want that light.

He pulled it onto his head and flicked it on. Intense white light flooded the ash at his feet. Turning his head, he looked for a flat spot to set up the tent. There were plenty of places that would work, but they were covered in wildfire ash and volcanic ash.

Deciding to retreat a short distance back down the hill, he found a good spot beside the road in the area that hadn't burned. Under the boughs of cedars, the volcanic ash was thin, too. This would work.

He unrolled the tent and shook it. Danny helped him pull the corners out square on the ground. He pounded in the stakes and raised the tent, then entered with all his gear and the kid.

As soon as he rolled out their beds, he flicked off the light, plunging them into total darkness. Another cold night on the hard ground.

This time with wolves.

And never-ending hunger as their only companion. A hollow ache opened in his mid-section at the thought of food.

They did still have two green apples. He should save them for breakfast, because they'd wake up ravenous. But his mouth watered when he thought of the big, juicy, tart fruit.

His stomach rumbled.

Plus, he was thirsty. The juicy apples would help with that, too.

He scrambled for the pack and rummaged until he found the old paper bag. Yanking it out, he reached inside, his fingers finding the hard, smooth fruit.

In the darkness, he felt for Danny's arm.

"Here." He pressed the smaller apple into the child's hand. "Eat slowly."

They munched in silence.

This might have been a bad idea. They might get sick from this acidic assault on their empty stomachs. In the morning, they'd surely wish they'd saved the apples for breakfast.

But, oh – at the moment, the fruit was a godsend.

Jacob forced himself to chew slowly, rather than gobble down the crispy goodness.

He ate it all. Even the core, but he spit the seeds into the paper bag. Danny dropped his core in there, too.

A new pain twisted his stomach, but his mouth was happy. The tart flavor lingered on his tongue. And the crisp fruit seemed to have cleaned his teeth, too.

He tucked Danny in, then crawled into his own sleeping bag.

In the morning, he'd be faced with a big problem – where to go, and what to do next. The Andersons had disappeared. Should he go see if Willow's group was still at their cabin? Most likely, it had been destroyed by fire, too.

Maybe they had all perished.

He shuddered. Their faces filled his thoughts – Raven, with her lovely Native eyes, dark complexion and glossy black hair; auburn-haired Willow's tall, slender form and sharp eyes that didn't miss a thing. Then there was Candy, with her bright blue eyes and cute blonde curls.

And the guys, Josh and Matt, and the new family.

When the Andersons left Ponderosa, Willow's mom went with them, to join her children. Had she found their cabin destroyed by fire when she arrived? Had she found their corpses?

Where was she now? And where were the Andersons?

Should he even bother looking for them, or was that a waste of time?

He needed to find food and a home for himself and Danny immediately. Maybe he should focus on that, rather than trying to chase down Willow's group or the Anderson family. Looking for them could turn into a huge waste of time.

He and Danny might starve if he wasted much more time.

He'd have to sort that out in the morning. For now, he closed his eyes. The best thing to do would be to get a good night's sleep, so he could think clearly when dawn broke.

"I gotta go," Danny's little voice whispered.

"Are you kidding? Now? Can you hold it?"

"No! I gotta go!"

DAYLIGHT REVEALED A DRAB, grey world burdened by volcanic ash. Jacob climbed out of the tent and grimaced. The familiar ache chewed away at his stomach. And there were no more apples.

Danny was still asleep, and that was fine. Good, actually.

Jacob needed time to think.

He built a small fire to warm his hands and chase away the morning chill. Standing with his back to it, he let the heat soak through his clothing and skin, clear to his bones.

Soon, it wouldn't just be the mornings that were cold. Winter was coming, with its short, bone-chilling days, and freezing nights.

But the immediate problem was food. He had to find some for him and the kid. Maybe he could hunt a deer?

Most of the deer within miles of any road had been hunted out already. He'd have to go way back in the backcountry to have a hope of finding any game.

And what would he do with Danny while he did that?

He could hardly leave him here in the tent. The kid was four years old! Nothing Jacob could say would make Danny stay in the tent while he was gone. Who knew what kind of trouble he'd get into?

He could wander off, or get killed by a bear. Or one of those wolves they'd heard last night.

But Jacob couldn't take the kid hunting, either. Miles of hiking through rough, mountainous terrain? He snorted. That'd never happen! It'd been tough enough to get him up the Forest Service road, where the going was easy.

Three whole days they'd wasted, getting here. He could have done it in one, if he'd been alone.

He turned and squatted beside the fire, warming his hands.

Maybe he should've stayed in Ponderosa. There, at least, they had a little food, and a babysitter when needed.

Perhaps he should go back. Apologize to Marcus, and get his old job back on the Litton farm. That had to be better than starving in a tent in the mountains.

MARCUS STOMPED onto Josh Miller's front porch. Stein and Carlson trudged up the steps behind him. It'd been a long night. Not as productive as he'd hoped.

He banged on the door, and moments later, heard footsteps thumping down the stairs from the second floor.

Miller opened the door, wiping sleep from his eyes. He was wearing pajamas and slippers.

"How'd it go?"

"Could've been worse." Marcus brushed past him. He pulled off his ashy boots and left them in the entry way. "Most of the homes are occupied."

"I could've told you that." Miller led the way to the living room. "But you got some stuff?"

"I think we're going to have to push farther south. Branch out away from the highway, too."

Stein took off his backpack. "We got some fruit."

"Apples and plums." Carlson tossed his pack to Miller, then sank onto the sofa. "Man, I'm so tired! What's for breakfast?"

Miller looked in the rookie's pack. "Plums and apples."

"For breakfast?" Carlson scowled. "No, man, you gotta do better than that. We need real food!"

"Everything gets shared, remember?" Marcus stared at Miller. "You'll need to contribute."

"Let's dig some of those potatoes, and fry 'em up!" Stein said. "Hash browns or whatever."

Miller frowned slightly. "I guess we could dig up a few. We don't have many, and they're still growing."

"That settles it then," Marcus said. "Hash browns and fruit for breakfast."

Light footsteps padded down the stairs, and Melanie appeared moments later, looking cute in snug blue jeans and a white cotton shirt. Miller filled her in on the breakfast plan, and handed her some of the fruit.

"Good job, guys!" She smiled at them, then headed for the kitchen.

"So, as I was saying, most of the homes here are occupied." Marcus focused on Miller. "Also, they're close together. Even if we come to one that looks vacant, it could be dangerous to scavenge there, because the neighbors might see us."

"In the dark?" Miller asked. "Not likely."

"We use flashlights and headlamps. Obviously." Condescension dripped from Stein's tone. "They would see that through the windows."

"So, what are you saying? You aren't going to check out the houses that look vacant?" Miller looked to Marcus. "I thought that was your whole plan."

"I'm saying we need to move farther south, where the homes are on larger acreages and are farther apart." He glanced at his team. "When we do that, we might not want to hike back here every morning. We might hole up somewhere for a day or two if things look good."

"So you'll just come back here when it's convenient or you're hungry?" Miller's eyes blazed. "In the meantime, you might not bring back all the goodies you find out there?"

"If you come with us, you don't need to worry about that," Stein said. "We need another guy. Three isn't enough."

"But I have a wife and kids! You want me to just leave them here while I go out scavenging for days on end? No way!"

"Melanie is a big girl. She can take care of herself for a couple days." Stein glowered at his host. "Besides, she needs you to go out and drum up some food for the kids, not sit around here worrying and fretting about stuff that might never happen. You need to man up and provide for your family!"

WILLOW WASHED the last of the breakfast dishes and set them on a towel to dry. It'd be great to have a drain rack. Maybe someday.

Most of the group had already left to work on a project at the new cabin. She and Raven planned to head over there in a few minutes.

"We had a hard frost last night." Uncle Tony's voice boomed as he entered the cabin. He was wearing a plaid flannel shirt over a black Audio Adrenaline t-shirt from the 1990s.

Willow turned her face to hide her grin. That man had quite a collection of ancient Christian band shirts!

"Yeah, it was really cold," Raven agreed. "Did you have any luck hunting?"

"Who cares about hunting?" Tony grabbed the sourdough pancakes Willow had saved for him, rolled one up like a crepe, and took a big bite out of the end. After he swallowed, he eyed the girls. "What're you waiting for? We gotta harvest whatever we can! Today!"

"You think it killed the garden," his niece said.

"Yeah! You bet it did!" Tony glanced at her. "Most of it, probably. We'll find out quick, that's for sure."

He swallowed another bite. "So clear your schedules of all your plans for today. We've got a harvest to bring in!"

When he finished wolfing down the pancakes, the three of them walked out to the garden.

"The tomatoes are finished, for sure," Uncle Tony said, pointing a stick at their frosted leaves.

"But they're not ripe yet!" Willow protested.

"Makes no difference." Tony planted the end of his stick in the ground to emphasize his point. "You'll harvest them today, or you'll watch them rot tomorrow!"

Willow looked at the rows of tomato vines. Some of the tomatoes had blushes of red or orange on their skins, while others were still fully green.

Raven knelt down and pulled one from the vine.

"I guess we'll be eating fried green tomatoes," she said.

"Maybe you can let the reddest ones finish ripening after you harvest them," Tony said. "You could can those when they're ready. Green ones could be canned in a salsa or relish, if you want."

Willow stared out over the rest of the garden. The corn had struggled, but was trying to ripen. Carrots were going gang-busters. The potato plants had been looking healthy.

"What about the rest of it?" She asked.

"You can leave the carrots in the ground." Uncle Tony pulled one up anyway, rubbed off the dirt, and started eating it. "They'll only get sweeter over time."

"Corn and potatoes? Onions?"

"Let's leave 'em for now. I don't know how cold it actually got, maybe they'll survive. But you gotta get the tomatoes."

He turned to leave. "I'm going up to the new place. Gotta get them started on a root cellar for all your garden goodies."

So, Willow and Raven spent the morning harvesting toma-toes and sorting them by ripeness. The day grew warm as they worked. Willow stopped to stretch her back. The sky was still grey, but not a normal-looking overcast grey. It was more like a heavy, high-level atmospheric haze.

She yawned and surveyed their progress. They were almost finished. They ended up with two boxes full of tomatoes that were nearly ripe and would be canned later. And lots of green ones that would soon be fried or turned into salsa.

Gilligan let out a low, rumbling growl, followed by a bark.

Willow scanned the clearing and the forest that hemmed it. There, at the far end, she saw movement.

Instinctively, she reached for her Smith & Wesson. The grip felt warm under her grimy fingers.

A man stepped out into the open, waving his hat in the air with one hand, while grasping the hand of a small child with the other.

"Hello!" he yelled. "Hello!"

Oh, no! Somebody had found their little refuge in the wilderness. Who was he? How many others were traveling with him, hidden back in the trees somewhere?

Was he harmless, as he appeared, or was he actually a threat?

10

"Stop right there!" Willow raised her weapon, knowing she was too far for handgun accuracy. She might get lucky.

The man froze.

"It's me!" He yelled. "Jacob! Don't shoot!"

She squinted. Was it? His hair was longer. He was about the right height, but skinnier.

Then again, everyone had gotten skinnier this summer. Her own pants barely stayed up with her belt on its tightest notch.

"It *is* him!" Raven breathed. She started forward, first at a walk, then breaking into a run.

Willow stood back and watched, lowering her gun.

Jacob?

What was he doing here? And why?

And why was Raven so happy to see him?

He'd abandoned them. Now he was just gonna come wandering back? Right at harvest?

How convenient!

Plus, he'd brought at least one more mouth to feed with him, too.

Forcing her feet to move forward, she holstered her weapon.

As she approached, Raven wrapped Jacob in a quick hug, then knelt to meet the youngster. He was a cute little kid, with black hair. His skin was the same color as Raven's.

"Hello, Willow." Jacob's voice was subdued.

She turned her gaze to him. "Jacob."

"This is Danny."

She glanced down and found huge brown eyes studying her. The boy was thin as a fence post. She offered him a smile.

"Hi, Danny. I'm Willow."

He stared at her. "I'm hungry."

Raven glanced at Willow, then offered her hand to the child. "Of course you are! Let's get you something to eat."

He slipped his hand into hers, and the pair started off toward the cabin.

Returning her attention to Jacob, Willow noticed how thin his face had become. And haggard.

"Why are you here, Jacob?" She crossed her arms.

He swallowed and watched Danny and Raven. Then he touched his tongue to his lips and turned his eyes to Willow.

"Things are bad in town. Marcus wanted to chip Danny." His gaze shifted toward the boy, who was nearly to the cabin. "Jeannie really liked him, wanted to keep him. So I brought him up to their retreat, but they were burned out."

His stomach whined and he swallowed again. "I didn't know where to go. I figured you guys were burned out, too – but here you are."

"Yes. Here we are."

She almost began to tell him where the Andersons were living, but caught herself. If Jacob was untrustworthy, her group was exposed already, but the Andersons were still safe. She needed to guard their privacy until she could figure out what Jacob was really up to.

"So now what?" She asked. "What are your plans?"

"Now, I don't have any plans." He inhaled slowly, then sighed. "I was hoping to work for the Andersons and stay with them at their retreat. They were all stocked up for the apocalypse, and they were shorthanded after the first gunfight with those marauders. Plus, they liked Danny, so – "

"So, you figured they'd take you in."

He frowned slightly. "In exchange for work, yeah."

She fell silent.

Jacob lowered his head slightly and looked into her eyes. "Are they okay? The Andersons? Do you know where they are?"

"They're fine." She decided to change the subject, and quick. "You look hungry."

"I'm starving!"

"Let's get you a bite to eat." They started toward the cabin. "When was your last good meal?"

"I dunno... maybe three weeks ago?" He picked up the pace. "In town, we were living on potatoes. The last few days, we had nothing but apples."

They entered the cabin.

"You'll need to start with a small amount of something bland, so you don't upchuck it all. A little rice should be okay."

"I'll take whatever you've got!" He rubbed his stomach.

"Today, you'll take rice." She glanced from him to Raven and the kid. "Same for Danny. Just a little boiled rice. We have some left over from yesterday."

Jacob's head turned as he looked around the cabin, then his gaze settled on the loft, where he'd slept while he lived with her group earlier in the summer.

"Everything looks the same around here. Except, where is everybody?"

Raven smiled at him. "Uncle Tony has them working on a root cellar up at the new cabin."

"That's good," he said. "They got much to store in there?"

"You've sure got a lot of questions," Willow answered before Raven could. She looked at him. "I don't trust you, Jacob Myers. You'll need to mind your Ps and Qs while you're here."

His jaw flexed. "I wasn't trying to be snoopy. And you *can* trust me."

"Really?" She stared him down. "If that's true, you'll have to prove it. And that will take some time!"

He cocked his head. "I've got all the time in the world."

Willow glanced at Raven and received a glare from her. *"What?"*

Raven shook her head.

"We'll talk about it later." She held out plates with tiny portions of rice for Danny and Jacob. "Why don't you take these outside? We've set up some stumps for chairs around the fire pit."

After Jacob and Danny went out, Raven turned to Willow.

"What was all that about?"

"All what?"

"All the hostility and distrust!"

"I wasn't hostile! And he sure hasn't earned our trust." Willow frowned and turned away. Fighting with Raven was miserable. And usually, a losing proposition, too.

"You certainly weren't gracious or hospitable. How do you think God wants you to act?"

"I think he wants me to protect my friends! Including you. And you're awfully trusting, by the way."

"That's not the worst thing I've ever been called." Raven's countenance flickered from indignation to amusement, then back again. "What are you so worried about? That he'll bring Marcus here to round us up?"

"I don't know. Maybe."

"He said he's protecting Danny from Marcus. From getting the mark!"

"What if that's not the truth, Raven? People lie."

"Sure. But has he lied before?"

Willow wasn't sure. Had Jacob lied? He'd disappeared, twice. But had he actually ever lied to them?

"I don't know."

Raven threw up her hands. "You don't know? Sheesh, Willow! What could he possibly say or do, to make you feel better?"

"He could leave."

"You'd condemn him to starvation, because – because what? You don't trust him? Don't like him?"

"I never said that."

"It's *so* obvious!" Raven moved into Willow's personal space, her face inches away. "So again – what would make you feel better?"

"I'd feel a whole lot better if I knew he didn't have the mark himself!"

Raven pulled back. "Are you kidding? You think he has the mark?"

"Maybe! I don't know." Willow paused for effect. "And you don't know, either, Raven!"

Without another word, Raven whirled around and stormed out of the cabin, leaving the door open.

Willow gulped. Had she ever made Raven this mad before? Her heart pounded as she moved toward the doorway and looked out.

Near the fire pit, Raven spoke to Jacob, who then extended his right hand. Raven took it in hers and examined it. Then, she moved to Danny and did the same. She said something to them, then strode back to Willow.

"They don't have it. I just checked." Her brown face was tinged with red.

Willow cleared her throat. "I'm sorry."

"I'm not the one you need to apologize to!" She grabbed her water bottle with its built-in filter. "I'm outta here. Can I trust you to be civil while I'm gone?"

Willow nodded meekly. "Where're you going?"

"Away from you." She walked out, said something to Jacob, then jogged to the end of the clearing, disappearing into the trees.

Willow slumped into a chair. Her eyes grew watery. She'd never made Raven so mad.

Maybe she was right, maybe Willow was hostile and suspicious. But maybe she was that way by necessity. Or maybe she was just plain wrong, and Raven was right.

Warm tears slid onto her cheeks, and she let them flow.

Maybe she should go after Raven. Mend fences and bring her back. But Raven clearly couldn't stand the sight of her. And if Willow said anything wrong, she'd make things so much worse.

No, she'd just have to wait until Raven cooled down and returned. She swallowed, wiped her face, and stood up.

She had guests.

The least she could do was "be civil," as Raven had put it.

Jacob looked up as she approached. "You want us to leave."

"No. I mean, not yet." Slowly, her eyes found his dark brown ones. They were grieved. She gulped. "I'm sorry, Jacob."

"For what?"

He certainly wasn't going to make this easy. She lifted her head.

"For being rude."

"Were you rude?" He picked the last grain of rice off his plate and popped it into his mouth. "You were suspicious. Maybe not rude."

"Okay."

"Okay?" His eyes studied hers.

"Whatever. I'm sorry for not being nicer."

At this, a long, slow smile spread across his face. It turned into a grin.

"Willow." He looked like he couldn't contain his amusement. "I'm not sure I've ever seen you be nice."

"What?" Never been nice? Of course she was nice! Maybe she hadn't been too nice *to him*, but she was nice. Right?

"Hey, don't take it so hard." His face was relaxed, his tone friendly. "Look, we're living in terrible times. I've done some things that you didn't understand. It's natural to be suspicious."

Willow sat on a log across from him. He was extending an olive branch, and she should take it. She sighed.

"Maybe we can start over." She met his glance. "I'll try to be nicer, and you –"

"I'll try not to do anything that'll make you shoot me." He winked.

Winked! She couldn't decide whether to be charmed or infuriated. So she stood up, then took his plate and Danny's.

"We should go up to the new cabin. The guys will be happy to see you."

"Well. At least *they'll* be happy."

She refused to respond to that, pushing open the cabin door. "You can leave your gear here."

Jacob set his pack and gear in the cabin, then the three of them started up the trail to the new place.

"Wow, they did a nice job," Jacob said when he saw it. "It looks good."

"Yeah." Willow didn't see anyone at the house. "I guess we can go up to the root cellar."

"Since Raven already spilled the beans about that," Jacob teased.

It wasn't that funny. If Willow needed to be less suspicious, then Raven needed to be more cautious. Loose lips sink ships.

Willow led the way around a small hill. Her friends were digging on the north side, where it'd stay cooler.

"Hey, everybody! Look who's here," she called out as she approached.

The group thronged them. There were hugs, handshakes, backslaps and lots of questions.

Jacob introduced Danny, who shrank back from all the commotion. He kept a firm grip on Jacob's hand. Delia and Beth sweet-talked the boy as he watched Maria playing with Gilligan. Eventually, the girls persuaded Danny to come play with them.

Willow stood at the periphery of the group. Mom came over to join her.

"Tony said you girls were picking tomatoes. Is Raven still working on that?"

"No, we got them all picked and sorted."

Mom shot her a quizzical glance. "So where is she?"

Willow's shoulders slumped.

"We got in an argument. She took off to cool down."

"So she doesn't know Jacob's here?"

"She knows." Willow frowned. "Let's not talk about it now, okay?"

Mom studied her with those clear, discerning eyes. "Fine. We'll talk later."

Jacob's arrival marked the end of the work day. Everyone wanted to hear all the first-hand news about town and Marcus, and how Jacob chased the black-clad ninja guy to Ponderosa, and eventually came to stay in Raven's house while taking in Danny and working at the farm.

When Jacob asked where Candy was, the group filled him in on the sad story of her death during the lightning storm. His shock and sadness appeared genuine.

Eventually, Willow left to return to the old cabin to begin

dinner. As she walked through the forest, she wondered if Raven was back yet. She needed to apologize and make things right.

What *had* she been thinking? They didn't need to have a fight over Jacob! Raven would be glad to hear that Willow had taken her advice and was nicer to him this afternoon. More or less.

Anyway, the rift in their relationship was crushing her spirit. Reconciliation could be humiliating, but folks always felt better once they achieved it. She picked up her pace, eager to resolve the problem and be on good terms again.

But when she reached the cabin, Raven was nowhere to be seen.

It'd been well over an hour, probably two. She must have been really mad!

Willow dug some potatoes from the garden and brought a basin of water outside to scrub them. She sat on a log where she could see Raven as soon as she came out of the forest. As she scrubbed, her eyes kept searching the trees at the edge of the clearing.

No Raven.

Or maybe she was sitting just out of view, observing Willow's apprehensive watching, and getting a chuckle out of it. Willow stood and dumped out the dirty water at the base of the old plum tree.

No, Raven wasn't like that. She was kind. That was why Willow loved her so much. Why everyone did.

She started a fire and put the potatoes on to boil, then began frying green tomatoes. Soon, everyone would be coming down to dinner. Not long after that, the sun would be setting.

Where was Raven?

Had she gotten lost?

She was a runner, a marathoner. With a terrible sense of

direction. What if she'd gone running, got turned around, and couldn't find her way home?

Willow swallowed. That was all her fault. If only she'd been nicer! If she hadn't argued with Raven. If she'd listened to her.

Then, Raven would've never left. She'd be home. Safe.

Willow pressed her fingers to her lips. For the second time this afternoon, her eyes misted, then formed tears. She blinked. Then prayed.

Jesus, I'm sorry! Please bring her home!

She stood in the doorway of the cabin, watching for her friend. Suddenly, she saw motion in the shadows at the edge of the clearing.

But it wasn't Raven. It was grey. She squinted to make it out.

Was it a coyote?

Or a wolf?

11

Willow slipped into the cabin to get her rifle. When she came back out, the grey beast had ghosted into the trees. Moments later, she heard voices on the trail from the new cabin. The hungry group was ready for dinner.

"Where's my niece?" Uncle Tony looked around for Raven.

"I'm not sure." Willow's voice quavered as she avoided looking into his eyes. "We got into an argument, and she took off."

"She take her rifle?"

Willow shook her head. "Just her water bottle. I think she was wearing her pistol."

"How long ago?" Uncle Tony stared at her.

"Couple of hours." Her lip trembled.

"Her sense of direction is worse than a blind cat! Why'd you let her run off?"

She bit her lip as her eyes grew moist.

"She was mad." Willow choked. "I thought she'd be back before now."

"That girl moves quick, like a deer. By now, she could be anywhere."

Willow nodded.

"Let's eat. If she isn't back when we finish, we'll go find 'er."

"Okay," Willow whispered.

Clark prayed a blessing over their food, and everyone dug in. But as word spread about Raven, conversation died down. They were in a hurry to finish.

"We need to find her before dark," Jacob said, looking at Uncle Tony. "How are we going to do this?"

"In four teams," Tony said. "Minimum of two people per team, because of wolves or cougars or slip-n-falls. I'll try to track her, but even with the ash, it'll be hard at night. And one team should head over to the Andersons to see if she went there."

"That is eight people," Clark said, looking at the assembled group. "Alan and I, Jacob, Matt, Josh, and Tony. We will also need two women."

"I'm going," Willow said. "Mom can't, because of her foot."

"It's almost better," Mom objected.

"You'll slow us down," Willow argued. "Jaci?"

"Yes. I'll go," she nodded, her brown hair bobbing around her shoulders.

"You'll be on my team," Clark said. "That will leave Deborah, Laura, Beth, Delia and the children staying home. I suggest they all wait here, together at this cabin, until we return."

"Good." Uncle Tony eyed the members of the search party. "The rest of you, team up!"

Minutes later, the teams were formed: Clark and Jaci, Matt and Josh, Alan and Uncle Tony. Which left Jacob and Willow.

She grimaced as she gathered her gear – backpack, water, rifle and flashlight. Maybe it could've been worse. She could have been paired with Uncle Tony, whose very presence would make her feel even more burdened by her guilt.

As the sun set, the search party gathered outside the cabin. Alan led them in a prayer for success in finding Raven, and safety as they searched. Willow chewed her lip and blinked back her tears as he prayed.

"Okay, here's the plan." Uncle Tony's voice sounded strained. "Matt and Josh – can you find your way to the Andersons in the dark?"

"No problem." Josh sounded more confident than he looked.

"Good. You two head over there. If she's not there, or even if she is, you guys stay put and come back in the morning. I don't want you out with the wolves twice tonight. Got it?"

The boys nodded.

"Alright, then. Skedaddle!"

They headed out.

"Now, the rest of you." He turned his eyes to Willow, who wilted under his gaze. "We'll start out together. I'll track her as far as I can. Maybe our teams won't have to split up. But if I lose her trail, we'll have to branch out in different directions."

They fell into a single-file line, with Tony at the front and Jacob bringing up the rear, right behind Willow. She didn't like having him behind her where she couldn't see him, so she dropped back to walk alongside him, which was almost as bad – but not quite.

"Her tracks are pretty clear in all this fresh ash," Jacob said. "We should find her in no time."

"I hope so." They entered the forest, where the shadows grew dark and deep as dusk strengthened its grip on the landscape.

They followed Raven's trail to the creek, stopping several yards back as Tony examined her prints.

"She stopped here. Probably filled her water bottle, or got a drink." He looked up the creek, then down. "She crossed over there."

He started across the water, while the others waited until he found her trail on the far side.

"Looks like she headed east. And she was moving at a good clip. Almost a dead run."

Willow followed the others across the creek. If Raven continued east, she'd end up in the burned-out area. The wildfire hadn't left much but blackened snags and charred logs all over the place. That'd slow her down.

Willow frowned. Why hadn't Raven come home?

Was she still mad?

Was she truly lost?

Why couldn't she follow her own trail though the ash back to the cabin?

What if she had fallen and hurt herself?

Or what if she'd been attacked by wolves?

Willow's throat constricted. She had to stop thinking like that. Put her faith in God. He knew where Raven was. He'd bring her home.

Wouldn't He?

"Penny for your thoughts." Jacob's voice was hushed.

She rolled her eyes before she answered. He wouldn't notice. It was getting too dark.

"I just want to find her."

"This isn't your fault, you know."

"Yes. It is."

"Maybe the argument was your fault, but Raven's reactions were her own. We all make our own choices."

"It never would've happened if...." Willow sighed. If she had been nicer to Jacob when he'd arrived. If she'd been nicer to Raven. If she'd listened. *If, if, if.* "Look, I don't want to talk about it, okay?"

"Suit yourself."

Ahead of her, Clark and Jaci came to a stop behind Alan and Tony.

"She's veering off to the north," Tony said. "Maybe she made a big loop to come back home."

Willow wanted to cheer. Maybe her best friend wasn't totally directionless after all! If she'd traveled a bit south, then a ways east, then north... she could turn west and get home. Or west, then south, depending on how far north she ran.

"Maybe she'll get home long before the rest of us," Jaci said.

"I hope so!" Willow smiled for the first time since Jacob had arrived this afternoon.

A cold breeze lifted her long, fine hair and swirled it around her face. Far in the distance, she heard something like thunder.

As darkness engulfed the land, they followed Raven's tracks through the ash, losing it a couple of times where the forest was dense and the ash was sparse. When that happened, they'd stop while Uncle Tony made some wide circles to find it again.

To save batteries, they only used three flashlights – one per team. Willow had to stick pretty close to Jacob so they could both see where they were going and avoid rocks, roots and other obstacles.

A wolf howled. Willow paused and turned her head, listening for the direction it had come from. South, she thought.

Raven's path led north.

But Josh and Matt had headed south, toward the Andersons. If they'd hurried, they might be halfway there by now.

Another canine voice raised its mournful dirge. She shivered. How far away were they?

"You cold?" Jacob asked. "I brought a sweatshirt if you want it."

"No." Willow stepped over a log. "I'm fine."

She scowled. She'd have to be freezing before she'd accept a kindness from Jacob. Trudging along behind her friends, she wondered about that.

Why did she dislike him so much? Sure, there had been questions about his loyalty, but those seemed to be resolved for the most part. Her last big question, about whether he was marked, was resolved today.

Everyone else seemed to like him just fine. Raven welcomed him back like an old friend. But maybe she had a crush on him. He *was* a real looker, with his nice tan, dark hair and deep brown eyes. He was self-confident and hard-working. Candy had found him charming, as had Raven.

Only Willow resisted his efforts at friendship. Only she found him irritating.

She tripped on a root, and he caught her arm, stopping her fall.

"You okay?" Jacob asked.

"Fine." After a long pause, she forced herself to add, "Thank you."

"You're welcome." He sounded truly surprised at her thanks. Why did he think she was an ingrate?

"I *am* nice," she blurted.

He chuckled. "Where did that come from?"

"You said I wasn't."

"That was hours ago. Are you obsessing about it?"

"No!"

Grrrr. It was exactly this kind of exchange that made her so annoyed at him. She clenched her teeth and refused to continue the conversation.

A few minutes later, Uncle Tony called a halt. They stopped in a clearing. Willow saw Raven's tracks in the ash. They were spread out, long strides. When she got this far, she was still running.

Oh, Raven. Willow hung her head. I'm so sorry!

"Let's take a minute to rest," Uncle Tony said, his breathing labored.

That was odd. Raven's uncle spent his life in the forest, hunting and hiking all over the place. But now he was winded.

Did it have anything to do with the heart trouble he had last month?

So, in addition to driving Raven away, now Willow was going to cause Uncle Tony to have a heart attack, too?

He sat on a stump, and she walked over to him.

"Are you alright?" She asked.

"Fine. Just need to drink some water." He took a sip from his bottle. "That girl sure can cover some ground."

"Yeah." Willow nodded. "She's quite a runner."

"My little bird started running the day after she learned to walk. She's never stopped since." He capped his water bottle. "She'd fly, if she could figure out how."

"Is that true?" Willow asked. "The day after she learned to walk?"

"Pretty close." He stood up. "That's what her mother said."

A wolf howled, not very far away. It sounded like it was ahead of them. Where Raven had gone.

As they followed her tracks, more lonely voices joined the chorus. Their cries resonated with the mournful feelings Willow was experiencing. If no one else were around, she'd lift her chin and howl her grief, too. Ahhwwoooooooh!

Please come back, Raven!

The wind kicked up, moaning through the tree limbs overhead. Willow shivered.

Why hadn't she thought to bring a jacket?

Jacob hadn't put his sweatshirt on yet, and she was tempted to ask for it. Her pride held her back. She still didn't want to be in his debt – not for the slightest favor.

"We're gonna get some rain," Uncle Tony announced. "That wind is bringing in a storm front."

"When do you expect it to arrive?" Clark's accent almost masked the concern in his tone.

"Hard to say." Tony paused. "Half hour, maybe?"

The wind began coming in gusts, blowing the volcanic ash in swirls highlighted by the beams of their flashlights. Willow bent her head against the stiff breeze.

Eventually, she felt a rain drop on her shoulder. Then a couple on her head. Within minutes, the heavens opened up and cried in earnest.

They took refuge under a stand of cedars, but Willow was already drenched.

The wind plastered her soaked clothing to her skin and sucked all the heat out of her body. She wrapped her arms around herself and shivered.

"We need to turn back," Clark said. "We are not going to find her tonight."

"You go ahead," Uncle Tony agreed. "I'll press on. I can find her."

"It would be best to return to the cabin, get dry and warm, and begin the search again in the morning," Clark pressed. "We don't want anyone to get sick."

"But we might be close to her now!" Uncle Tony argued. "In the morning, we might not be able to pick up her trail."

"You all go back," Willow said. "I'll continue on with Tony."

"I'll stay, too." Jacob's voice was husky. "If Alan, Clark and Jaci return to the cabin, Willow, Tony and I can keep up the search."

The rain began to let up.

"Can you guys find your way home?" Willow asked.

Navigating in the mountains in the daylight was tricky

enough. It was much harder at night, when one couldn't see any landmarks at all. And this family was new to the wilderness.

For a moment, no one answered.

Finally, Alan spoke up.

"I'm not sure we can find our way. How about if we search for one more hour? If we find her, great! If not, we'll go home, get some rest, and tackle it in the daylight."

Uncle Tony grunted.

"That sounds good," Willow said. "But we all have to agree. Tony?"

"Okay. Fine."

"You'll come home with us in an hour, right?" She wanted a little more confirmation.

"Alright. One hour."

"Good. Anybody have a watch? What time is it?"

A tiny light illuminated Jacob's wrist. "It's 11:15."

"Tell us when it's 12:15," Willow said. "Lead on, Tony!"

Her shivering dropped off as they hiked and circulation warmed her body again.

An hour. Hopefully that would be long enough to find Raven. She must have stopped running when it got dark. She wouldn't be able to see, since she hadn't taken a light. They should be able to catch up with her.

The rain picked up again as they walked. Willow shivered. Oh, what she'd give for a rain coat! Or an umbrella!

Her rifle was soaking wet, too. It'd need some serious attention when they returned to the cabin.

Willow nearly bumped into Jaci, who had stopped abruptly ahead of her. Uncle Tony's flashlight beam was swinging wildly across the ground.

"This darn rain!" His voice shook with cold and worry. "I've lost her tracks!"

12

W illow circled the area with her own flashlight. After the wind had blown through, the rain had soaked the ash, washing it into the landscape. It created rivulets, humps and bumps around rocks and shrubs, and a wet, ashy concrete-like sludge in the low areas.

The only visible tracks were their own, in the soaked ash. Tracks made before the storm arrived had washed away.

"We can't find her in this," Alan said. "We need to go home and get some rest. Come back out in the daylight."

Willow didn't know if she'd be able to sleep, but Alan was right – the group needed to get rest. They were all soaked and shivering.

"Okay, let's go home," she said.

A flashlight beam caught Uncle Tony's face. His nose was red, his eyes set in a pained stare. He dropped his head.

"Okay." His voice was barely above a whisper.

The walk home sapped all of Willow's energy and body heat. They approached from the northeast and arrived at the new cabin first.

"Tony, why don't you sleep here tonight, with us?" Alan

asked. "Willow and Jacob can head on down to the pioneer cabin and let everyone know we're okay."

"Raven's not okay." Uncle Tony's voice was hoarse. "And what, you don't think I should sleep in the barn when I'm soaked to the bone?"

The gruff old guy followed Alan, Clark and Jaci into the new cabin, leaving Willow and Jacob to walk down the trail to the original cabin.

When they reached it, Willow pushed open the door and stumbled inside. A single candle on the table bathed the tiny cabin in soft light. Everyone was asleep except Mom, who was sitting up by the warm stove.

Willow knelt beside it, holding her icicle fingers up to its heat. Jacob went to the opposite side of the stove and turned his back to it, getting so close that water started steaming off his pants.

"Any luck?" Mom asked, pouring two mugs of venison broth.

Willow shook her head. Her teeth chattered.

"Here. Take a sip." Mom held the mug to her lips. "When you stop shaking, you can hold it and warm up your hands."

The broth tasted bland, but Willow gulped the warm liquid. "Needs salt."

"Everything does. But we have to use it sparingly." Mom handed the other mug to Jacob. "Go easy on this. Your stomach isn't ready for too much yet."

"Thanks." He took a sip and closed his eyes, swaying slightly in front of the woodstove. "I guess the attic's available, since the boys went to the Andersons?"

"Absolutely." Mom nodded. "Your gear is in the corner."

"It'll be pretty warm up there." He picked up his backpack and started up the ladder. "Tonight, that's a good thing."

"Good night, Jacob." Mom turned to Willow. "You need to get out of those soaked clothes."

"Yep." Willow glanced at the bunks. The teen girls had taken the top beds, while Danny and Maria shared a lower one, and Deborah slept in the other. "Looks like we'll be sleeping on the floor."

She changed into dry clothes and pulled her sleeping bag and pillow near the woodstove. When she closed her eyes, all she saw was Raven. Upset, sad, running through the forest, chased by wolves, climbing trees and pursued by cougars.

When she fell asleep, the images turned to dreams.

She woke up shouting.

"Are you okay?" Mom asked from the other bunk.

"Fine." Willow cleared her throat and wiped her eyes. "I'm fine."

Pale grey light in the window proved that morning had arrived. Today they would find Raven. Willow prayed she would be okay.

She put wood in the stove, ran out to feed the goats, rabbits and chickens, then gathered the eggs and hurried back to the cabin. She'd leave the watering and milking to Mom, who would be staying around the homestead today.

Breakfast was a hurried meal. Clark and Alan arrived from the new cabin and announced that Jaci was staying home with Uncle Tony, who had a bad cough. Willow cringed at the news. There wasn't much that could keep Tony from searching for his niece, so he must be pretty miserable.

Concern etched Mom's face.

"I hope he didn't catch his death of a cold out there last night." She glanced at Jacob as if to ascertain whether he was getting sick, too, then put her hand on Willow's forehead, checking for a fever.

"I'm fine, Mom!" Willow ducked away. "Sheesh!"

Alan looked around at the assembled faces. "Are Matt and Josh back yet?"

"Not yet," Mom said.

"Then it appears that four of us will be searching today," Clark said. "Alan, Jacob, Willow and myself."

"We can come, Dad," Delia volunteered.

Beth grabbed her dad's hand. "Yeah, Dad, let us come! We've got good eyes and ears."

"No doubt you do, little one. No doubt you do!"

"We can come, then?" Delia asked, a smile warming her dark face.

Clark glanced at his father-in-law. "Jaci is going to kill me for this."

Alan shrugged. "Let them come along. We'll be back before dark."

THAT MORNING, the search party followed their own tracks back to the spot where they'd lost Raven's trail the previous night. But the only visible tracks were the ones left after the rain. Raven's, left before the rain storm, were washed away.

They spread out, about fifty yards apart, searching and calling her name. Around noon, they ate the boiled eggs and potatoes Mom had sent along for lunch, saving a few for Raven. Then they continued on, searching all afternoon.

They found no sign of her.

As the sun sank low on the horizon, they were miles from home.

"I'm sorry, Willow, but we have to turn back," Alan said. "It'll be dark soon, and we haven't seen a single footprint of hers today."

"So you want to give up?" Willow's voice quaked. For the past hour, she'd sensed that their search was fruitless, but she couldn't admit it.

Couldn't believe it.

"We can try again tomorrow," Clark said, laying a big hand on her shoulder. "I need to get my girls home."

Willow glanced at Jacob. He said nothing, just gave her a sad look and a shrug.

"Just ten more minutes," Willow said. "She's out here somewhere!"

Twenty minutes later, the sun began to dip behind the mountains. Clark and Alan exchanged a significant look.

"Willow." Clark's dark eyes fixed on hers, his accent evident in every word. "We must return. It will be dark soon."

She looked away and lowered her head. A branch lay in front of her feet, and she kicked at it.

"Okay." Her voice was barely audible. "Lead the way."

Clark took the lead, with Delia at his side. Behind him walked Alan and Beth, with Willow and Jacob bringing up the rear.

Tears obscured her vision. She'd failed her best friend.

Would she ever see her again?

Or had she fallen into a ravine, or been killed by wolves or cougars or a bear? Even when times were good and search teams were equipped with ATVs, drones and technology, plenty of folks got lost in the wilderness and were never found.

She stumbled over a root and fell, scraping her hands. The procession stopped. Jacob reached out a hand to help her up.

"Just leave me alone!" She sobbed, her tears falling freely now. She slumped forward, the ashy earth cold and indifferent to her misery.

"Just leave me here," she whispered.

Yes, she knew it was irrational. But at the moment, her grief was so deep she didn't care. As she cried, she heard Jacob speak quietly to the others.

"Go on ahead. We'll catch up."

Footsteps fell as they moved away. After a minute, she sat up and wiped her cheeks. A few feet away, she saw Jacob's boots and pants legs. She didn't look up to his face. Couldn't bear what she might find there, whether it was pity or loathing or concern. Whatever it was, she didn't want to see it.

Taking a deep breath, she stood up.

"Let's go," she mumbled.

He fell in beside her, and together they hurried to catch up with the group.

The sun set, and twilight left the forest in its grey shadow. Then dusk turned to darkness, but by then they were close enough to the cabin that Willow recognized the landscape and was able to lead them home.

First, they stopped at the new cabin. Jaci flung open the door as they approached.

"Oh, thank goodness!" She wrapped her arms around Beth, then Delia. "I was so worried!"

Her eyes scanned the group. "Raven?"

Clark shook his head. "Not yet."

"I'm sorry." She looked sadly at Willow, then hugged her husband. Her dad moved toward the door.

"Wait!" Jaci blocked the entrance. "I think you all should go to the other cabin tonight. Tony has a real bad cough. I don't want anybody to catch it."

"What about you?" Clark asked, concern in his voice. "You could catch it."

"I've already been exposed. No sense in anybody else exposing themselves." She kissed his cheek. "Besides, Laura made us a Vitamin C concoction from rose hips, so Tony and I are both boosting our immune systems. Plus, he's drinking usnea tea from a lichen he calls 'old man's beard' – smells gross, but I guess it's got antibiotics."

"I will go lay hands on him and pray for him," Clark said, slipping past her. A minute later, he returned.

Inside, Uncle Tony coughed, a deep heavy cough that sent him into a coughing fit.

"Sounds like a chest cold, or bronchitis," Alan said. "Jaci's right, we should take the girls down to the other cabin."

"And you guys stay there," Jaci insisted. "I don't want my men catching this, either!"

She hugged her dad and kissed her husband. "Now, off you go!"

They started down the trail, with Willow's heart sinking lower and lower. Raven still missing, maybe dead. Uncle Tony still alive, but very sick. All of it, her fault.

She was bad luck. Or a curse on the group. If she had anywhere to go, she'd leave and spare everyone any more grief.

They reached the cabin, and she trudged inside.

Mom had saved some dinner for the search party, and her eyes scanned the faces as they came into the cabin. Somber faces. Without Raven. Her gaze came to rest on Willow's face.

The sympathy in Mom's eyes nearly killed her. Willow averted her gaze so she wouldn't burst into tears.

At least Josh and Matt were back. They hadn't been killed by wolves or anything.

After Alan and Clark told the group about their unsuccessful day, Josh and Matt told everyone about their experience going to the Andersons the previous evening.

"I shot at a wolf!" Matt said, his eyes fixed on Delia.

"What?!" She and her sister exclaimed in unison.

"It's true," Josh said. "On the way over, just as it was getting dark, we heard wolves. And they were close!"

Mom's hand fluttered to her chest as she watched her son's excited rendition.

"And then we saw them," he continued. "First, Matt saw one, then I saw another one."

"Maybe a hundred yards across a burned out area," Matt added. "They stopped howling, and started moving toward us."

"Just two?" Jacob asked.

"Well, there was probably a whole pack around there," Matt said. "But we only saw two."

"So, when they started moving toward us, we had to do something," Josh added.

"So I took aim at the closest one, and fired," Matt said. "I think I hit the ground right in front of its paws. Anyway, it turned and ran."

"And we hurried to the Andersons, watching our backs the whole way!" Josh said.

"In the dark," Matt added.

"My goodness!" Mom exclaimed. "It's a good thing you have strong guardian angels!"

"Totally," Josh agreed. "But that's not all!"

"Not even close." Matt took a moment, as if making sure he had everyone's attention. "Some looters were scoping out the Andersons' place, and we saw them and ran them off!"

"WHAT?" Now Mom looked truly alarmed.

"Yep!" Josh grinned at her, then turned his eyes on Clark, and his words began rushing out in a torrent. "Remember those guys we saw coming up the road when we were all out scavenging at that one house, with John? The ones that went in the driveway where we were?"

Clark nodded. "Of course."

"Well, those were the same ones!" Josh sent a quick glance Beth's direction, and seemingly satisfied, continued. "Four of them, with empty packs. Matt and I saw them this morning, in the trees just behind the barn, scoping the place with binoculars. We ran them off!"

Mom's face paled. "Thank God you're okay!"

"Yeah, well, John was pretty upset," Matt said.

"Yeah, well, we would be, too!" Willow interjected, only slightly mockingly. She turned to Jacob. "Maybe they *will* be happy to have you come over and help guard the place."

He nodded soberly before speaking.

"Sounds like they could use some extra help. There's only four of them, and they have to sleep sometime." He looked at Danny with concern in his eyes. "It might be more dangerous over there."

"It's dangerous everywhere," Willow said. "But you can leave him here, if you want. For a while, anyway."

"I'll give it some thought." He appeared a little sad as he spoke. "First, though, I want to take another day to search for Raven. Who knows, maybe I can pick up her trail tomorrow."

"I'll be going, too," Willow said.

"There's one more thing," Matt said. "John wants to make another scavenging trip. He still needs oil and gas for the chainsaws."

"And we need all kinds of stuff," Mom said. "But with those other scavengers running around, it's not safe, and the empty homes are likely to be picked clean."

Slowly, faces began to turn toward Willow.

"We need to pray about it," she said, finally. "I hope you'll all do that tonight and tomorrow. We can discuss it over dinner tomorrow night."

13

Marcus stepped carefully through the dark field, keeping his flashlight beam on the ground just ahead of his feet. Soren Stein walked to his left, and Josh Miller was on his right. The rookie, Dalton Carlson, trailed a few yards behind them.

The full moon, dimmed by the high grey overcast, barely illuminated the barn and farmhouse ahead of them.

Stein stopped, and the others halted too.

"What?" Marcus whispered.

"Turn off your lights," Stein hissed.

The flashlights blinked out. Marcus waited for his eyes to adjust to the darkness.

"I thought I saw a light in that upper window," Stein said. "Just for a second, then it was gone."

"Let's get around behind the barn, then!" Marcus started moving. "We're sitting ducks out here!"

Moments later, they reached the back of the barn.

"I'm going in." Stein reached for the latch on the rear door.

"Right behind you," Marcus said. "Miller, you're with us. Carlson, keep watch out here."

Inside, the barn smelled of sweet hay and cow manure. Marcus flicked on his light. Its beam caught the huge eyeballs of a Jersey cow.

In the next stall, a horse snorted. Marcus turned his light that way. A big blue roan tossed its head, its nostrils flared.

At the front of the barn, some chickens clucked as their sleep was disturbed.

"It's like Christmas!" Stein breathed. "We've struck the mother lode!"

"We can't just take all their animals," Miller said.

"Sure, we can," Stein retorted. "I'll ride the horse, you can lead the cow, and the other guys can round up the chickens."

"And leave nothing here? You want to steal everything this family has?"

"What about your own family?" Stein scoffed. "You want them to starve?"

"Don't be an idiot! I'm just saying, maybe we can take some of the chickens." Miller swung his light around. "And maybe the cow."

"You didn't even want to come with us! Now you want to sabotage our scavenging!"

"This isn't scavenging!" Miller hissed. "This is theft!"

"Okay, that's enough." Marcus stepped between them. "You two start fighting, and you're gonna wake up the folks in the house, if they're not awake already, and we'll all get shot."

"I'm taking the horse." Stein found a halter, bridle and other tack hanging opposite the stall. "You guys get whatever you want."

Miller stared at the cow. "Melanie would love to have some milk and cream for the children."

"Bring the cow, then," Marcus said. "I'm going to round up some chickens."

The chickens began waking up and didn't want to be

rounded up. Marcus grabbed one and tucked it under his arm. He reached for another, and got a sharp peck for his efforts.

The clucking turned to squawking.

A huge bird flew straight at his face. Marcus flung his arms to shield himself, releasing the one hen he'd caught.

He batted away a big red rooster, but not before it had put its spurs to use, scratching his cheek and slicing his hand.

A string of obscenities flew from his mouth as pain ripped through his hand.

The big rooster circled around for a second attempt, and Marcus kicked at it.

The chickens were in a full uproar now, squawking like banshees.

"Make them shut up!" Stein growled. "They're gonna wake the dead."

"Or get us shot dead," Miller said.

The back door swung open, and the rookie stepped inside.

"Gotta go! I'm seeing flashlights in the house!"

Stein shoved the bit in the horse's mouth and leapt onto its bare back. "Open that door wide, Carlson!"

He leaned low over the horse's neck to clear the door frame.

Marcus gave up on the chickens. He headed toward the back.

"You got that cow, Miller?"

"She won't budge!" Miller had the stall gate open, and was putting all his weight into dragging the cow toward it.

"Gotta go! NOW!" Carlson yelled from the rear of the barn. "They're coming!"

"Leave her!" Marcus ran toward the exit. Miller's footsteps pounded the floor behind him. Stein's horse thundered away in the distance.

They burst through the door and sprinted toward the cover of the trees behind the pasture. Rookie Carlson, perhaps a dozen yards ahead, ran like his pants were on fire.

A shot rang out.

Marcus was nearly to the trees. He poured on the speed.

Another shot. This one seared his left arm.

Three more strides, and he was in the forest. He darted behind a big pine. Somewhere in the darkness, a horse galloped away.

Ahead, Carlson crashed through the brush deeper in the forest.

Miller?

He'd been right behind Marcus.

"Miller!" he hissed. "Miller!"

No response. Marcus's left arm felt warm. His sleeve was wet.

The wound was on the outside of his arm, halfway between his shoulder and elbow. It hurt like the dickens.

He let out a low curse.

A moan rose from the pasture, maybe a dozen yards back.

"Miller?"

Another moan.

A flashlight flicked on, then off, behind the barn. The residents were smart. Checking what they had to, but not leaving their lights on. It made them harder to target.

How many were there?

Would they see Marcus if he came back out to grab Miller and drag him to safety? If they saw him, they'd surely shoot him. Again.

WILLOW'S NIGHT was filled with nightmares. Every time she woke up, she prayed for Raven. Morning brought little relief, but she was glad to stop dreaming.

Maybe Jacob was right. Maybe they'd find her today.

Since Uncle Tony was sick and Jaci had sent her family down

to stay in Willow's cabin, the tiny one-room home was filled to the rafters. And noisy when everyone woke up and rolled out of bed. Clark, Deborah and Alan walked up to check on Jaci and Tony, and had news when they returned.

"He's on the mend," Deborah announced with a big smile. "Still has a cough, but Jaci says he slept quietly and his color is better. She says he's almost well."

A great sigh of relief escaped Willow's lungs. She sent a silent prayer of thanks heavenward.

"Praise the Lord!" Mom said. "That's great news!"

"Now, if we can just find Raven," Willow added. "Everybody keep praying for that! And about another scavenging run with the Andersons."

They got an early start searching for Raven that morning. Willow prayed as she walked. For Raven's safety, and that they'd find her quickly.

Mom and Deborah had stayed at the homestead to care for the animals and the little children, while Jaci was taking care of Uncle Tony.

Willow glanced upward. The sky was grey, the same weird high overcast that it had been ever since the volcanic ash fall days earlier. She hadn't seen a blue sky or normal clouds since that happened.

She studied the sky and thought back to her freshman earth science class. If volcanic particles were trapped in the upper atmosphere, how long would it take until they settled out? If they were too high, they wouldn't fall with normal rain, which formed lower.

This ugly sky could be around for a long time. And worse, the temperatures had dropped significantly more than normal for this time of year. Days were much cooler, and nights were downright cold for early September.

Willow led the group northward again, and eventually split

up the search party, with Alan, Clark, Matt and Delia heading northwest, and herself, Jacob, Josh and Beth heading northeast.

"Everybody meet back here at this spot before the sun sets," Willow said. "We'll all walk home together. With Raven, hopefully!"

Willow and her group spread out about eighty yards apart, looking and calling Raven's name. They crossed into the area where the forest fire had burned, but soon re-entered the non-burned areas.

The ash was deep in the burned area, and Willow doubted Raven would have traveled there. Especially considering the ground obstacles of downed, burned trees and broken off stumps. It looked like a war zone, filled with black ash and covered with lighter grey volcanic ash.

Uninhabitable. Barren. Desolate.

Pale light illuminated the living forest. Willow ducked under branches and walked around brush, calling Raven's name until her voice was hoarse. Her stomach whined, then growled.

Finally, she called a halt for a late lunch.

Jacob stared at the potatoes as she handed them out. He accepted his like it was a golden coin, then took a huge bite.

"Hey!" Josh objected. "What about the blessing?"

Jacob looked embarrassed as he chewed. "Sorry."

"I guess you get to ask the blessing, then," Josh said.

"No. You go ahead."

Willow watched him. What was that expression – confusion? Remorse? Uncertainty? Whatever it was, she didn't think she'd seen it on him before, and why now, when he was just asked to bless the food?

Josh began praying, and Willow closed her eyes.

When she opened them, she looked at Jacob. Whatever it was, was gone. And he glanced her way, catching her watching him. She averted her gaze and bit into her potato.

"We need to decide how much longer we can keep going, if we're gonna get back to the meet up spot before sunset," Jacob said.

Willow turned it over in her mind. To be safe, they should plan to meet the others around six o'clock. They had split up about three hours ago.

"I think we can do another hour," she finally said. They wouldn't be able to cover much ground in that time.

She prayed, again, that Raven would turn up. Then she urged her group to finish eating, so they could get on with the search.

An hour later, Jacob reminded her they needed to turn back.

They hadn't seen a trace of Raven.

She led her group about a quarter mile west, so they were in an area that hadn't been searched yet, then they spread out and began moving south toward the point where they'd meet the others.

Her heart felt like lead.

She called Raven's name every few minutes, until she was fully hoarse.

Where could she possibly be?

Perhaps the other group had found her. She hoped so. Her eyes turned heavenward.

Oh, please, God! Let them find her. Help us find her!

Right at sunset, they reached the meet up location. A few minutes later, the other party arrived.

Without Raven.

Oxygen escaped Willow's lungs and she sank to her knees in the grey ash. Where could she be? She covered her face with her hands as tears filled her eyes.

They'd searched for days, with no sign of her.

They couldn't keep doing this. Her group had to get ready

for winter. Which by the looks of it, would be very early this year.

But where was Raven?

How could she vanish without a trace?

And why hadn't God brought her home?

She sniffled. A warm hand fell on her shoulder. She blinked and saw the boots. Josh's. A good brother, sometimes.

He patted her shoulder awkwardly.

She needed to pull it together. Get her group home safe before dark.

She coughed, then sputtered, then wiped her eyes with her sleeve. Taking a deep breath, she took the hand Josh offered and let him pull her up. Compassion and pity filled his gentle brown eyes, sending her into a tailspin.

Quickly, she looked away, but not before a fresh round of tears raced to the surface.

Turning away from the group, she focused on taking deep breaths and calming herself. She had to get it together. She swallowed and blinked, then turned around.

"Okay," she whispered. "Let's go home."

As they hiked back, Jacob made a point of staying close to Willow, but not so close she'd notice and be annoyed. He just wanted to be close enough to lend a hand if she tripped or slipped in the darkening forest.

Raven was gone. She'd been so mad at Willow when she left the day he'd arrived, but she'd told him she was going for a run.

She'd never intended to be gone very long.

Now, it appeared she might be gone forever.

Vanished without a trace.

He called out her name, just in case she was near enough to

hear them. Josh echoed her name a moment later, followed by Alan. Then, silence.

Willow tried to call her, but just choked out a hoarse whisper. She'd been calling and calling, until she wiped out her voice.

It was sad. He'd really liked Raven. She, unlike Willow, was always nice. Friendly and pleasant and smiling, her perfect teeth setting off her bronze face and bright brown eyes. That's how he wanted to remember her, not mad like she was when she took off.

Although Willow carried more weight on her shoulders because she'd taken on leadership of the group, she could afford to be more pleasant. It was as if her concerns and burdens made her hostile and suspicious, rather than just cautious and careful.

Still, he had to admire her tenacity and leadership skills. Until recently, she'd done a good job keeping her group together and on task.

As far as he knew, the only older adult to really challenge her role of leader had been Matt's mom, who got killed. Maybe Candy had challenged her a little, too – those two seemed to have some other issue he'd never figured out – but she hadn't challenged Willow very much.

No, it was like Willow was a modern-day Joan of Arc, getting her instructions straight from God and guiding her followers accordingly. And, they'd done pretty well with that, considering the state of the world.

Maybe that's why the other adults pretty much let her lead. Even her mom, which did seem a little odd. Except that Willow was already the established leader for some months before Laura arrived. And Laura had to recognize that Willow was special.

She was gifted.

Everyone could see that.

Now, though, she trudged hang-dog toward home. The few times she lifted her face, it was filled with grief, mixed with despair. Failure.

Hopefully, she could overcome that. Maybe Jacob didn't depend on her, but everyone else did.

She'd have to pull it together to get her group ready for winter.

In the meantime, he had his own problems to figure out. Number one – should he go live with the Andersons? If so, should he take Danny with him, or would the kid be safer in the wilderness with Willow's group?

Number two – these were all Christians. And Jacob wasn't, really. After his parents were killed in an accident, he'd been adopted by his aunt and uncle, Jewish converts to Christianity. Jacob didn't see himself as religious, so he'd put off a decision about all that.

He stepped around a tree, ducking under the branches.

No, in reality, he had made a decision – to live as he liked, until he changed his mind about religion. The only reason he hadn't gotten the mark was because his adoptive parents were so freaked out that it was the "mark of the beast" in the Bible.

If they were right, and he got it, he'd drop straight into hell when he died.

So he'd put that off, at significant personal risk, the same way he'd put off the religion thing.

Eventually, though, he might be pressed to make decisions. Major ones. Because he couldn't live in this limbo state forever.

And, if he was honest with himself, he didn't want to.

After dinner, when everyone wandered off to do their own thing, Willow sat alone with her thoughts in front of the fire ring. The fire had died down to coals, flickering red and glowing orange. The growth rings in the wood stood out brightly in the coals, thin and evenly spaced, and curved like trout bones. It was as if they were highlighted by heat into red neon lines in each coal.

She sighed. Wanted to pray, wanted to ask God where Raven was and why he hadn't answered their prayers and brought her home, but she couldn't.

All she could do at the moment was stare at the coals and wallow in her misery.

"Hey." Mom's soft voice and warm touch on her shoulder pulled her attention upward.

"Hey." Willow's voice was still hoarse.

Mom sat down beside her. She pulled Willow's hair away from her face and draped it over her shoulder.

Now she was exposed to Mom's inspecting gaze. Willow refused to meet those eyes, though. She stared harder at the dying coals.

Mom rubbed her back.

"You did your best."

Willow's mouth puckered and her eyes clamped down. No more tears! No more!

In spite of her efforts, a sob escaped, and she let herself be drawn into Mom's arms. There, she cried freely. Couldn't help it.

"I'm drowning you," she gurgled as her tears soaked Mom's shoulder.

"Not the first time." Mom hugged her tighter.

"It's all my fault!" Willow wailed in her hoarsest voice. "I was so stupid!"

"You have to let it go, honey. Give it to the Lord." Her fingers smoothed Willow's hair. "Give her to the Lord."

"My best friend," Willow sobbed. "Oh, Mom!"

Mom rocked her gently as she cried herself out, her breath coming in ragged gasps between her sobs. Finally she calmed enough to speak.

"I'll never forgive myself," she whispered.

"You will. You have to."

Eventually, Willow spent all her emotion. She pulled out of Mom's embrace, taking her hand and giving it a squeeze. Though Mom was silent, Willow knew she was praying. She could feel the peace and comfort seeping into her from her mother's prayers.

Together, they watched the fire's embers.

Until Jacob came over and sat near them. Willow bit her tongue. What did he want now?

Finally, he spoke.

"I've been thinking."

Slowly, Willow's eyes found his face in the dim orange light cast by the dying fire.

"About what?"

"Well, first, about the scavenging trip. We were going to discuss that tonight, but –"

"Doh!" Willow winced. "I forgot."

"It can wait until tomorrow," Mom said. "There's no rush."

"Sure," Jacob agreed. The orange glow reflected in his brown eyes. "Also, I've been thinking about Danny. And the Andersons."

"And?" Willow watched his face. Something was bothering him. She could see it as he turned his gaze to the fire.

"I'm not sure what to do. I think Danny might be safer here, because you're off the road system."

"You can leave him with us," she said. "No problem."

His shoulders relaxed.

"Good." A moment later, he added, "Thank you."

Willow almost smiled. "You're welcome."

She noticed Mom watching Jacob, her sharp eyes studying him. She put two fingers over her lips as her gaze moved across his face. Then she folded her hands in her lap.

"Jacob." Mom's voice was soft, but Willow knew that tone. It was direct. Mom was onto something. "How's your spiritual life?"

"What?" His reply was sharp, his tone higher than normal. "What do you mean?"

"Your prayers. I never see you read your Bible."

"You haven't been around me much," he said.

But Mom was like a terrier with a bone. She wasn't dropping it.

"Are you a believer?"

Willow's breath stopped.

What? She stared at Jacob. He turned his eyes to the embers. *What?!*

He didn't have the mark. Surely he must be a believer! Finally she found her breath.

But Jacob didn't answer. Mom fixed him with her trade-marked gaze, the one that always made Willow and Josh squirm.

Willow expected a retort. Or maybe he'd jump up and leave in a huff.

But strangely, he just sat there. Willow stared. What was going on?

His Adam's apple bobbed.

"Not exactly," he admitted, his eyes fixed on the coals.

A cold chill ran through Willow's body, starting at the back of her neck and working its way down her spine.

A nonbeliever! A traitor in their midst! She'd known she couldn't trust him, she'd known it all along!

But now what? He was here, and he knew all about her group's secrets. Location, supplies, food storage, weapons....

The air leaked out of her lungs.

Still, he didn't have the mark. Raven had checked. And he hadn't betrayed them yet, as far as Willow knew. She sucked in a breath.

"Would you like to be?" Mom asked. Willow's eyes veered toward her. Then back to Jacob.

"I've been thinking about it." His voice was low, almost a whisper.

Willow couldn't wrap her mind around this. Jacob wasn't a Christian! No wonder she'd had so many doubts about him!

"You know, Jesus says, 'Today is the day of salvation.' If you hear Him, don't harden your heart. You don't know what tomorrow may bring," Mom continued. "Especially now, when life is so precarious. If Raven died, she went straight to Heaven. Where would you go?"

His eyes turned toward Mom.

"If there's a Hell, I might go there. According to my aunt, anyway. She raised me and preached at me a lot."

"You'll certainly go to one place or the other. And the only

way to go to Heaven is to accept Jesus here, before you die."
Mom's voice softened. "I can show you how."

Jacob's gaze flickered to Willow, then shot back to Mom.

"I really have been thinking about it."

"Don't put it off," Mom urged. "It's the most important and
best decision you'll ever make. Do it now."

"Right now? Here?" Jacob asked. "I mean, shouldn't it be in a
church or something?"

"No. Right here," Mom said. "This is the perfect place, the
perfect time."

Jacob's gaze turned to Willow, and she felt like an intruder.
Maybe she should leave and give them a little privacy.

But she couldn't pull herself away from this moment. The
experience was too momentous. She wished she could be invisible. Her spirit began praying for Jacob's.

Jacob's eyes turned back to Mom. "How do I accept Jesus?"

Mom explained the story of Nicodemus and being born
again. She told Jacob that he should recognize and confess that
he was a sinner, that he believed Jesus was the Son of God and
had given his life on the cross for Jacob's sins and had risen to
life again, and Jacob should ask Jesus to be his savior and come
into his life.

"Romans chapter ten, verses nine and ten say, 'that if you
confess with your mouth the Lord Jesus and believe in your
heart that God has raised Him from the dead, you will be saved.
For with the heart one believes unto righteousness, and with the
mouth confession is made unto salvation.'"

Mom paused. "Do you believe that Jesus is God? That he
died for your sins?"

Jacob stared into the coals. "I do think he is God. I don't like
the sin part."

"That you commit sin? Or that he died for your sins?"
Mom asked.

"Both?" Jacob expelled a big sigh. "I know I'm a sinner. No doubt about it. But I hate thinking God died because of *my* sins."

"It's a hard truth," Mom agreed. "But if you accept it, you'll eventually come to see it as a beautiful truth. His love for you was – is – so deep and overwhelming, he would die to save you."

Jacob pressed his lips together and nodded. Finally, he turned to Mom.

"How could I reject a sacrifice like that?"

"Exactly!" Mom smiled. "Are you ready now?"

He nodded again, then spoke slowly.

"Yes. I believe I am."

As he prayed with Mom, tears seeped down Willow's face for the umpteenth time. This time, though, at least they were happy ones.

The angels rejoiced that night, and so did she. And for the first time all week, she fell right asleep moments after her head hit her fluffy new pillow.

MARCUS, Stein and the rookie were armed for war when they hiked back to that farm again. They each carried a rifle, two handguns, and practically enough ammo for a small infantry unit.

Marcus had told his guys he didn't know what happened to Miller, that he'd yelled for Miller but got no response. Stein had ridden off, and Carlson had run off, and Marcus himself was shot. So, getting no response, and seeing the residents headed his way, he'd retreated.

That was all they needed to know, anyway.

Melanie had spent the whole day crying, and the kids picked up on that and joined her. It grated on his nerves and disrupted the sleep he was trying to get.

His wound wasn't bad. Just a flesh wound. Stein had cleaned and dressed it. Then he'd offered to try stitches, but Marcus had passed on that and got butterfly bandages instead.

So now, they closed in on the farm from the forest, coming up behind the barn in the dark. Marcus had said they needed to come in this way for concealment, but it was also because that's where he hoped they'd find Miller, if he was still out there.

Again, the moon, though just past full, barely helped. That grey overcast dimmed the world.

They paused at the edge of the trees.

"Okay, let's go over this again," Marcus said. "We're gonna find Miller, and take the cow and the chickens. That's it."

"Roger that." Stein swung his rifle off his shoulder and gripped it with both hands.

"Got it," Carlson said.

"Okay, then. Nice and slow." Marcus stepped into the pasture. "And spread out a little, in case anyone takes another shot at us."

Miller couldn't be far. Marcus flicked his flashlight on, swinging it over the grass, then turned it off again.

The other guys, not knowing what happened to Miller, were striding toward the barn, their lights off.

Marcus flicked his light on again.

There! Twenty feet ahead, Miller's red hair blazed in the bright light.

"Guys!" Marcus hissed. "Get back here! Got something!"

The men reversed course and hustled toward him. Marcus strode toward Miller. He lay on his stomach, blackened blood crusted on the back of his flannel shirt. Lifeless eyes stared at the earth, and his mouth gaped.

Stein let out a string of profanities.

Carlson knelt down, feeling for a pulse.

"He's gone, you idiot!" Marcus growled. "Close his eyes."

He couldn't bear the sight of those dead eyes. They screamed silent accusations and curses. Miller had never wanted to come scavenging. He'd wanted to stay home and take care of his family. And now he was dead. Because Marcus had left him there to die.

Stein whirled toward the house. "I'm gonna kill those –"

"Now hold on!" Marcus grabbed his arm. "Let's think this through."

"There's nothing to think about." Stein yanked away from him. "They killed Miller, now they're gonna die!"

Stein glared at Carlson. "You coming, rookie?"

With a curse, Carlson stood up and strode toward the house. Stein overtook him and moved into the lead.

This was gonna happen. Marcus couldn't stop it. And maybe he didn't really want to.

Stein and Carlson took positions at the back door of the house, so Marcus went around to the front door. Ten seconds later, he heard them bash through the door and enter the home. He took a firing stance a few yards from the front door and waited.

A man shouted.

A woman screamed.

More shouts, then a shot fired. Then lots more screaming.

His heart pounded way too fast. His hands trembled. He stared at the door in the dark, waiting for the slightest movement of the handle.

Stein yelled inside. Carlson responded.

Good. Both his guys were still alive.

The woman wailed, piercing, heart-rending shrieks.

Marcus sidled up to the door and tried the knob. Locked. He'd wait a little longer.

A single pair of footsteps thudded around in the house. Probably one of his guys, clearing the other rooms. Or possibly a loose subject, running around in there. The footsteps stopped near his door.

He backed away three paces and got ready.

"Laramie! You out there?"

That was Stein.

"Yeah!"

"Don't shoot!"

He heard the deadbolt turn, then the handle. The door swung in, and Stein stood there, gun and flashlight in hand.

"Two alive, plus one nearly dead upstairs," Stein barked. "I haven't found the basement yet."

"Take the lead," Marcus said, stepping in beside his officer. "The rookie has the ones upstairs?"

"Yeah. Good training for him."

Marcus flipped on his light, and the two made their way down a hall, checking the rest of the rooms but finding no one. There was some old mail on a desk addressed to Thomas and Mary Smith. And a magazine addressed to Tom Smith, Jr.

Which one had killed Miller? Thomas or Tom? Or maybe Mary? Marcus clenched his jaw. One of them, that was for sure! And Stein would make sure they paid for it.

Moments later, they found a doorway with stairs to the basement, so they scuttled down.

No one was there. The basement held a family room, a storage room and an area with dusty exercise equipment.

Returning to the main floor, Marcus paid more attention to the home's layout. He followed Stein through the hall to the stairs that went up to the second floor. A cross hung on the wall at the top of the staircase.

There was an empty bedroom, a second bedroom with a guy in his thirties bleeding out on the floor, and a master bedroom with a couple who might be in their early sixties. They were kneeling on the rug beside the bed, their hands shaking in the air.

Carlson held them at gunpoint, his bright light making their skin appear ghostly pale. The woman, in a cotton nightgown, sobbed bitterly. The man beside her wore a white t-shirt and a pair of shorts.

Stein stormed into the room.

"Which one of you killed Officer Miller last night?" he demanded.

The man squinted in the bright light, but looked surprised.

"I don't think anybody killed anybody," he said. "Are you police?"

"Josh Miller is dead behind your barn! You shot him last night!"

A flash of recognition registered on the man's face.

"We shot at some thieves. They stole our horse."

Stein rushed toward him, leveling his gun at the guy's eyes. "You shot an officer of the law!"

The man glanced toward his wife and said nothing.

"What I want to know, is who shot Miller!" Marcus seethed. "Was it you, or that dying guy down the hall?"

The woman sobbed and rocked forward.

"Or maybe it was your wife, here?" Marcus turned the gun on her.

"No!" The man reached toward the woman.

"Keep your hands up!" The rookie yelled.

The man's hands lifted toward the ceiling. "No, it was our son."

The woman yelped as if she'd been kicked. She glared at the man through her tears.

"Go see if he's still alive," Marcus ordered Carlson.

He skittered out of the room and down the hall, returning a moment later.

"Nope." The rookie took position, his gun trained on the man. "Dead as a doornail."

The woman wailed at the ceiling.

"Shut up!" Stein stuck his gun in her face. "Or I'll shut you up!"

The woman closed her mouth, sobs burbling in her throat. Her cheeks were shiny with her tears. Her eyes shifted toward the wall.

Marcus swung his flashlight to the point where she was looking.

A white cross hung there.

"They're Christians," he muttered.

"WHAT?" Stein's voice rose an octave. "Check their hands, Carlson!"

The rookie rushed forward, grabbed their right hands and checked.

"No chip," he said. "Neither one!"

Stein rocked back on his heels. "Now, this is gonna get good!"

RAVEN HOBBLED toward the dark house, leaning heavily on her makeshift walking stick. Her ankle, now eggplant purple, had swollen to twice its normal size. She was beyond exhausted, beyond famished. But at last, she'd walked out of the forest.

She dragged herself onto the porch and pounded on the door with her stick.

It might get her killed, but she didn't care. If this didn't work, she'd probably just lie down and die anyway.

Movement and rustling in the house told her someone was home.

"Who is it?" A gruff voice demanded.

Good. He still lived here. Raven almost smiled.

"It's Raven! Open up, you nuthatch!"

The door flew open.

"Get in here, you idiot!" Her cousin's voice thundered. "What in tarnation are you doing way out here?"

She limped inside. "Got lost."

"You look like death. How long you been out there?" His eyes scanned the forest before he shut the door.

"Four days?" Raven hobbled to the sofa and collapsed onto it. "I'm starving."

"Everybody's starving." Denis lit the stub of a candle in a holder on the coffee table. He stared at her in the flickering light.

He puffed out his chest.

"Lucky for you, I snared a rabbit."

Raven lifted her feet onto the sofa. Pain shot up her leg.

The room spun for a second before everything went black.

15

Willow stepped out of the cabin. Another grey day. And cold. She glanced at Mom, who was carrying a bucket of water from the creek.

"Mom, what's up with the sky? Think we'll ever see the sun again?"

"I'm not sure." Mom set the bucket on the ground and turned her face upward. "There are some prophecies in the Bible about the weird things that happen in the end times."

"Yeah, I know... the great earthquake, the sun turns black, the moon becomes like blood, stars fall to the earth – but I don't think there's anything about the sky turns grey."

Mom sighed. "Maybe a great earthquake set off a massive volcano. It's happened before. They called it the year without a summer."

"Great." Willow patted Gilligan, who pressed against her knee. "Our summer is over, all the sudden."

"And we might be in for a dark, cold winter." Mom picked up the bucket and went inside.

"Great," Willow said again, to herself. "That's just great."

Her eyes turned to the edge of the clearing, searching the trees for any sign of Raven. A sad sigh slipped from her lips.

"Penny for your thoughts."

She whirled. Jacob had come up behind her.

"Sheesh, Jacob! You could get shot, sneaking up on people like that."

"There was no sneaking involved. You were just standing there, staring into space, and you didn't hear me. Obviously." He cocked his head and studied her. "What were you thinking about?"

She frowned. "Raven."

"Yeah." He turned and looked toward the mountains, then patted Gilligan. "I thought so."

"I want to keep looking for her, but...." Willow shoved her hands in her pockets and didn't finish her sentence.

"But we haven't seen hide nor hair of her, and we need to be focused on getting ready for winter." He glanced at her. "That about sum it up?"

She nodded. "Yeah."

"So... this prayer thing is new to me, but I've been praying for her."

Willow looked into his eyes. "You have?"

"Sure. I mean, maybe I'm not doing it right, but – "

A smile crept across Willow's face. "You can't do it wrong. Prayer is just talking to God. Like you're talking to me."

"I do *that* wrong all the time!" He grinned, and she laughed.

"God is more patient than I am," she said.

"Everybody is more patient than you are." But he winked when he said it.

"Maybe you're right." Willow looked again toward the forest. Jacob was quick to point out all her faults, but he usually did it lightheartedly. Maybe it was God's way of holding up a mirror in front of her.

Anyway, Jacob was a Christian now. Maybe he'd shape up and be tolerable.

Going forward, maybe she'd be able to trust him.

"So..." He nudged a dirt clod with his boot. "Are we going scavenging with John?"

"I've been praying about that." She glanced sideways at him. "Have you?"

"Man, there's a lot of stuff to pray about when you become a Christian!"

"I'll take that as a no."

"Not yet," he admitted.

"Well, I think we'll be going. Tomorrow. So I'll need someone to run over to talk to John about it today, to make sure tomorrow works for him." She watched his face. "You want to do that? They're living right down the road from their original retreat, in the house where the ninjas held you captive."

He shrugged. "I guess I could."

"And that brings up Danny. What do you want to do with him? And are you going to move over to John and Jeannie's, or are you going to stay with us?"

He didn't meet her gaze. "Is that an option?"

"Staying?"

Jacob nodded.

"I guess so," she said. "Now that you're a believer."

"There's a lot to think about."

"And *pray* about."

"Right." He turned and stretched, his muscles rippling as he moved. "I guess I can think and pray as I hike over to talk to John."

"Good." She started toward the cabin door. "Try to be back by dinner."

∽

Willow's group rose early the next morning. Matt, Josh, and Jacob wanted to join her for the scavenging run, as did Clark. Alan and Deborah planned to work on the root cellar with Jaci, Delia and Beth. Mom would stay home and watch the little kids. Uncle Tony was still recuperating, and decided to take the day off.

"I'll be up to snuff tomorrow," he said. "Today, I'm gonna be a lazy bones and snooze like a bear."

The sky was dark grey as Willow set out with her team. By the time they reached the Andersons' place, a breeze had picked up, cutting through her jacket. She eyed the ominous sky.

"Hope it's not gonna rain on us," she said.

"Sure is cold!" Josh zipped up his coat. "Feels like October!"

"Or November," Matt said.

John came out of his house dressed for winter, with gloves and a hat. Willow grinned. It seemed a bit early for all that. But at least he'd stay warm. She was chilled already.

"So, I scouted out a place about a mile down the road," he said. "Pretty sure it's vacant."

He untied his bay gelding from a hitching post he'd set up beside the house. The horse was already saddled up.

"Julie is coming with us, but Mike is staying back with Jeannie." He led the horse to the driveway. "We had those looters hanging around the other day, when Matt and Josh were here."

"Have they come back?" Willow reached up and patted the gelding's neck. He took a step closer and nuzzled her arm.

"I haven't seen them, but I can't be sure."

She could understand his concern. She'd be really unhappy if strangers were scoping out her cabin. Actually, unhappy would be an understatement! She'd be spitting mad, plus worried sick. Something would be done about it, that's for sure.

Julie came out the front door in a heavy black cardigan and blue jeans, with an empty pack on her back. She smiled shyly and said hello to Willow and her group. And that was all she said. She was probably the quietest person Willow had ever met.

"Let's say a prayer before we head out," John said. Everyone bowed their heads, and he prayed for safety and success in their mission. Then they headed down the road, letting John lead the way, both out of respect and because he was the only one who knew where they were going.

They traveled silently, in single file. Willow scanned the trees on both sides of the road, as well as the upcoming curves and each driveway.

The volcanic ash had settled a lot in that first heavy rain, but she could see some tracks in it. A few deer tracks crossing the road, a rabbit, a bicycle, some boot prints, not very distinct. It was easy to tell the older tracks from the fresh ones.

John's tracks, and his horse's hoof prints, were sharp and clean. All of her group's prints would be the same. Not good.

"You know we're leaving a bunch of fresh prints that lead right back to your place, right?" She asked John quietly.

"Yeah, I know." He walked a few more steps before continuing his thought. "But on the bright side, it makes it look like a whole bunch of people are living at that house. An overwhelming force!"

He had a point. Anybody following their footprints would think a lot of adults were living in the Andersons' home.

"Except... my group all left tracks coming down to your place," she said. "And we'll leave matching ones going out tonight. That'd make it pretty clear we aren't living at your place."

He shrugged. "But who would know that? It'd just look like five people left my place, went up the road, and then returned later. To a casual observer, it'd look like everyone was home again."

"I guess you're right." Willow fell silent. She hoped he was right, but she wasn't sure.

And she wasn't too happy that her group was leaving tracks that could easily be found and followed by anyone on this road. She should have thought about that before she'd decided to go on this scavenging expedition.

There wasn't much to do about it now. She'd pray no one decided to follow them back to the cabin. And that their tracks would be obliterated soon by the weather.

She glanced over her shoulder and caught Jacob's eye. He gave her a solemn nod and a thumb's up sign. In return, she gave him a thin smile.

It would be good when today was over, when they were home safe in their snug cabin with whatever goods they'd managed to rustle up today.

Eventually, John came to a stop just before a driveway that wound back into the forest.

"This is it," he said quietly. "We should post a couple of look-outs here at the road, like we did last time."

There were no tracks in the ash covering the driveway, which Willow hoped was a good sign. Either the home was vacant... or maybe the residents were home, and they were holed up on the property.

"Okay." She glanced over her shoulder. "Volunteers?"

She hoped Josh and Matt would volunteer, because it might be safer out here by the road. But of course, they didn't. And she decided not to make them.

Julie raised her hand tentatively. "I'll stay."

"Thanks, Julie. One more?"

"I will, as well," Clark said.

"Good man," John said. "Thank you."

He turned to the others.

"Just like last time. Single file, absolute silence, I'll go first."

Josh and Matt hurried to fall into line right behind him. Willow went next, hoping to keep an eye on everything, and Jacob followed her.

Today, she didn't mind having him back there. Before, she didn't like it because she didn't trust him. But now, she just wanted someone to "have her back." Even if it was Jacob.

The gravel driveway was narrow, and curved into a switch-back as it climbed away from the Forest Service road. Trees crowded it on both sides, their branches pressing in to close out the sky. The driveway was longer than she expected.

They'd walked about an eighth of a mile before the house came into view. An old, ratty-looking two-story home with blue siding and darker blue roof, it had obviously seen better days. Maybe forty years ago.

Willow's mouth grew dry.

Her chest constricted.

Instinctively, she moved left, where she was closer to the forest if she needed to take cover there. Behind her, Jacob's safety clicked off.

John stopped, and the boys almost ran into him. The big bay shook his head, rattling his bit over his teeth. John glanced back.

"I see tracks in the ash around the house," he whispered.

Not good! They had to be recent. The ash hadn't been here a week yet.

"Want to turn back?" John asked.

Willow sent an instant prayer, asking for direction. And got an instant answer.

"No," she said. "Wait here. I'll go first."

He led his gelding to the side, and Willow waved Josh and Matt into the trees. But Jacob didn't budge.

"I'm with you," he said.

She took a deep breath. "Okay. Stay close."

Rather than approach the front, she decided to circle around behind the house and scope the place out first. Maybe she'd be able to tell if people were actually living there, or if the prints were left by scavengers.

Slipping into the trees, she circled the home, with Jacob right behind her.

A dilapidated double carport served as a woodshed, and there appeared to be about a cord of wood stacked in it. This house would probably need close to six cords to heat it through the winter, so maybe that was the remainder of last winter's wood.

From a hill overlooking the house, she could see lots of footprints around the rear door. Strangely, they led in scattered directions into the forest. Whoever had been here had been leaving the house, but only through the forest, never out the driveway.

Why would they do that?

She glanced at Jacob, a question on her face.

He shook his head and shrugged.

All her questions remained. Was anyone actually living here? Or had the home been looted? Most importantly – was anybody in that house right now?

There was only one way to find out.

And she might get killed doing it.

16

"Watch my back." Jacob stepped past Willow before she could object. He moved down the hill toward the back of the house.

Oh, dear Lord! Please don't let him get killed.

She considered following him, but she had a good vantage point where she was. She could see anyone who came out of the back of the house, or the woods that surrounded it. And they'd be in range of her rifle.

Jacob moved like a cat, sure and stealthy. He paused briefly at the edge of the trees before moving swiftly into the back yard and up to the door. It swung open when he put his hand on the knob.

He stepped inside, disappearing from view.

Willow strained her ears, but couldn't hear anything. She prayed hard. Prayed he was alone in that house.

Her heart thumped as she stared unblinking at that back door.

After a lifetime passed, Jacob re-appeared. Willow drew in a deep breath. He was unharmed.

Looking her direction, he beckoned for her to join him.

She hurried down to meet him at the rear of the house. His expression was weird – not worried, but unsettled.

"Well?" She looked past him, through the door. "What?"

"Don't go in yet." He held his arm across the doorway.

"Why?"

"Just listen for once, okay?"

She looked at his face. "What?"

"I think someone was killed in there. Two people, actually."

Her stomach sickened. "Are they in there? Dead?"

"No, but there's blood spatter and... stuff."

"A murder/suicide?"

"Could be. But the bodies are gone. So somebody moved them." He lowered his arm, and Willow slowly stepped into the house.

It smelled funny. Not like death, but like an old house that hadn't been kept up. Musty, maybe mold or mildew.

She sneezed. Then, as her eyes adjusted to the dim light, she took in her surroundings.

This was the dining room. The table and chairs sat in the center of the room, but there was nothing else – no decorations or photos or artwork. A china hutch claimed the corner, but it was barren. No dishes or knickknacks or anything.

She moved into the living room. Again, the furniture was there. Sofa, rocking chair, recliner, loveseat and end tables. And there it was – the blood spatter Jacob had found.

It was around the rocking chair, and around the recliner. Small dark blotches stained the chairs and the carpet near the chairs, too.

Willow stood back and scanned the room. There were some small holes in the window glass. She approached for a closer look. They were about the right size for rifle bullets.

The rocking chair and the recliner were more or less in line with those holes.

"JACOB!" She yelled. "Check this out!"

He rushed in. "What?"

She pointed at the chairs, then the windows.

"Somebody outside the house shot the people who were sitting in those chairs." She turned to face him. "They were murdered!"

Jacob examined the glass. "You're right."

"Go tell John what's going on. I'm going to check out the house, but I think the murdering looters took everything except the furniture!"

As he left, Willow hurried through the house. The kitchen was cleared out. Same with the bathroom. Not much left in the bedrooms, either, but there were personal photos there. Grand-children, graduations, weddings, and such. Whoever had lived here had loved their family, before they were murdered. Right here in their own home.

A chill raced up her spine. This place was getting creepier by the minute!

She had to check it all out, though. After the effort to get here, she was going to find anything worth taking.

The attic held boxes of books. She would love to have books to read this winter, but didn't want to pack them out now, when her group really needed food, canning equipment and hand tools.

Down in the basement, rows of heavy shelves now stood bare, but the dust patterns on the wooden shelves indicated a recent disturbance and removal of cans and boxes. She hurried back upstairs.

Was there nothing useful left in this house?

She'd been through every room. And no, there really wasn't.

Walking out the front door, she found a broom and a shovel. She grabbed them. Pathetic little, but still better than nothing.

Jacob and John were looking at an area in the forest near where John had waited with his horse.

"I think we found the grave," Jacob said as Willow approached. "John noticed this fresh dirt that'd been turned up."

Willow circled around a couple of trees to see what they'd found. A mound of crumbly brown dirt, maybe eight feet long and four feet wide, was partially hidden from the driveway. John had happened to stand there long enough to notice it. A passerby probably wouldn't have.

"It doesn't have any ash on top of the soil," Willow pointed out. "That means it's only a few days old!"

Excited voices from the opposite side of the driveway told her Matt and Josh had found something interesting. The boys burst out of the trees.

"Good thing you sent us into the woods there, Willow!" Matt said, grinning. He carried a big white pail with a red lid, and its contents appeared heavy.

Josh had a matching one.

"Check this out!"

"What is it?" she asked.

"There's a bunch more where this came from, too!" Matt said.

"Mine's labeled 'white rice,' and Matt's is 'black beans.'" Josh set his bucket down in the driveway. "C'mon, you gotta see this!"

He grabbed Willow's hand and pulled her up the hill into the trees. After clawing through some brush, they came to a small trail. It looked bigger than a game trail, but narrower than an old skid road. Probably wide enough to get an ATV through, if you didn't mind getting some scratches from tree branches.

They followed it about a hundred feet, and Josh stopped.

"There! See it?"

Willow looked around. She saw trees, brush, grey sky, the trail... she looked at Josh.

"See what?"

He pointed. She squinted.

There, in the hillside not more than a dozen feet from the trail, and camouflaged by brush, was a dark spot in the side of the mountain. She stepped closer.

"A cave?" She asked.

"Nope!" Josh grinned and hurried past her. "This is awesome! It's an old shipping container. They buried it in the side of the hill."

He leaned against the door, pushing it open a little further. Willow peered inside. It was dark in there. Really dark.

"And check this! A bicycle, right?" Josh hopped on, and started pedaling what looked like a stationary bike. As he pedaled, lights flickered on inside the container.

Now she could see shelves, boxes, and pails matching the ones the boys had brought out.

"Ingenious, right?" Josh couldn't be more pleased. "You pedal the bike, and it's set up to harness that energy to power those little LED lights."

"A battery would be a little more ingenious," she said.

The cargo container smelled like dank earth. Willow scanned the shelves. There could be a lot of food here, if all the boxes and pails contained food.

"We never would have found it, if you hadn't sent us off to wait in the trees," Josh said.

Willow stepped outside. Matt was bringing John and Jacob up the trail.

"How much can your horse carry, John?" Willow asked. "I think we might have a real haul right here."

"Couple hundred pounds, no problem." John looked around, obviously uneasy. "But based on what Jacob told me, there are murderers in the neighborhood. And I have to wonder if they're the ones who were scoping out my place a few days ago."

"I have to believe they're the same people," Jacob said. "Three or four people, scoping out inhabited homes from the forest behind them – sounds like the same method and group."

John winced. "We're going to have to do something about that."

"I agree." Jacob ducked into the storage container. "But first, we need to get all these supplies out of here and back to your place and the cabins. Someone is bound to follow our tracks and find this place, taking anything we leave behind."

"Right. Let's load up," John said.

"We'll need to make several trips to get all this up to your place," Willow said. "And we'll need to post guards here while we do that."

"We've already got Clark and Julie at the end of the driveway." Josh picked up a box and carried it outside.

"I want somebody here, too, in case the bad guys come back through the forest. That's how they came in before," Willow said. "But I guess we could get by with just one at the driveway entrance."

John began loading supplies onto his horse. "We should have the guys carry this stuff up the road. Sorry, but they're just stronger than you ladies are."

"You're right," she said. "I'll stay and guard here, and Julie can stay put at the end of the driveway."

It took the guys all afternoon and four trips to relocate all the supplies to the Andersons' house. Jeannie took inventory as it came in, and divided it according to the number of people in each home.

Afterward, Willow surveyed the supplies. There was a lot of food, but it had sat in storage for quite a while. There were also cases of canning jars and lids, plus two old-fashioned kerosene lanterns, and some fuel for them.

"Nearly all of this food is expired." She opened one pail. "Red beans. Expired four years ago."

"Those beans will just need a good, long bath." Jeannie's blue eyes twinkled. "Nobody's gonna complain when they eat them!"

"True. And this rice is white, so it probably hasn't gone rancid like brown rice would have." Willow turned to John. "What are you going to do about the murdering looters?"

"For now, we'll switch up patrols around the house. There are four of us, so each person takes six hours a day. We'll be circling around the perimeter of the property at least once an hour." He shook his head. "It's just not good."

Willow glanced at Jacob. Was he going to move to the Andersons' home? She hadn't talked to him about his final decision. And no one had mentioned anything about it, so she decided not to bring it up at the moment.

"We'll be praying extra for your protection," Willow said. "You know you're all welcome to move out to our place."

"You're crowded already," Jeannie said.

"We can make room." Willow turned to John. "Seriously, if you want to come out, it's not a problem. I think it's safer there. Especially now."

"I appreciate that. We'll consider it and pray about it. But I have to say, we're pretty comfortable here, with real bedrooms and furniture, and the barn for our cows and horses – but we will think about it."

"If you decide to join us, just come on out. Any time."

"Thanks." John smiled. "In the meantime, do you want to borrow our horses to haul some of your loot home? I think the boys are tired of being pack animals."

"Amen to that!" Josh exclaimed. "My arms are mush!"

"You need to build up some real muscles," Matt said, flexing his.

Josh promptly bared his arm so they could compare.

"Okay, you guys!" Willow rolled her eyes. "Seriously. That's enough!"

She glanced at John. "And yes, we'd love to borrow your horses. We should be able to return them tomorrow."

"Yes!" Josh grinned.

"Not so fast," she said. "There's a lot here. We'll all be packing as much as we can carry tonight."

A cold breeze blew in from the west as they divided the goods and loaded the horses and backpacks. After handshakes and hugs with the Anderson group, Willow and her team headed for home.

It'd been a long day, but a good one. She couldn't have dreamed they'd make this kind of haul. She felt truly sorry for the couple who'd stashed this food away and then been murdered, but she was so glad the killers hadn't found the supplies.

Jacob fell in beside her as she hiked.

"Feels like winter's coming," he said.

"It's only September!" She glanced at the sky. Still grey. "But you're right, it does feel like it."

"We've had snow in September before. It's not normal, but neither is that volcanic sky."

"True." She glanced sideways at him. He seemed happier somehow. Less burdened. "You've changed, you know."

"Have I?" He smiled. "Your mom says the Bible says I'm a new creature since I accepted Christ."

"That's right." Willow paused. "Do you feel different?"

"I guess I do." He walked in silence for a while, then added, "I feel like... like I'll be okay. No matter what happens. In the future, if bad stuff happens, God will take care of me. Or take me to Heaven. It's good either way."

"That's a huge weight off your shoulders." Willow walked around a boulder. "I think that way about Raven. I hope she didn't die, but if she did... well, I know where she went. If she did die, she's better off than we are."

Tears came to her eyes. "I miss her, though."

"I know you do," he said softly. "We all do."

"I miss her all the time!" She was going to start bawling if she didn't change the subject. "Let's talk about something else."

Jacob didn't miss a beat. "How about all the food we got today? That's amazing, right?"

"Yeah."

"I mean, we got to the place, and it'd been ransacked. There was nothing there worth taking."

"Except the shovel and broom," she said.

"It was like God had hidden that stash so the bad guys didn't find it, but we did!" Jacob couldn't contain his excitement. "Right?"

Willow smiled. "I've never heard you talk so much about God before."

"I wasn't a Christian before." Jacob kicked an ashy pinecone. "I don't know why I waited so long. It's like, now I see everything, and it's so clear! Looking back, it was like I had blinders on – I missed out on so much!"

"We need to get you a Bible, so you can start catching up on what you've missed," she said.

"That would be awesome. I'd love that!"

Willow smiled to herself. The guy really was changing, right before her eyes. Maybe he'd turn out okay, after all.

As the sun set, the wind picked up. She was glad for the heavy backpack. It kept her back warm.

Ahead, Josh and Matt led the horses toward home. She

could hear the boys' banter, but couldn't make out their conversation. Probably about girls – specifically, Clark's daughters.

Glancing back, she checked on Clark. He was a big man, but he was weighed down with two pails and a pack. He didn't look up from the trail.

"Is it snowing?" Jacob's tone carried disbelief.

Willow glanced around. There – a flake. And another. And a few more. She shook her head.

"Nah – it's just some volcanic ash."

"Are you sure?" Jacob stopped and held out his hand.

A white flake landed. And disappeared.

"That's snow!" He exclaimed.

Since they'd stopped walking, Clark caught up with them.

"It is too early for snow!" His breathing was labored.

"It won't stick," Willow said. "You want to take a break?"

"No." Clark shook his head and began walking again. "I want to get home to my family."

Willow followed him down the trail, with Jacob beside her.

"You know, we should hold a Thanksgiving feast, once we get the harvest in," she said. "I feel like God has blessed us so much this year, in spite of everything horrible that happened."

"For sure. I've been the most blessed of all," Jacob said. "We should invite the Andersons and have a celebration before winter sets in."

"Maybe we'd better plan it for the next week or two," Willow laughed. "If we're going to beat winter!"

Daylight dimmed as they continued toward home. The snow stopped, but the wind grew worse.

A hair-raising howl trembled through the evening air.

Wolves! Ahead, the horses skittered sideways and tossed their heads.

"Get a firm grip on the reins!" Willow yelled. "We can't risk the horses running off! Especially with all our food!"

17

Another wolf howled. Willow whirled around. It sounded like it was right behind them! She didn't see it, but daylight was fading fast.

The big bay reared, pawing the air. Josh scrambled to avoid the flailing hooves.

"Hold onto him, Josh!" Willow yelled.

The mare that Matt was leading whinnied and leapt sideways, pulling Matt off balance.

Willow and Clark rushed forward, spooking the horses even more. The mare reared, then bucked.

A wolf howled.

Clark reached the mare first, so Willow ran to Josh's aid. The bay snorted, then pinned his ears back.

"He's gonna run!" Willow grabbed a rein. "Hold on!"

The gelding reared and struck, but Willow dodged his hooves. They could get killed doing this! Maybe she should let him go.

But all that food!

"Jesus, help us!" Her voice rose above the wailing wolves.

"Peace, be calm!" Clark spoke to the mare.

The horse tossed her head, wild-eyed.

"Hang onto them!" Jacob ordered. Moments later, his rifle boomed.

There was a yelp. Then silence.

The bay sidestepped and snorted. He shook his head. But he didn't run.

"Jesus, help us," Willow repeated, more calmly this time. She put her hand on the gelding's shoulder as she clutched his left rein. Josh still had the other one.

A quick glance over her shoulder told her Clark had a good grip on the mare and she was settling down.

"You okay, Matt?" she asked.

"I think so. Slammed my shoulder into a tree."

"Jacob?" She could barely see him in the gathering darkness. "What's going on?"

"Got one," he said. "Let's get out of here."

With Willow on one side of the bay and Josh on the other, they continued toward home. Matt led the mare, with Clark close by. Jacob brought up the rear.

After what seemed like the longest hike ever, they finally emerged from the forest into the cabin's clearing.

A single candle lit the window. Relief washed over Willow. They'd made it!

"Let's get the supplies in the cabin, and the horses in the barn," she said. "Then thank God for getting us all home safe!"

IN THE MORNING, Willow bridled the horses for the return trip to the Andersons' place. Jacob had volunteered to come with her. He tightened the gelding's saddle cinch.

"You're up for this, right?" Willow asked. "I mean, I know you're not really a horse person."

"It'll be fine. We've done it before."

"Once." She smiled. She'd invited Josh to come along, but he'd opted to stay home. Or, probably, to stay around Beth and Delia.

She stepped into the left stirrup and swung into the mare's saddle. Jacob led the bay to a stump, which he climbed on, then clumsily flung himself astride the gelding. The bay grunted and sidestepped.

Willow turned away so Jacob couldn't see her grin.

"Alright, then. We're off!"

The day was grey, but didn't feel as cold as yesterday. Willow took the lead, riding in silence with her thoughts.

It'd be awesome to have a horse or two of their own – for transportation, hauling wood and water, maybe even plowing, if they could find or design an old-fashioned horse-drawn plow.

Man, with a plow, they could cultivate the entire clearing around the cabin, turning it into a regular crop field. Maybe potatoes.

But she was dreaming. They didn't have any plows. Or any horses. Or anything to feed horses. Although, if they did have the horses, along with the proper tack and equipment, they might be able to put up enough hay to feed them through the winter.

Yeah. She was still dreaming.

She glanced over her shoulder. Jacob's shoulders swayed to the rhythm of his horse's steps. He appeared lost in his thoughts, too, until he noticed her looking at him.

"Everything okay?" he asked.

"Yep. Just checking on you."

"You thought I'd fallen off or something?"

"Nah. You would've hollered." She grinned.

As they approached a little stream, she stopped her mare. "Let's let them get a drink here."

Jacob rode up beside her. His horse dipped his head to the water. Willow decided to ask the question she'd been turning over in her head.

"Are you coming back with me, Jacob? Or are you going to be staying with the Andersons?"

"I'm coming back." He stared off at the mountains for a minute before he continued. "John and I talked about the possibility of my staying there to help out. I told him I couldn't bring Danny, though, because it's too dangerous."

"But you're not – "

"No."

She waited. He didn't volunteer any more. She was too nosy to let that go.

"Why?"

"You said I could stay with your group."

"That's true."

"So I'm staying." He backed the gelding away from the stream. "If that's still okay."

"Yeah." Puzzled, she started her mare back up the trail. Jacob obviously didn't want to tell her why he'd decided to stay with them. Maybe she could pry it out of him some other time.

Later, as they arrived at John and Jeannie's place, the wind kicked up. Willow watched the sky. Looked like storm clouds were forming below that high grey overcast.

The Andersons came out to meet them, with Julie.

"Where's Mike?" Willow asked.

"He's patrolling the back of the property," John said.

Jeannie zipped up her jacket. "Would you like to come in? We've got hot coffee."

"That sounds wonderful!" Willow dismounted in one smooth motion.

John held the gelding's bridle while Jacob scrambled down.

"Thanks for letting us use your horses," Willow said.

"No problem." John smiled. "It's good for them to get some exercise. Why don't you let Julie take the mare, and you two go inside and warm up?"

Julie took her reins and smiled shyly when Willow thanked her. Jacob followed Willow and Jeannie into the house, where the fragrance of fresh coffee filled the kitchen.

"It smells so good in here!" Willow inhaled deeply. "Do you have any cream and sugar for that coffee?"

"Sure do." Jeannie poured two mugs. "The cow is starting to dry up, so that will be the end of the cream, though."

John came in and joined them. "Looks like a storm's brewing. You two want to hole up here and wait it out?"

Willow wanted to get home. But she glanced at Jacob, who just looked at her and shrugged.

"Up to you," he said. "I'm fine either way."

"I think we'll head back. We brought rain gear."

Jeannie stood up. "Let me at least make some cheese sandwiches to take with you."

Willow savored her coffee.

"Thanks, Jeannie. This is delicious!" She glanced from her to John. "We were thinking it'd be neat to get together after the harvest is in, for a Thanksgiving celebration. Would you guys like to come over?"

"Sounds good," John said. "I guess you mean in a couple weeks, rather than the actual date in November?"

"Yeah, I don't think we'll want to travel that late in the season, with all the cold and snow we'll have by then. And the very short days."

"Speaking of snow, we had a little last night," Jeannie said.

"We saw some, too." Willow shook her head. "It sure is early!"

"I think it'll be a long, cold winter," John said. "Anyway, do you want to set a date now, or firm something up later?"

"Let's say three weeks from today," Willow suggested. "Would that work?"

John and Jeannie exchanged a glance.

"I don't know why not." Jeannie looked at Jacob. "I'll sure be glad to see that little Danny boy!"

"It's a date, then!" Willow drank the last of her coffee and stood up. "We should probably be heading out."

Jeannie wrapped the sandwiches in a newspaper page and handed them to her. "Maybe we should have Thanksgiving here, at our place. It's more spacious. And you could all stay the night, if you want."

Willow considered it. Mom's foot was nearly healed. In three weeks, she'd be fine to make the hike. With the whole group of teens and adults, there wouldn't be a problem carrying Maria and Danny when they tired. They could take turns riding piggyback.

"I think that'd be alright." She looked to Jacob. "What do you think?"

"Sounds good to me."

"Maybe you could plan on an overnight, then," John said. "Maybe we could do one more scavenging trip the first day you're here, then have the feast around noon the second day. I'd sure like to get some gas and oil, if there's any to be had."

"Maybe you could spend two nights," Jeannie said. "It'd be great to fellowship with everybody before winter sets in."

"We'll have to think about that," Willow said. "I was only thinking of a one-afternoon festivity."

She looked at John. "I know you need the gas and oil for your chainsaw. But with those crazies in the neighborhood... I don't know. You and Jeannie should talk with Julie and Mike about moving out to our place."

"You guys are way too crowded already," John said.

"We can make room," Jacob said. "We could add lean-tos onto the cabin. It wouldn't be a problem."

Jeannie wiped her hands on her apron. "We're comfortable here. If we die, we die. We're not afraid."

Jacob nodded slowly. "I'm just coming to understand that perspective."

"Did he tell you?" Willow smiled. "He got saved!"

Shock registered on John's face. "I didn't realize you weren't!"

"Do you have the mark?" Jeannie asked. "I didn't think anyone would convert, if they had the mark of the beast."

"I never got it." He held his hand out to her so she could see for herself.

"Why not?" John asked. "Everybody did. Except believers."

"Almost everybody," Jacob said. "I put it off because although I'm Hebrew, I was raised by Jewish relatives who converted to Christianity. They were sure we'd be sent to hell if we got the chip. I wasn't sure they were wrong."

"Wow." Jeannie sank into a chair, but she was beaming. "Just, wow!"

"Welcome to the family!" John slapped Jacob's back.

Grinning, Willow stood up. "I hate to break this up, but we really need to head out. I'd like to beat that storm home."

John and Jeannie walked them to the door, still smiling. Jeannie gave Willow a warm hug.

"I can't wait to see you guys again, for our Thanksgiving. And you just stop by anytime! You're always welcome here."

"Thanks, Jeannie." Willow smiled at the kind lady. "We love you."

"Love you, too, kids!" Jeannie waved as they left the porch. "We're praying for you!"

Warm contentment filled Willow's chest as she and Jacob walked out the driveway. She glanced at Jacob.

"It's good to have friends," she said. "And they've become like family."

"They're good folks," he agreed. "I feel like my family is expanding exponentially."

"I love that about Christians." Willow felt a raindrop on her nose. "Hold on, I gotta get out my rain jacket."

Before she got it zipped, they were getting pelted with rain.

"We could go back," Jacob said. "Wait this out."

"Nah. We won't melt." She stopped and looked at him. "But if you want to – "

"I'm fine. Let's go home."

They walked in silence up the road to the Andersons' original retreat, then veered off into the blackened forest and over the ridge. Willow thought of Raven. How she missed her warm smile and good advice! Losing her was like losing a sister.

Somehow, it didn't seem like Raven was really gone, though. Willow felt a calm assurance that she'd see her friend again. In heaven.

But she wasn't ready to give up hope of seeing her here on earth, either. It was still possible she was alive, out there somewhere.

Willow glanced at Jacob. He had his hood pulled well over his head in an effort to keep out the rain. His pants were getting soaked, though, and muddy black ash covered his boots.

She glanced down at her own boots and saw the same. Yuck!

A few minutes later, the rain let up, but a huge gust of wind swept over the landscape and plowed into Willow's back, nearly bowling her over.

Jacob reached over and caught her hand.

"You okay?"

She nodded. "That was crazy!"

Then, a flash of lightning.

But no thunder. And the rain stopped entirely.

Jacob dropped her hand. A brilliant light illuminated the blackened landscape, and Willow shielded her eyes. She knew what it was, she'd seen it before.

Seen *him* before. It was her angel, the tall lightning one with the gold hair.

"Jacob." The angel's voice rolled like the waves of the ocean. "It is time."

What? He was talking to Jacob? Willow moved her fingers away from her eyes, letting herself be blinded by the apparition.

Jacob had fallen to his knees, and the angel reached down and touched something to his forehead.

"Rise and stand!" The angel thundered. Jacob bolted to his feet, his face glowing like molten gold.

The angel spoke words Willow couldn't understand. Then he spoke in English again.

"As it is written, so it is accomplished!" The angel's timeless voice echoed across the land. In the next moment, he disappeared, and the dazzling light faded.

Willow stood there, transfixed. Jacob's face was still glowing.

What just happened?

18

"Jacob." Willow's voice sounded foreign in her ears. "Jacob!"

He just stood there, staring into the sky where the angel had disappeared.

"JACOB!" She wanted to grab his arm and get his attention, but she was afraid to touch him. He was still glowing.

What was going on? How could he be glowing like that?

"Jacob." It was just a whisper now, but he finally turned his eyes toward her.

She nearly fainted. His eyes glowed, too, like coals of fire! She trembled, but couldn't take her eyes off him.

"What is going on?"

As if he would know. He'd only been a believer for like, two days!

"You're glowing! You're freaking me out!"

Jacob swallowed, then touched his face. His hands were glowing, too!

Had she ever glowed like that after talking with her angel? No. She'd certainly remember that!

"Can you talk, Jacob? Are you okay?"

He nodded, but said nothing.

Then, he took a long, deep breath and opened his mouth.

"I...." His voice was boomy and echo-ey, like the angel's. He looked at her, dumfounded.

"Maybe you better sit down." She pointed to a stump, afraid to touch him or lead him to it.

He moved toward it like he was floating, but instead of sitting down, he leapt up on it. Turning his eyes to the grey sky, he lifted his arms toward heaven.

Then he began to sing!

His voice was deep and melodious, but she didn't understand any of the words. Jacob closed his eyes and sang the most beautiful melody Willow had ever heard.

If she thought she couldn't be more astonished after seeing the angel, she was now.

Here, this usually annoying, pretty-much average guy was glowing and singing on a stump, hands reaching toward the sky, with no thought or concern for how he might appear. He was filled with joy and wild abandonment, and all she could do was stare.

Had she ever felt like that?

Ever?

A twinge of jealousy bit her heart, but she rejected it. No, this was Jacob's moment. And she was blessed just to be here to witness it. Even if it was *her* angel who visited him.

He was having a spiritual experience like none she'd ever had.

Sure, she'd felt buoyant and uplifted during particularly good worship services at church, but nothing like Jacob was getting now.

He was physically glowing!

And his song – in some language she couldn't understand – was brilliantly beautiful. She watched and listened in awe.

Finally, he reached the end, and the last strains rolled over her in waves of joy. He lowered his arms. He opened his eyes.

She had no words.

It was like they'd been transported – no longer on this tortured, painful earth, their spirits were swept up, away from all this. Away from the darkness. Away from the ash. Away from the hunger and the wolves and the evil running rampant everywhere.

Willow closed her eyes, replaying the last part of Jacob's song in her head. Such beauty! She could listen to that for the rest of her life.

At last, she opened her eyes.

Jacob had come down from the old stump. His glow was beginning to fade. He looked at her, amazement on his face.

"Whoa." His eyes darted around, as if looking for the angel. "Whoa!"

He looked like he might topple over, then hurriedly sat down on the stump.

"That – " He looked at Willow and shook his head. "That –"

"Was amazing!" She rushed toward him. His glow was nearly gone. She grabbed his hand and felt electricity shoot up her arm. She yanked her hand away.

Unable to resist, she reached for his hand again. Felt the electricity again. This time, she held on and let it zap her clear to her toes before she released his hand.

Her heart skipped a beat, then another, before it settled back into its normal rhythm.

"Jacob," she said, staring at his fading glow. "That – that – what was that?"

He turned his eyes toward the sky.

"I think I died and went to heaven." His voice was low and filled with awe. He took a deep breath and released it, and the rest of his glow faded, leaving his skin its normal tanned color.

"Did you see anything?" Willow asked. "Did you actually see heaven?"

"No. I just felt joy – like I've never felt before." He turned his eyes to her. "Pure joy. I don't even know how to describe it."

She watched him as he spoke, and noticed something on his forehead.

"Is this what it's like to be a Christian?" he asked.

Willow reached tentatively toward his overgrown locks, and moved his dark hair off his forehead. Yes. There it was. Something like a little brand.

"Jacob." She stared. "There's something on your face."

He reached up and touched his forehead, then jerked his fingers away.

"It's a little sore," he admitted. "That's where the angel touched me."

"He left a mark, Jacob."

∽

THE RICH AROMA of rabbit stew pulled Raven from her slumber. Her eyes felt dry and gritty as she opened them. Hunger gnawed at her stomach.

As her surroundings came into focus, she pushed away a homemade quilt. She was on a couch, across from a wood stove with a big pot on it.

A pot of her cousin's stew. Her mouth watered as she pulled herself into a sitting position.

Her feet touched the cold floor, and she realized her boots and socks were gone. She spied them in the corner near the door.

"Denis?" She looked around. Was she alone?

How long had she been here?

She started to stand up, and pain shot through her left ankle.

Hollering, she sank back to the sofa. She'd twisted that ankle, sprained it bad, while climbing through a rain-slicked rock slide in the forest a few nights ago.

Was it just a few nights?

How long had she been here? How long was she passed out?

She had no idea, and there was no way of knowing. At least until she found Denis. He'd know.

Bending over, she inspected her ankle. It was still swollen and purple, but the color had changed from bright purple to dark, and shades of yellow blended across her brown skin.

It had been healing, then. Maybe for a few days, maybe longer.

Where was Denis?

The simmering stew called her name, and her stomach rumbled a reply.

Carefully this time, she rose to her feet. She found her walking stick leaning against the wall. Reaching for it, she put her weight on her good foot, then hobbled to the kitchen in search of a ladle, bowl and spoon.

Her mouth watered in urgent anticipation.

Back at the wood stove, she lifted the lid off the hot stew and ladled some into a bowl. Besides the rabbit meat, there were carrots, potatoes, and some kind of greens in the pot. She couldn't tell what those greens were, and didn't care.

She blew on her first spoonful, then sipped it off the spoon, savoring the rush of flavors. And then she prayed over the rest of the bowl, asking the Lord's blessing on it. And her. And her friends.

The greens in the stew were tangy. Perhaps they were wild greens. Denis knew a thing or two about foraging wild edibles.

Their grandmother had taught him, but she'd never had the time of day for Raven.

She finished off the bowl and set it on the coffee table beside the candle stub that Denis had lit the night she'd arrived. Drowsiness and fatigue overcame her, and she stretched out again on the sofa, enjoying the warm cabin and her full stomach.

Her eyelids grew heavy, and she let them drift closed. The best strategy now was to eat, rest, and wait for her ankle to heal itself. She yawned and slipped into oblivion.

WHEN THEY ARRIVED HOME, Willow and Jacob gathered everyone. Eyes grew wide as the group heard Willow describe what she saw. Then Jacob described what he experienced. He lifted the hair off his forehead and let everyone get a good look.

Clark let out a low whistle.

"You were sealed, brother!" He stared at Jacob. "What did the angel say?"

"In English, he told me to stand up, and that what was written was accomplished. But in Hebrew, he told me I was sealed." Jacob's eyes swept the group. "I don't know what all that means, but I hope he'll come and do it again!"

Mom laughed, her eyes dancing with joy. "Jacob. You won't need it again."

He looked at the friends around him.

"You all don't have seals," he said. "Why do I?"

Alan stepped closer to inspect Jacob's forehead. He shook his head and smiled.

"We are already sealed, Jacob. According to the New Testament, believers are sealed by the Holy Spirit when we accept Jesus. You already had that invisible seal. Today's seal is special. Different."

He looked around. "Somebody bring me a Bible?"

Willow raced into the cabin, grabbed hers, and ran it back to Alan.

"Okay, so the passages about the sealing of all Christians are in Ephesians chapters one and four, and some related verses elsewhere. But your seal, Jacob, this physical mark on your head, is prophesied in Revelation chapter seven, beginning at verse two."

He looked again at Jacob's forehead, shaking his head in amazement, before he began reading the passage.

"Then I saw another angel ascending from the east, having the seal of the living God. And he cried with a loud voice to the four angels to whom it was granted to harm the earth and the sea, saying, 'Do not harm the earth, the sea, or the trees till we have sealed the servants of our God on their foreheads.' And I heard the number of those who were sealed. One hundred and forty-four thousand of all the tribes of the children of Israel were sealed –"

Alan paused and looked up. "The next verses go on to reveal that 12,000 were sealed from each of twelve tribes of Israel."

Jacob took the Bible from Alan and looked at the passage for a minute.

"So, that's 144,000 Jews." He handed the Bible back. "How did I get picked?"

Alan smiled. "I have no idea. I guess God had a special plan for you."

"Like what?" Jacob asked. "What does all this mean?"

"The Bible doesn't explain it all," Alan said. "There's a little more, though, in Revelation chapter fourteen. You should read that sometime. Soon."

"I will!" Jacob grinned and looked around the group. "Guys! This is amazing!"

MARCUS KICKED back in the recliner. Stein was right, this was a great place to be. Besides the chickens, cow and horse, the family here had raised a huge garden, and the wife had started canning the veggies.

Stein had intended to kill the whole family the night they'd discovered Miller dead behind the barn. To Marcus's surprise, the rookie was on board with it, too.

But things had taken a drastic turn when the guys had rounded up the family and discovered something surprising – none of them had the chip! Of course, the younger guy died from his wounds when Stein and Carlson stormed the house, but the older couple – his parents – were uninjured.

Until Stein got ahold of them. He was determined to take them clear back to Ponderosa and chip them. Or actually, he wanted to torture them until they eventually capitulated and accepted the chip.

But Marcus had no intention of hiking clear back to Ponderosa, where the cops were hated, to deal with this.

So Stein decided to just torture them until they begged for the chip, then kill them.

It was noisy and messy, so Marcus demanded Stein take them out to the barn.

Today was the third day of all that. Marcus didn't go out to see it. He'd seen enough, when Stein did it at the jail, back when they still had electricity and running water. Carlson went out to watch and help, though.

Marcus was a little surprised the rookie had the stomach for that kind of work.

Anyway, the recliner in the meticulous living room was a perfect place to take a little nap. Marcus closed his eyes and waited for sleep.

Boots stomped up onto the back porch. And then through the door.

"Marcus!" The rookie yelled. "You in here?"

"Living room," Marcus responded.

"You gotta do something about Stein. That body is starting to stink something awful, and he refuses to let them bury it."

So much for the nap.

Marcus would have gotten rid of the son's corpse the first day, but Stein thought refusing burial would bring more misery on the parents. So he'd drug it out to the barn where they could see it. And now smell it.

Marcus cursed and climbed out of the recliner. The torture was one thing, but the dead body was another. It was going to become a health hazard.

Walking out to the barn, he could smell it well before he reached the building. He gagged as he opened the barn door.

"Stein!"

Stein rose from the kitchen chair he'd taken out there, and swaggered over to Marcus. His eyes looked bloodshot and a little crazed.

"Yeah?"

Marcus covered his nose with his arm. He released a few expletives, then added, "Get rid of that body! This afternoon!"

"It's just starting to get ripe," Stein protested. "Plus, it's gonna work. Just you wait!"

"We're done waiting! That thing's gonna stink us out of here. Get rid of it!" Marcus turned to Carlson and jabbed a finger in his face. "You help him!"

He whirled and stormed out of the barn before Stein could say another word. And before he lost his lunch from the stench.

19

T he next morning, Marcus was awakened by the sound of gunfire. He scrambled from the comfortable bed and grabbed his Glock.

Jamming his feet into his boots, he heard a third shot. Sounded close!

"Stein?" He yelled. "Carlson?"

He rushed into the hall and down the stairs. Where were his guys?

He yelled for them again, but got no response.

Racing out the back door, he heard shouting in the barn. He headed that way. Angry yelling continued as he reached the door and yanked it open.

Inside, Stein had Carlson by the throat and was strangling him. Marcus flew toward them.

"Break it up!" He grabbed Stein from behind, pinning his arms to his sides and pulling him away from the rookie.

But Stein responded with superhuman strength, shaking Marcus off like he was a piece of lint and going after Carlson again.

"ENOUGH!" Marcus barked, grabbing Stein. The officer

flung him off with such force that Marcus flew into the railing of the nearest stall. Then Stein reached the rookie and continued choking him.

That did it.

Marcus drew his Glock and fired a round right through the roof.

"I said, ENOUGH!"

Stein relaxed his grip but didn't release Carlson. Marcus leveled the handgun at him.

"Let. Him. Go." Marcus stared Stein down.

Stein didn't comply. But he wasn't choking the rookie, either.

"Now!" Marcus ordered.

Slowly, Stein released Carlson's throat. But then, just as the rookie was scrambling away, Stein landed a powerful punch on his jaw.

Carlson fell backwards and dropped in the hay. Probably blacked out, which was better than dead, as Stein intended.

Keeping his gun trained on Stein because he was acting so nuts, Marcus launched a string of profanities. Stein crossed his arms and leaned back against the barn wall. He stared at Marcus with crazy eyes.

Seconds ticked by, and Marcus began to calm down. Maybe Stein would, too.

"What was all that about?" Marcus asked.

"He killed the prisoners!" Stein growled.

"So you were going to kill him?"

"They never recanted!" Stein's red eyes practically glowed. "They never begged for the chip! They died as *Christians!*"

He spat out the last word like a curse.

"Where are they?" Marcus asked.

Stein jerked his head toward the back of the barn.

"Last stall." He glared at Carlson's motionless body.

"Go get some fresh air," Marcus ordered.

Stein hesitated.

"Now!" Marcus stared him down.

Stein spat in Carlson's direction, then moved toward the door. Marcus waited until the hothead was clear of the building before he went to check on Carlson.

The rookie's breathing was ragged. Red marks circled his neck from Stein's grasp. The throttling would leave bruises.

His pulse was fast but steady.

He'd probably be okay. Eventually.

Marcus slapped Carlson's cheek. "Hey!"

"Dalton! Wake up!" Another slap.

Carlson's eyes opened. His pupils dilated, then contracted. He focused on Marcus, then looked wildly around the barn.

"Where is he?" The rookie jerked into a sitting position, reaching for his handgun.

"Whoa, there, calm down!" Marcus got in his face. "He's gone."

Carlson scrambled away from him. His eyes jerked unevenly as he searched for his nemesis.

"I told you he's gone," Marcus said. "Calm down."

The rookie touched his throat. He winced as he swallowed.

"He tried to kill me." Carlson's voice was hoarse from the injured vocal chords. "That –"

"Now calm down!" Marcus stared at him. "He said you shot the old couple. Why'd you do that?"

"I couldn't take it anymore!" His eyes widened. "When I tried to sleep, the woman, her face, her cries – I couldn't get it out of my head!"

His gaze shot to the back of the barn. "They were never gonna recant their religion. It was obvious after the first day. But Stein, he just kept going and going – no sleep for three days – he went plum crazy!"

Carlson's gaze ricocheted to the door Stein had exited. "He's nuts, man. I mean, seriously nuts. He tried to kill *me!*"

"He'll calm down," Marcus said. "Give him some time. He needs to get some sleep. In the meantime, you stay away from him!"

Marcus started for the door, then looked back at the rookie. "And you better bury those bodies. It'll tick him off if he has to help you!"

RAVEN WOKE up suddenly when she turned over on the sofa and moved her ankle the wrong way. Pain reminded her of the injury. She glanced around at her surroundings.

Dirty windows filtered dim grey light into the room.

The pot of stew still simmered on the stove. Her stomach gurgled. She was hungry. Always hungry. It was hard to remember the last time she wasn't hungry.

"Denis?" She called softly, not wanting to wake him if he was home and sleeping in the bedroom around the corner.

No answer. But her soup bowl was gone from the coffee table, so if he wasn't home now, he had been recently.

She got up, hobbled into the kitchen, and found a clean bowl.

Back in the living room, she put another piece of wood in the stove and ladled stew into her bowl. The stew looked thicker now. She put the lid back on, sat down, and prayed – not just a blessing for the meal, but also for healing for her ankle and for a safe return to her friends.

She wanted to go home as soon as she could. Now that she was at Denis's place, she knew how to get back to the cabin – she'd follow the highway south a ways, then turn east on the road the Andersons lived on – maybe stop in and say hello, then travel north through the wilderness to the cabin. She'd made that trek often enough that she wouldn't get lost. Hopefully.

But she wasn't going anywhere until her ankle was strong enough to bear her weight. How long would that take?

The swelling was going down, so that was good. The bruise colors were muting, so that was also good.

She couldn't wait to go home! To clear the air with Willow, to fellowship with her friends, to check on her uncle and just be where she belonged....

She hung her head. She'd been foolish, running off like that. She could've died.

Worse, she might have put her friends in danger. No doubt they'd gone looking for her. If anyone was injured or lost because of her stupidity – how could she live with that?

Her soup was cooling. She ate a spoonful.

As she ate, she prayed for her friends. And that she'd be able to get home to them soon.

Later, she began carving her walking stick. It was a nice one, and she decided to carve a raven in the wood. It was an awkward depiction, but not terrible. She added her initials, then sprawled out on the sofa for another nap.

WILLOW STEELED HERSELF. She hoped this was a good idea.

"Can I talk to you?"

Jacob looked up as she approached. He was seated on a log, gazing out over the clearing, with Raven's Bible in his lap.

"Sure. Have a seat." He scooted over to make room for her. "What's up?"

"There's something bothering me. Normally, I'd talk to Raven about it, but...." She sighed.

He waited.

She picked up a pinecone and turned it over in her hands. Maybe this wasn't such a good idea. Why would he have any good advice? Well, he had been chosen by God, and sealed by an angel.

"Can you keep a secret?" She peered into his dark brown eyes. They looked clear and honest.

"Sure." He watched her expression. "Really, Willow. I won't tell a soul."

She took a deep breath.

"Okay." Playing with the pinecone, she tried to figure out how to begin. "I – there's something I want to tell my mom and brother, but I don't know how."

He closed the Bible, then waited.

"I... well...." She coughed, then blurted, "Maria is our half-sister!"

His eyes widened, his mouth frowned, and his face turned directly to hers. "But nobody knows?"

She shook her head.

His brows tightened. "How...?"

She covered her face with her hands.

"Candy... and my dad. Had an affair." Willow's posture slumped and she stared at the ground. Jacob put his hand on her shoulder.

"I'm sorry," he said.

"Yeah. Well, so am I. I mean, how *could* they?" Slowly, she turned her eyes to meet his. "Anyway, Mom and Josh never found out. Dad died. And now Candy's dead. So me and Raven are the only ones who know. Unless she's dead, too."

Willow choked. Jacob patted her shoulder.

Awkward! Why had she decided to tell him? Ugh!

"Hey." His voice was gentle. "You do need to tell them."

"I know," she whispered, staring hard at the ground. "But I don't know how."

"Want me to do it?"

She almost laughed. "No!"

Then she grew somber again.

"The thing is, Mom and Josh both have this wonderful image of Dad. They wouldn't believe he'd stoop this low. It'd destroy their memories of him. It'd crush them."

"But Josh has a right to know he has a sister." He paused. "I mean, another sister."

She turned to meet his eyes. "I know! That's why this is so hard!"

Willow turned and hurled the pinecone at a nearby tree.

Thunk! It fell to the ground and lay there, lonely and abandoned. Just like she felt.

She rested her elbows on her knees and propped her chin in her hands. They sat in silence for a few moments.

"It's a tough situation," Jacob finally said.

"Mmhmm."

"Do you want to pray about it?" He asked. "With me?"

Pray with Jacob? The image of him standing on the stump, singing his heart out, flashed through her mind.

She nodded. "Yeah."

He offered his hand, and she took it, then closed her eyes. He began praying aloud, stilted at first, then like he was really talking to his father. Willow pressed her eyes closed so no tears would come, because it felt like they were going to.

When he finished, he squeezed her hand and released it. She bumped his shoulder with hers, and sniffed.

"That was pretty good, for a beginner," she said, trying not to smile.

He wrapped his arm around her shoulders for a moment, then stood up. "Go get 'em, Tiger!"

She gulped. Then stood up. She would, soon... but not right now. She still wasn't ready.

THE NEXT WEEKS PASSED QUICKLY, and the weather turned cooler as the band of believers prepared for winter. Food was harvested and put up, wood was split and stacked, and work continued on the cache and the root cellar.

One evening, Willow was pulling carrots and digging potatoes for dinner when the breeze picked up. It was cold, too – so very cold for this time of year! She stood and stretched her back. These dark grey days were starting to get to her. There was never a bright moment or a shaft of sunlight breaking through that terrible ashen overcast.

Would she never see a blue sky again?

Even Gilligan was depressed. He lay beside her row of carrots, looking at her with big mournful eyes. He'd been sulking for weeks. Ever since the skies turned dark.

No. That wasn't quite true.

It was since Raven had disappeared.

Willow's heart weighed down her chest. It'd been weeks since Raven left. And Gilligan was never going to let Willow forget that it was her fault.

She piled potatoes into a basket.

Everyone else was up at the new cabin, putting the finishing touches on the root cellar. And just in time, too. Frost had been heavy on the grass the last few mornings. It almost felt like November.

As she worked, a light snow began falling. It wasn't the first. They'd had several already, but none had stuck.

It was a good thing they were having Thanksgiving soon with the Andersons. One of these days, the snow would stick. And it would stay until April.

Ugh! She shook dirt off the carrots.

She was not looking forward to winter. Why hadn't she grown up someplace warm and sunny, like Arizona or Florida?

But those states surely had their own problems now. Overpopulation in urban areas, crime, lack of water and resources... at least here in Montana, she had a wilderness and a place to hide. She looked over her shoulder at the cabin.

God had blessed them with a home, and friends to share it with. But her best friend, Raven –

Gilligan let out a low growl and rose to his feet. Willow jumped up and followed his gaze.

Her blood turned cold.

There, just beyond the garden, coming out of the trees, was a huge Canadian grey wolf!

20
—————

Willow froze. Her rifle was in the cabin!

The wolf took a step forward, head low and eyes focused on her.

Gilligan growled, every hair along his spine standing straight up.

Willow reached for her trusty Smith M&P. The handgun was better than nothing. Her fingers landed on her jeans instead of her holster.

What? She glanced down, shocked.

Then, with a sick feeling, she remembered – she'd taken it off in the outhouse an hour ago. And must have forgotten to put it back on!

Her mouth dried like the desert. Glancing over her shoulder, she calculated – could she make it to the cabin before that beast overtook her?

No. Not a chance.

The outhouse? The barn? Probably not.

Gilligan's low rumble grew louder.

Her eyes cut toward the wolf. Another one emerged from the

grey forest behind him. If there were two, there was probably a whole pack.

Gilligan whined, then barked, his hackles making him look inches taller that his true height.

She had no weapons! But she had a shovel, and a hoe. Grabbing the shovel, she screamed and flung it at the first wolf.

It fell short. The wolf was about fifty feet from her, and the shovel only traveled about thirty feet.

Willow snatched up the hoe. She wouldn't be throwing this tool. It was all she had left.

She moved closer to Gilligan, whose rumbling growl continued non-stop.

Shaking the hoe at the beasts, she began yelling.

"GET OUT of here! SHOO!"

It was ridiculous, she knew. But she couldn't think of anything else to do.

Except pray.

"God, save us!" She yelled. "PLEASE, GOD!"

The larger wolf took a step forward. He stared at Gilligan and snarled.

"NOOOooo!" Willow took a step forward, too, and shook the hoe. "God, help us!"

The wolf leapt forward, its fangs bared. It bounded over the garden, covering yards in single leaps. Suddenly, every moment passed in slow motion.

Willow screamed.

A shot rang out.

The other wolf sprang forward, focused on Gilligan.

The first wolf stumbled. Its head turned toward its shoulder.

Again, Willow screamed. She couldn't help it, the sounds just erupted from her throat.

Gilligan launched at the first wolf, each movement of his muscles captured in the frame-by-frame slow motion of terror.

The second wolf closed in on them, latching onto Gilligan's throat.

Willow brought the hoe down squarely across the smaller wolf's back. It yelped and whirled toward her, fangs snapping.

She swung the hoe again. And connected powerfully.

Gilligan attacked the first wolf, who skidded into the earth.

The smaller wolf turned from Willow and went after Gilligan.

"Noooo!" Willow whirled, striking the smaller wolf's flanks with the hoe. She yelped and tumbled.

"Get out of the way!" Someone shouted.

From the corner of her eye, Willow saw Uncle Tony. She moved perpendicular to him, to get out of his line of fire.

His rifle boomed. The smaller wolf jerked, mid-air, and fell to the ground.

"GILLIGAN!" Willow screamed. The larger wolf, though obviously bleeding and injured, was tearing into him.

There was no way Tony could get a clean shot. The dog and the wolf were locked in a spinning, snarling, tangled fight to the death.

Not thinking, Willow raised her hoe and rushed in.

Moments later, rough hands grabbed her arms and yanked her back.

A handgun boomed, deafening her.

The big wolf fell. Gilligan pulled away from him, crying in pain.

Gun in hand, Jacob stepped closer and made sure the wolf was dead, then checked the smaller wolf.

The hands holding Willow back released her. She rushed to Gilligan.

The border collie's black body was torn, his white markings covered in red. Crimson stains soaked into the snow and ash on the ground. His cries tore her heart.

"We're going to have to put him down," Tony said.

"No!" Willow reached for the dog. "No, we can save him!"

"He's all torn up. It would be merciful."

"Noooo," Willow wailed. She was already responsible for the loss of Raven. Now she'd be responsible for losing her dog, as well?

How could she bear it?

Clark crouched beside her. It had been his rough hands that'd pulled her away. Slowly, he reached toward the crying dog.

"Let us pray for him."

Willow closed her eyes as tight as she could, locking back the tears as Clark prayed. Gilligan's crying turned to whimpering. After Clark finished, they examined the dog.

He was in bad shape. A long gash sliced down his neck. Blood poured from his ears and oozed from his front legs. He refused to let Willow handle his left front foot. His flanks were covered with bite marks and gashes, and his lower right rear leg was ripped open.

He pressed his face against Willow's shirt. Her tears slowed and hindered her examination of his wounds.

"Oh, Gilligan!" She laid her hand gently on a spot that wasn't bloody. "You're such a good boy."

She looked at her friends through her tears.

"We can save him," she blubbered. "We just need to get him patched up."

Tony shook his head.

"Maybe, if we had a vet clinic, or even a bunch of sutures and needles and gauze and stuff." He looked sadly at the dog. "But we don't. And what we do have, we need to save for emergencies for people. Besides, he's in pain. And you'd need anesthetic, at least, to stitch him up. Ideally, you'd knock him out before you try doing anything for him."

Willow laid her hand on the dog's head. Maybe Tony was right. Besides, what if the wolves had rabies? Gilligan would contract that, too.

But no! She couldn't – wouldn't – let him go without a fight. She straightened her back and shoulders.

"I'm going to see what I can do," she said. "And we prayed."

Jacob stood beside her. "What do you want me to do?"

"I'll try to clean his wounds and close up the worst ones. Would you haul more water?"

He nodded, retrieved buckets, and headed for the creek, rifle over his shoulder.

With the snow falling heavily now, Uncle Tony gathered the scattered potatoes and carrots. He put them back in the basket and took them inside. Clark stayed with Willow and the dog, watching the edge of the forest.

"Do you see something?" Willow asked.

He shook his head. "No. But there might be more out there."

"Let's get to the cabin."

Willow walked slowly, with Gilligan hobbling beside her. He was a tough little dog, but no match for a wolf. Another minute, and he'd have been killed. And then Willow.

"Where is your gun?" Clark asked.

She hung her head. "In the outhouse. Would you mind getting it for me?"

He turned wordlessly and started toward the outhouse. Willow led Gilligan to the cabin. The grey day was fast fading into night, even earlier than normal because of the snow storm.

Mom, Josh and the others hurried down the trail from the new cabin, and Clark told them what had happened. The teenagers ran to see the dead wolves, and Mom rushed to Willow. Clark brought her handgun and holster to her.

"You were unarmed?" Mom's voice was almost hysterical, which Willow had only heard one other time in her life –

when they'd learned about Dad's death. "What were you thinking?"

"I forgot! I took it off to go to the bathroom...."

"You could've been killed!"

"I know, Mom!" Willow looked down at Gilligan. Mom stormed into the cabin. Willow kneeled beside the dog. "I'm sorry, boy. I'll do my best, I promise."

After heating water on the wood stove, Jacob helped Willow clean Gilligan. She used her own towel to dry him.

"We don't have many first aid supplies," Jacob said. "I'm going to have to agree with Tony about saving them for human emergencies."

"I know." Willow bit her lip. "But we've got to do something with some of these bigger cuts."

Gilligan whimpered and laid his head on the floor.

"Oh, I know!" Willow turned to Jacob. "We can try duct tape. And super glue! Would you check in the toolbox in the barn?"

Raising one eyebrow, he stood up. "Okaaaay."

He left and returned quickly with both items.

Because she couldn't shave Gilligan's fur, Willow gave up on the duct tape. But the super glue worked as messy, make-do stitches.

"Hold his head, so he doesn't lick anything until it's dry," she told Jacob.

When they finished, Jacob leaned back to inspect her work.

"Huh," he said. "That actually might work."

Willow stood up. Maybe it would. She didn't have any better ideas. Anyway, Gilligan was bearing the pain pretty well. He wasn't whining or whimpering. She gently patted the top of his head, which wasn't torn up.

"You're a good boy, Gilligan. A good boy."

Uncle Tony came into the cabin and studied the dog. "Well. Maybe he'll live."

"Of course he will." Willow's words sounded surer than she felt. But she'd done everything she could. She looked up at the mountain man.

"How did you get there so quick?"

"Where was your gun?" he countered.

She lowered her eyes. "In the outhouse."

"Willow!" His voice thundered. "You can't make mistakes like that! People could get killed. You nearly did!"

His words moved tears to her eyes. She couldn't look at him.

"I know," she whispered. "I know!"

Tony took a deep breath and huffed it out. "Lucky for you, I was just coming back from deer hunting. I was able to shoot the big wolf once, but after that, you and the dog and the wolves were all flying around and I couldn't get a clean shot off, until you finally moved out of the way."

He looked at Jacob. "You must have been nearby, too."

"Not exactly." Jacob exchanged a look with Clark. "We were up at the new cabin, and the strangest thing happened."

"What was that?" Tony asked.

"I heard a voice. In my head." Jacob glanced at Clark, then at Willow. "An audible voice, and it told me to get Clark and run down here. Something bad was about to happen."

Clark nodded. "That is what happened. Jacob grabbed my arm. He told me what he had heard, and the two of us began running down the hill immediately."

"Praying the whole way," Jacob added. "I didn't even know what to pray for, so I just prayed for help!"

"As we approached the cabin, we heard Willow screaming." Clark's somber eyes looked at her. "When we entered the clearing, we saw why."

"God spoke to you!" Willow looked at Jacob. "First, you were sealed by an angel, and now you're hearing from God."

What was next? Would he become a miracle worker or

something? His obedience to the Lord's voice had been critical. What if he'd thought he'd just imagined it, and stayed up at the new cabin?

She looked at Gilligan's wounds, then glanced from Jacob to Tony to Clark. "You guys saved our lives."

"Just barely." Tony turned to the door, then stopped and spoke quietly. "I'm glad you're okay, Willow."

"You're going out?" She asked. "It's dark and snowing."

"I'm gonna skin those wolves," he said. "Gonna have me a nice fur ruff this winter."

RAVEN'S COUSIN had snared another rabbit and brought it home to her. She cleaned and butchered it in the woodshed, then carried it into the house, shivering as the snow fell on her shoulders. It seemed like they'd been eating rabbit stew for months. In reality, it had only been weeks.

The other day, Denis had brought home a bunch of apples. Most of them, Raven sliced thinly and hung to dry. They'd be heavenly this winter.

For Denis, not her. She'd be home at the cabin by then. She glanced at the snow piling up on the grass. Hopefully.

Raven had saved two fresh apples for her final night with her cousin. Tonight, she'd cook them slowly with a bit of sugar and cinnamon she'd found in his cupboards. Her mouth watered. She could almost smell the sweet aroma already. Mmmm!

If she wanted to get home before winter set in, she needed to start her journey. And at first light, that's what she would do. The swelling had gone out of her ankle, and it was pain free.

She'd go slow and rely on her walking stick when she needed it.

But she needed to get going. If she waited another week, it

might be too cold and snowy to hike home. Plus, she couldn't wait to see her friends.

And her sweet buddy, Gilligan.

How she longed to see his perfect face and run her fingers through his shiny black fur!

MARCUS SURVEYED THE DEAD GARDEN. It was a shame Carlson had killed the woman who lived here. She'd begun putting up the summer harvest, but hadn't gotten too far on that when Marcus and his guys showed up. There were some jars of green beans and some pickled beets, which he hated.

For the past few weeks, he and the guys had lived high on the hog off the remains of her garden, but none of them knew much about canning or preserving food. So they hadn't. Now it was busy rotting, killed off by the frost.

If they'd kept the woman alive for a few more weeks, she could have preserved all that food, and maybe it would have gotten them through the winter.

Now, they'd have to go back to scavenging. It was dangerous and he hated it. But how else would they survive?

He kicked at a dead corn stalk.

Next time they came across a place as good as this one, they'd keep the homeowner alive if she knew how to do stuff, like gardening or canning or milking cows. Next time, they wouldn't let a winter's worth of food rot on the vine.

The other thing they'd done wrong was eat all the root crops first. For two weeks, they'd gorged themselves on carrots and potatoes, when they should have been eating the veggies that had a shorter shelf life. The root crops would have been easy to harvest and store for months, and didn't require prompt canning or drying.

He pulled up a rotting onion.

Live and learn.

They just needed to stay alive long enough to learn more.

Tonight, he and the guys would start scavenging again. If they were lucky, they'd hit another gold mine like this place. And not let so much of it go to waste. He didn't want to be scavenging all winter.

Behind him, the front door banged open. By the sound of the boots stomping down the steps, it was Stein.

"Thought we could make vegetable soup for lunch," he said as he approached.

Marcus handed him the rotted onion.

"Good luck with that!"

21

M arcus found a pair of warm gloves in the closet. It would be cold tonight. Might even snow.

Hopefully, he and the guys wouldn't have to travel too far to find a good house to scavenge. Maybe they'd get lucky and find a place like this one, all set up. Maybe they'd be really lucky and find one with pretty girls who knew how to cook and can and milk cows.

Okay, that was probably asking too much. But a guy could dream, right?

He wondered what Heidi was doing. Probably not pulling on a wool hat to go scavenging in the cold night. Most likely, she'd found a new man by now. She was probably stirring a pot of chicken soup over a cozy fire in a warm house.

Then there was Melanie, Josh Miller's widow. She was a young, slender beauty with amazing green eyes. But she came with two kids. A man might be a fool to take that on during normal times, and insane to do it now. Too bad, though. She was nice enough, and pretty.

But he needed to focus. Get his head in the game. Stop dreaming about women.

"You guys ready?" he hollered down the hall.

"Yeah," the rookie answered.

Stein didn't respond, but he clomped down the stairs. He zipped a jacket over his body armor, then picked up his rifle and slung it over his shoulder.

"You're gonna want a hat and gloves," Marcus said.

"I'm fine. I've got good circulation." Stein checked his ammo.

Carlson joined them by the front door.

"Here goes nothing." Marcus opened the door and a blast of cold air swept over them. He switched on a headlamp he'd found in the house, and stepped out into the dark night.

They walked south along the highway for a quarter mile, then came to a likely-looking county road that went east, toward the mountains.

"Let's try up here," Marcus said.

The first residence they came to was dark, like pretty much all the homes were nowadays. The house was newer, with modern architecture, but it didn't have a barn or any outbuildings. Marcus and Stein circled around back. There was no evidence of a garden or chickens or anything worthwhile.

"Nothing here," Stein said. "Probably city people who wanted to live in the country. Probably starving."

"Moving on, then." Marcus started up the road to the next place. Cold wind nipped his cheeks as he walked, head bowed against the gusts.

The second home looked a little more promising. It was older, but had a little red barn and an assortment of outbuildings. It also had a small orchard, although there wasn't a single piece of fruit on the branches or even on the ground beneath the trees.

Whoever lived here must have preserved every morsel. If they hadn't eaten it all as it ripened.

Marcus headed to the barn. A small hen house was attached to the structure as a lean-to that'd been added on at some point.

Hens cackled as he shined his light in the window.

Good!

He followed Stein into the barn. There were four goats. Two big ones, and two little ones.

If they couldn't figure out how to milk them, they could eat them.

"Let's take the goats." Marcus looked around for collars and lead ropes.

"Nah. Let's leave them here," Stein said. "If this place has any food, we'll just move in."

"And the residents will just move out? Not likely!"

"A couple of bullets will move them. That and shovels." Stein found one, grabbed it, and mimed digging a grave.

Sometimes Stein was so stupid. Marcus took the shovel from him and hung it back on the wall.

"We can't just go around killing everybody!"

"Sure we can. We got plenty of ammo." Stein caught Carlson in the beam of his headlamp. "Right, rookie?"

Carlson shrugged. "Nothing to stop us. We gotta eat."

"That's why we're taking the goats." Marcus found a lead rope. "Besides, we're not invincible. Bullets will stop us as easily as them."

Stein hammered his body armor with his fist. "I'm invincible! C'mon, rookie! Let's see what's in the house!"

The two started out the barn door.

Seriously? Now they wanted to kill everyone just so they could find out if there was edible food in the house? They weren't even truly hungry. They'd been gorging themselves for over two weeks!

"You coming?" Stein stared at him.

Marcus stepped out of the barn. He couldn't let them get

themselves killed. He needed a team. At least for now, while they had to scavenge. Later, if they found a decent place... well, he wouldn't need a team anymore, would he? Especially not a half-crazy one.

"I'll watch the front door," he whispered. "You guys breach the back, like last time."

If all went well, this would work again. If not, the other guys were more likely to get killed than he was. In any event, they were the ones who wanted to do it. He was just going along to get along. And to try to keep them alive.

He hustled around to the front of the house. About ten seconds later, the back door crashed open. Marcus took aim at the front door and prepared to shoot anybody who tried to come out that way.

Muffled shouts filled the cold night air, then a single shot. His heart hammered.

The front door flew open, and a man burst out, wearing a white t-shirt – a perfect target.

Marcus dropped him with two shots to the chest.

Inside, Stein and Carlson exchanged shouts. As seconds ticked by, Marcus waited, focused on that front door.

With his adrenaline now on overdrive, he began to overheat in all the cold weather gear.

Finally, Stein came to the front door.

"All clear!" He barked, then retreated back into the house.

Marcus turned on his headlamp to make sure the guy he'd shot was dead. As the man's face came into the light, Marcus gaped. His stomach turned over.

He'd just shot Sgt. Greg Daniels of Montana Highway Patrol. Daniels had gotten his start at Ponderosa Police Department. They'd worked together for years.

Marcus cursed loud enough to bring Carlson and Stein running.

Stein recognized Daniels instantly and let loose his own string of profanities.

"What?" Carlson asked, looking from Marcus to Stein. "Who is it?"

"Highway Patrol," Stein said. "He lives in Flathead County! What's he doing here?"

"Probably same as us." Marcus stared at the blood seeping across Daniels' white shirt. "Just holing up somewhere."

"I guess that was his kid we shot, then," Stein said, looking back into the house. "A teenage boy."

Marcus cursed again.

The rookie fiddled with his handgun, then secured it in his holster. "We should move them."

Stein kicked the front steps.

"Man! We coulda used him! We needed a fourth guy!" He turned on Marcus. "Why didn't you recognize him before you shot him?"

"It was dark, you idiot! I never saw his face until after you came out and I turned on my light!"

Bile rose in Marcus's throat. Too bad Stein hadn't gotten shot, instead of Daniels. The highway patrolman would have made a much better partner.

"What's done is done," Carlson said. "Let's go see if there's anything good in the house."

Robotically, Marcus climbed the steps. Might as well. Maybe it'd make him feel better.

First, he looked for the kitchen. It was small and sparsely stocked. The pantry held some canned foods like applesauce and corn. Not much, though.

Stein stepped into the room and peered in the pantry. "I think we should move here."

"Why?" Marcus pulled open a drawer. Silverware. "We're fine where we are."

"Because it's a good base of operations, that's why." Stein closed the pantry door. "We can work the entire road from this house."

He had a point. There was no reason to stay at the other place. Being right on the highway, they were more exposed there. And they were about out of food, too.

"We'll need to bring the horse, cow and chickens over here," Marcus said.

"Obviously. We could do that tonight."

"Or tomorrow, after dark." Marcus didn't feel like making the effort right now. But the livestock shouldn't be moved during the day – that would be like moving a pile of gold in a horse cart – a stupid obvious invitation to get robbed.

"Whatever."

Carlson came into the kitchen.

Marcus glanced his way. "Find anything good?"

"Nah. But I dragged the kid outside."

"We'll bury them in the morning. Then we'll go back, get some rest, and move here tomorrow night."

AT FIRST LIGHT, Marcus and his guys buried Daniels and his kid behind the barn. Then they hiked back to the Christians' farm to get the animals and the remaining food there.

In the kitchen, Marcus divided the food into their packs, while Carlson and Stein went to the barn to feed the animals. They hadn't been gone a minute when Carlson burst into the house with a shout.

"They're gone!" He stormed into the kitchen, his face raging red. "All of them. Cow, chickens, horse!"

"What?" Marcus turned toward him. "Did you leave the doors open?"

"They were stolen!" The rookie racked a round in his hand-gun. "Let's go after them!"

Marcus wasn't sure that was a great idea. Animal thieves were probably armed and watching their backs. Just like Marcus and his gang.

"I don't know –"

Stein stormed into the house.

"I found tracks! Headed south!" He looked at Marcus, who stood motionless by the sink. "What're you waiting for? Let's go!"

Marcus pursed his lips. Five chickens, a cow and a horse. Not worth getting shot over.

Plus, the new place had chickens and goats. If they didn't get stolen before Marcus and the guys got back over there.

Of course, he'd really like to keep that horse.

Transportation was getting pretty rare these days.

"Well?" Stein demanded. "What's the hold up?"

"Let's take a minute to think about this." Marcus scratched his new beard. "There are thieves running around. If we don't get back to the new place pronto, they might take the goats and chickens that are there."

"I want that horse!" Stein grabbed his pack.

"That's fine. I do, too." Marcus tried to sound agreeable. "But I think we need to post a guy at the new place to keep an eye on the goats and make sure nobody moves in."

"Fine." Stein buckled his backpack's hip belt. "The rookie and I will go after the horse thieves, and you go wait at the new place."

"That'll work." Marcus didn't like Stein's attitude or the fact that he was bucking the chain of command, but he'd deal with that later.

If Stein and the rookie could retrieve the stolen animals and bring them to the new place, great. If they got killed trying, oh well. Marcus could set himself up pretty good at the new house anyway. In the meantime, he wouldn't be the one risking his neck for a horse.

WILLOW CLOSED her Bible and flexed her fingers. Now or never. With the wolf attack, she'd had another freakishly close brush with death last night. Her life was precarious – everyone's was – but even more so now.

She had to tell Josh and Mom about Maria before she ran out of time or opportunity. Climbing down from her bunk, she sent up another prayer.

Mom was on the bunk below, combing Maria's hair.

"I need to talk to you," Willow said. "And Josh. Do you know where he is?"

"He was out milking Sassafras." Mom glanced up with those keen eyes. "What's going on?"

Maria scooted off her lap and hurried towards Danny, who was playing with the toys he'd brought from town.

"I need to tell you something." Willow felt a frown forming. "Privately."

"We'll go outside, then." Mom reached for her coat. "Beth, can you watch the kids for a few minutes?"

Looking up from a novel the Andersons had sent over, Beth nodded, her black curls bobbing around her face.

Willow grabbed her own coat. She dampened her chapped lips. Could she really do this? Really say it? Put them through it?

Queasiness fluttered in her stomach.

Oh, Lord. Please help.

She led the way out to the barn. Matt was there, along with Josh and Delia. The milk pail was half full.

"Matt, would you and Delia mind going to the house?" Mom asked. "We need to talk with Josh."

Matt shot Josh a look like he was in big trouble.

"Okay." He picked up the pail. Delia followed him out of the barn and closed the door.

"I didn't do anything!" Josh began.

Mom held up her hand to stop him. "Your sister wants to say something."

Two sets of curious eyes turned on her. Willow swallowed hard. Oh, no. She couldn't do it. Just couldn't!

She pinched her lips together. Stared at the floor, but found no help there.

"Willow?" Mom waited until Willow's eyes reluctantly found her face. "What's going on?"

The breath was sucked out of her lungs. Her eyes grew wide and wet. "I..."

"Spit it out, already!" Josh said. "We haven't got all day."

Mom silenced him with a single look.

Willow's mouth trembled. She swallowed. "Maria."

"What about her?" Josh asked, cocking his head to one side.

"She's –"

Mom's chin dropped. She closed her eyes. Did she *know?*

"Mom?" Willow touched her elbow.

"Go on!" Mom snapped.

"What about Maria?" Josh demanded. He crossed his arms.

"She's your sister," Willow blurted. There. It was out. Her eyes snapped toward her brother, then her mom.

Josh stared at her, his mouth open. Then he turned toward Mom.

Mom's hand flew to her mouth. Her eyes sought Willow's for a moment, then jerked downward.

"That's – that's crazy!" Josh stammered. "Right, Mom?"

Mom didn't look up. She didn't say anything.

Josh grabbed Willow's arm, his fingers biting through her coat. "What are you talking about!?"

His face looked blurry through her drenched eyes, but there was no turning back now.

"Candy had an affair...." She could barely say it. Finally she whispered, "With Dad."

A little cry escaped Mom's throat, and she sank to her knees on the old barn floor. Rocking slightly, she covered her ears.

"That's a lie!" Josh's face flamed red. He jerked her arm. "Take it back!"

"It's not!" Willow stared into his anger. "I swear!"

A sob rose from Mom, still on the floor.

"You're a liar!" Josh yelled. "I hate you!"

He whirled and stormed from the barn, slamming the door on his way out. Leaving her alone with her mom.

"Mom?" It came out as a whisper. Willow knelt down beside her. "Mom?"

Her mother's hands covered her face. Another sob shook her thin frame. Willow put her hand on Mom's shoulder.

Mom recoiled. "Don't touch me!"

Willow stared at her trembling shoulders. What could she say? Anything? Her eyes turned toward Heaven.

She never should have said anything! What had she been thinking?

"Go away," Mom whispered.

Slowly, clumsily, Willow got to her leaden feet and moved toward the door. She turned and looked back.

"I'm sorry." Her voice trembled.

"Leave me alone!" Mom wailed.

Willow stumbled outside, tears distorting her world. She gulped the ones filling her throat. Needing to be away from everyone, she headed toward the creek.

Why had she thought this was a good idea? She was tormenting her loved ones! And she could never, ever take it back.

22

W illow cried until she ran out of tears. Coldness pressed in around her like the arms of death. And for a while, she wished she could die. Just lay down here by the creek, on the freezing ground, and quit breathing.

How could she cause so much pain to her mom? Her brother?

Why on earth did she tell them?

Was she stupid beyond belief?

They'd never recover from this misery.

It was bad enough that they'd lost Dad when he died. The family was just finally getting its bearings back, finding their way without him.

And now, it was like he'd died again.

Mom and Josh were suffering a fresh tsunami of grief and sorrow.

Only this time, she'd caused it. Could she be any stupider?

She lay on her back, staring at the grey sky through the grey branches. The frigid ground leached the heat from her body. Maybe if she stayed out here long enough, she'd succumb to hypothermia. She sucked in a deep breath of chilly air and held it as long as she could.

Okay, maybe she was being a little melodramatic.

They'd get over it eventually.

Wouldn't they?

Footsteps approached. Maybe it was Mom. Maybe they could fix this. Willow pushed herself up on her elbows.

It wasn't Mom. Or even Josh.

It was Jacob.

She dropped back to the ground.

Too late. He'd already seen her. Twigs snapped as he came near.

"Hey." A moment later, he towered over her. From her ant perspective, he looked like a giant, with very long legs and his head in the trees.

"Hey." She sighed.

He extended a hand, and she reluctantly took it, letting him pull her to her feet.

"Your fingers are icicles!" He wrapped two very warm hands around hers.

Against her will, her eyes turned toward his. She found pity there. He knew.

She pulled her hands away. "Mom told you?"

"Josh." He cleared his throat. "For what it's worth, I think you did the right thing."

"It's not worth much," she scoffed. "I might as well have taken a kitchen knife and stuck it in Mom's chest, then turned and stabbed Josh with it."

She sat down on an ashy log and rested her elbows on her knees. "I hate my life."

"Whoa, now!" Jacob squatted in front of her. "It's not *that* bad!"

"Feels like it." She coughed weakly. "I've destroyed my family."

"No, you haven't."

"Yeah. Pretty sure."

"Your Bible says the truth shall make you free. I just read that this morning."

She looked at him. His dark brown eyes watched her earnestly. "So. Non-believer to Bible-thumper in less than a week?"

A flicker of disappointment crossed his face, then disappeared.

"Look, I know you're hurting. But you did a brave thing, Willow." His eyes never left hers. "You always do."

"Brave? Looks like stupid, to me."

"Stupid? No. Tough? Yeah." He sneezed. "Come on, let's go back to the cabin. It's freezing out here."

She shivered. "I'm not ready to face them yet."

"You're going to have to." A tiny smile curved his lips. "It's not like you can go stay in a motel for the night."

Her shoulders slumped. "You should have seen their faces."

"It was a shock, I know." He wrapped an arm around her and rubbed her arm briskly. "They'll be able to deal with it. You did."

That was true. But she'd had a long time to sort through her thoughts and feelings about it. Mom and Josh were on the very first step of that journey.

"It's devastating." She dusted ash off her clothes. "I should have waited until after our Thanksgiving party, at least."

"What time are we heading out tomorrow?"

"Early. John wanted to make another scavenging run."

"You think that's a good idea?"

She turned to face him. "Focus, please! Mom and Josh."

"Okay." He took her hand and warmed it in both of his. "Why did you tell them now?"

"Because of the wolves last night." Her eyes widened. "If you guys hadn't shown up so quick, I could've died, Jacob."

"So you were worried that you'd die before you told them."

She nodded. "It could happen. Almost did."

"You made the right choice." He took her other hand and began warming it. "Sheesh, girl, you are freezing! Can we go home now?"

She frowned.

"If we must." Willow took a few steps, then stopped. "Jacob?"

"Yeah?"

"Thank you."

He offered her his arm. "Sure."

Sliding her hand into the crook of his elbow, she said, "I really don't want to go home."

"Sorry, Willow." He led her forward. "There's no place else to go."

As NIGHT FELL, Raven looked for a place to sleep. At this point, she was only a couple hours' walk from the Andersons' place, but she was tired and freezing and her ankle hurt. Better to get some rest, and finish the trek in the morning.

She was nearly to the Andersons' road, so she pressed on until she reached it. Maybe she could find a vacant home or an outbuilding.

The first home she reached was dark. It looked fairly new, but there were no outbuildings. Did she dare find out if anyone was in that house?

She sat under a tree and watched it for a few minutes. No lights, no noise, no movement. It actually might be vacant.

On the other hand, the owners might be home and, if so,

they were likely armed. Knocking on a door at dusk could be a death sentence. It wasn't worth the risk.

She'd move on and find something else.

A strong wind sliced under her jacket as she walked, shivering. Around the bend, she came to the next home.

It was older, smaller, and had plenty of outbuildings. She stole in the driveway and headed toward the little red barn.

Chickens clucked in an attached lean-to as she pushed the door open. Inside, her eyes adjusted slowly. It was warmer in here. No wind or drafts, and maybe some body heat.

Straight dark shadows indicated stalls. She felt her way toward them.

The palest moon glow through the windows revealed four goats – two adults and two juveniles. They seemed friendly enough, so she let herself into their stall. It'd be warmer in there.

She tucked herself into a corner, curling up on the dry bedding. As her body warmed, she grew drowsy. The quiet sounds of the contented goats lulled her to sleep.

MARCUS GLANCED OUT THE WINDOW, watching for any sign of Stein and Carlson. They'd been gone all day. Had they retrieved the horse and cow from the thieves? Had they gotten themselves killed?

It was a good thing he hadn't gone with them. Instead, he'd come back to this place, cleaned the boy's blood off the floor, found a creek nearby, fed and watered the chickens and goats, and mucked out the stalls. Those goats had nice clean bedding now, so they better produce some good milk.

Maybe he'd tackle the henhouse tomorrow – it reeked.

Or better yet, he'd make the rookie do that. The kid had lots of energy, and needed to earn his keep.

Soon, it was so dark he couldn't see a thing outside. He turned from the window and clicked on his headlamp. Time for some grub!

There were jars of homemade applesauce in the pantry, and they were calling his name. He opened a pint, grabbed a spoon, and made himself comfortable in the living room. After he gobbled down the first half, he slowed and savored the second half. It had more cinnamon than he liked, but it was still delicious.

Time to start a fire. The house had grown cold as the evening wore on, and Stein and Carlson would probably be chilled to the bone when they arrived.

With some effort, he coaxed a blaze in the wood stove. But before the fire really took off, cold air flooded down the chimney and pushed the smoke into the house.

He uttered a few choice words, then opened the windows and doors to let out the stench. And all the remaining heat.

Boots stomped up the front steps.

Marcus reached for his Glock. What'd he been thinking, leaving the doors wide open? He clicked off his headlamp.

"Marcus?" A young voice called from the darkness.

It was the rookie.

"Yeah, I'm here." He holstered his weapon, turned his light back on, and went to the front door. "Did you guys get the horse?"

He swept the front lawn and driveway with his light. Didn't see a horse. Or Stein, for that matter.

"No." Carlson stepped into the house.

"Where's Stein?"

"Dunno. We got split up." The rookie headed straight to the hot stove. "What's to eat?"

"What do you mean, split up?" Marcus turned his light on Carlson's face, and his brown eyes squinted closed.

"Get that outta my eyes!"

"Tell me what happened!"

Carlson took off his coat. "We were following the horse's tracks, 'cause they were easiest to make out, with all the other tracks along the highway. After a couple miles, the horse's tracks went one way, but the cow's went the other way, with several boot tracks going with each animal."

He turned around and held his hands above the stove.

"And then?" Marcus demanded.

"Then, Stein said he'd follow the horse, and he told me to go after the cow. I said that was stupid, but you know how he is."

Marcus glared at the rookie. "So that's it? You just split up, and haven't seen him since this morning?"

"Yep. I followed the cow tracks, and eventually they went to this farm, but there were a bunch of people there. Like a dozen or more. I wasn't gonna try to take them on!"

"So you just came back here?"

"I went back to where Stein and I'd split up, and I waited an hour or more." Carlson scratched his head. "Then I headed home."

Marcus sat down in the recliner. This presented a conundrum. Should they go looking for Stein tomorrow? Or just write him off and be glad to be rid of him?

He'd really like to have that horse.

"What's for dinner?" Carlson asked.

"Do I look like your momma?" Marcus growled. "Go find something in the kitchen!"

WILLOW TUCKED Danny and Maria into bed, then turned and studied Mom's face in the light of the single candle on the table. She wore a grim expression.

Her mother hadn't said a word to her all evening, and neither had Josh.

The boys had spent the afternoon and evening at the new cabin with the Wilcox and Collins family, coming home at dark and heading straight up to the loft. Josh hadn't even looked at her. Had he told anyone besides Jacob about Maria?

Jacob tried to act normal, and failed miserably, but Willow appreciated his effort. Eventually he, too, had climbed the loft ladder, but not before he shot a sympathetic look her way.

She moistened her lips.

"Good night, Mom."

After a moment of silence, there was a quiet, "Night."

It was the first word her mom had spoken to her since her disastrous revelation.

She scooted up the ladder to her bunk and dropped her head on her wonderful pillow. Across from her, Raven's bunk lay empty. And below it, Gilligan curled in sleep, his wounds slowly healing. Willow had checked them several times during the day, and saw no sign of infection. But it was too soon to tell.

A sigh slipped from her lungs.

She turned and faced the log wall. Tomorrow they'd head over to the Andersons' home for what was supposed to be a feast and celebration.

The last thing she felt like doing was celebrating.

How could she, when her mom and brother despised her, and her best friend was missing or dead?

23

S   traw poked Raven's neck. Slowly, she opened her eyes. Dim daylight revealed the old barn timbers and small, grimy windows.

Her vision filled with the face of a curious young goat. She pulled back, gently pushing the youngster away.

It bounced around the stall on stiff legs, looked at her, then approached with its head down.

"Git!"

She had no desire to play head-butting games with goats. She needed to get out of there as quickly and quietly as possible. Farm folks were early risers. No telling how soon –

And at that moment, it happened. Squeaky hinges indicated the barn door was swinging open.

Raven's breath stalled. She pressed into the corner of the stall.

Maybe the farmer would feed the chickens first. Maybe he wouldn't find her before she could slip out – how? The back, maybe? If there was another door there.

She lowered her head so she could look between the stall boards. This stall had probably been originally built for horses or cows, but wire fencing had been added to keep the goats from climbing out. That wiring covered the exterior stall door, too.

She wouldn't be able to sneak over stall dividers or between boards. She'd have to exit the front of the stall, through the gate.

A young man moved into view at the front of the barn. Early twenties, black hair, light skin. He seemed vaguely familiar, but she didn't actually know him.

He opened bins and lifted lids, like he was looking for something. Like he didn't know where things were kept.

Finally, he filled an old coffee can with some feed, and started out the door. Probably to feed the chickens. The goats would be next!

This was her only chance.

Raven stood and bolted out of the stall, hurriedly fastening the gate behind her. She scanned the back of the barn. There was a door, but it was blocked with stacked firewood.

The front was her only option.

And that guy was out there.

Her muscles tensed, then she sprang forward, toward that door and the free world outside. Just as she reached the door, it swung open and she crashed into it.

She fell backward. Pain seized her chin and forehead. Blinking, she forced her eyes to focus.

The young man stared at her, astonishment registering in his brown eyes.

"What are you doing here?" He demanded.

Raven skittered backward, then got to her feet. She lifted her hands, showing they were empty.

"I'm not stealing!" She calmed her voice. "I just needed a place to spend the night."

The man said nothing, but glanced over his shoulder.

"Please. I'm going now." She forced her feet to move toward him, toward that door and the freedom it represented.

"Hold on a second!" The man slammed his hand across the entry, blocking her way. He studied her with cold eyes.

Could she take him? He was taller than her, and looked muscular. So, no.

But if she could get around him, she could outrun him – or at least normally she could.

With this bum ankle, who knew?

She steeled herself. Straightened her back and shoulders, and put on her confident, dangerous face.

"Get out of my way." Her tone was forceful and authoritative. "Now."

Slowly, a look of amusement crossed his face. Then he laughed aloud.

"Or what?"

"Or you'll regret it." She sent up an urgent prayer for help. Her handgun was tucked in the back of her waistband, but she didn't have much ammo – and she didn't want to draw the attention of anyone else by firing it. They might be more of a threat than this young guy. The gun would be her very last resort.

He advanced toward her slowly. She moved left, her eyes darting from him to her surroundings, looking for a handy weapon. A pitchfork and a shovel leaned up against the wall.

She lunged for the pitchfork, snatching it before he could react.

"Don't make me use this!" She aimed the tines just below his center of gravity.

He eyeballed her. "You wouldn't."

Now it was her turn to be amused.

"Try me!"

His gaze shot from the pitchfork to her face. She stared him down with her best expression of crazed psycho woman. Slowly, he moved to the side.

"Fine. Get out of here."

She stepped toward the door, keeping the pitchfork aimed at him.

"And don't come back!"

Raven hurried outside, keeping her pitchfork ready. She hustled backward across the grass until gravel crunched under her feet, telling her she'd reached the driveway.

She got out of there in record time, taking the tool with her. In her haste, she'd left her walking stick in the goat stall. That was okay. She'd find a new one if she needed it.

WILLOW DRAGGED herself out of bed, only because she had to. It was time to head over to the Andersons' place. If only she had a sore throat or something, so she could stay home.

Mom was cooking breakfast. The boys came down the loft ladder, waking the children with their noise. She glanced at the little faces.

Danny, the little rogue, yawned and climbed out of bed. Jacob took his hand and led him outside. To the outhouse, no doubt.

Maria turned over in her blankets, her brown curls spilling over her shoulder. Willow decided to let her sleep until they were almost ready to head out. She combed her own hair, then approached the stove.

Mom's eyes were bloodshot. Underneath, dark bags spoke of lost sleep. Still, she didn't make eye contact with Willow.

A dry lump formed in her throat, and she swallowed.

"Mom?"

"What." Still no eye contact.

She wanted to ask if Mom hated her. If she'd ever forgive her. If she'd forgive Dad. But somehow, she couldn't ask those things.

It was like a sign was posted in front of Mom's heart, and it said, *No trespassing. Violators will be shot.*

Finally, Willow said, "We'll be leaving soon."

So lame! Her heart was breaking, and she wanted Mom to open her arms and comfort her, or let Willow do the comforting, or something – but there was an enormous chasm between them, and Willow wasn't allowed to cross it.

"I'm going to stay home." Mom's voice was hoarse. No doubt from crying.

"What? No."

Mom shot her a cautionary, reproving glance but didn't reply.

"Please – everyone is going. It's our Thanksgiving!"

"Someone needs to stay and take care of the animals."

"We'll give them extra food and water, and lock them in the barn. They'll be fine!"

Mom flipped the pancakes. Without looking up, she asked, "And who will milk the goats?"

Willow rubbed her forehead. That was something she hadn't considered. They were supposed to be gone for one night, maybe two – too long to leave milk goats! Her lip trembled as a frown formed.

"We can take them with us?" She'd meant it as an answer, but it sounded like a question.

Uncle Tony came in, with Jacob and Danny behind him. The child raced into the room and flung himself at Matt, who lofted him in the air and swung him around.

"Take that monkey business outside," Mom ordered. The boys went out the door.

Tony held out a plate, and Mom slid pancakes onto it. He looked at her, then Willow.

"I'm going turkey hunting today," he announced. "I'll join you for the feast tomorrow."

"Oh." Willow picked up a plate. Having a turkey would be nice. She tried to sound more upbeat by adding, "Sounds good."

Mom flopped a pancake on her plate without looking at her.

Would she ever get past this?

She ate her breakfast in silence, then got Maria up, dressed her warmly, and fed her breakfast. Finally, it was time to go. She felt only a tiny bit of relief as her group gathered outside.

Gilligan walked over and stood beside her. Like any dog, he didn't want to be left behind. Even if he was recovering from serious injuries. She got down and looked at his face, then touched his uninjured shoulder.

"I'm sorry, boy. You need to stay here."

He cocked his head at her, then sat down with a whine. Willow wasn't sure if that was an objection or an injury response.

She sighed, then led him into the cabin.

"Mom, can you keep him here? He'll follow us if he's outside."

Mom gave the slightest nod.

"Okay," she said in her most weary voice.

"I love you, Mom," Willow whispered.

Finally, Mom looked up.

"Love you, too." Then she turned away.

There would be no hugs, farewell or otherwise. Still, there was love. Somewhere, under all that grief and pain. It had to be enough for now.

Willow stepped outside and closed the door quietly.

Expectant faces turned toward her. With the exception of Tony, everyone had gathered. They were looking forward to a good time. She forced a smile.

"Let's say a prayer and be off." She turned her eyes toward Jacob. "Would you like to do the honors?"

He nodded and bowed his head. Willow did likewise. He

needed practice praying in public. And she had to admit, he did an okay job with it already.

Then they were off, minus Mom, Tony and the dog.

Matt and Josh hurried to the front of the pack, and the older girls joined them. Alan and Deborah were next, followed by their daughter and son-in-law. Danny and Maria chased after them, with Willow and Jacob bringing up the rear.

Willow shifted her pack to better accommodate her rifle sling. She watched Josh. How was he coping? He still hadn't said anything to her.

But he was obviously distracted by the girls, particularly Beth. It must be hard to be depressed when you're focused on flirting.

"How are you holding up?" Jacob's voice was low enough that the others wouldn't hear.

Shoulders drooping, she cast a glance his way. Concern etched lines across his forehead.

"I'm hanging in there." She stepped over a rock. "I wish Mom had come, but it's clear she doesn't want to be around me."

"She needs some time, Willow." Jacob's head turned away as he glanced around the forest. Always on the lookout for danger. "It's hard to find solitude, with everybody crowding each other all the time in that tiny cabin. Now she'll have time to herself, to process her thoughts and feelings."

"Maybe." It was the best she could say. She hoped he was right. Hoped Mom would spend her alone time in prayer, rather than in depression.

Dad's death had been so earthshattering, so unexpected. The grief cycle had been horrible for them all. And now, they were cycling through grief again.

She looked ahead, watching Danny and Maria. The little girl – her baby sister – was tiring already. Willow called for Matt and

Josh to wait up. They were strong and energetic. They could take the first turn carrying the little ones.

Josh swung Danny onto his shoulders, ignoring Maria's outstretched arms. Matt picked her up. Willow exchanged a significant look with Jacob.

He'd noticed, too.

$\sim$

Marcus looked up as Carlson entered the kitchen, carrying a basket of eggs.

"There was a chick in the barn." The rookie set the basket on the countertop.

"You mean in the henhouse?"

"No, a chick – a girl – was sleeping in the barn!"

"She pretty?" Marcus took his first sip of coffee.

Carlson shrugged. "Maybe. She's crazy, though."

"Where is she now? What'd she look like?"

"Native. Young, early twenties. I guess she'd be hot if she weren't nuts."

Marcus set down his mug. Native? Could it be his half-sister, Raven? Nah... what were the odds?

"Tall? Short? Fat or skinny?"

"What does it matter? She's gone."

His heart rate picked up. "I need to know!"

"Kinda athletic looking. Lighter skin, like mixed race."

That could totally be her! Marcus looked out the window toward the driveway. It was beginning to snow.

"She left? How long ago?" He gulped his coffee, burning his throat.

"Ten minutes, maybe fifteen."

"Get your gear on!"

Marcus grabbed his hat and coat and rushed out to the barn.

Maybe there was a clue out there, maybe she'd left some evidence of who she was or where she was going. He flung the door open and stormed inside.

Didn't see anything obvious. The goats peered through the stall boards at him. He walked over and looked in their pen.

There! In the corner. A long stick.

He entered the stall and picked up the stick. One end was dirty and worn, like a walking stick. And there were carvings, but it was hard to make them out in the dim light.

As he stood up, he saw two long strands of dark hair caught in the corner boards. Carefully, he pulled them free. They were long. Really long, like Raven's.

He strode outside where the light was better. The strands were black and straight, like his sister's. About three feet long. For a moment, he fought his police training to save and catalogue all evidence. Then he opened his fingers and released the strands in the wind. It's not like he could get the state lab to run a DNA test!

Turning the walking stick in his hands, he examined the carvings. There was a bird. And some letters.

He wiped off the dust. "R.D."

Raven Deepwater!

His heart pounded so hard he thought he'd explode. His blood pressure must have blown off the charts!

Raven was here. She'd slept in his barn, right under his nose all night!

Did she know? No, she couldn't have. He'd only moved in yesterday.

Besides, if she'd known, there was no way she'd have stayed here, that was for sure!

He ran for the house.

Today was the day! He'd catch her for sure this time. She was only fifteen minutes ahead of him, she was alone, and she didn't know he was coming!

This was almost too good to be true.

"Carlson! You ready to go?" Marcus hurriedly grabbed his rifle and extra ammo for it and his Glock. "Let's move!"

24

Tiny snowflakes drifted down as Willow trudged toward the Andersons' place. Jacob walked silently beside her. This was supposed to be their Thanksgiving, but sadness filled her heart instead of joy.

If only she hadn't told her mom and Josh about Maria! If only she hadn't argued with Raven about Jacob!

If only... things would be so much different.

Now, Jacob was becoming a friend. In the end, Raven had been right about him. Willow *could* trust him, now that he was a believer.

But Raven was gone, probably forever.

And who knows when Mom and Josh would forgive her. Or when their re-broken hearts would heal.

"Penny for your thoughts," Jacob said.

She nearly smiled. "You always say that!"

"Because I'm broke. Can't afford more than a penny."

"That's about all my thoughts are worth, anyway." She shot a glance his direction. There was hope and encouragement in his eyes. "I don't want to talk about them. Instead, how about we play a game?"

His eyebrows lifted. "Like what?"

"*What If.* I'll go first. What if you could have one thing that you don't have now? What would it be?"

Willow had dozens of answers for this. Chocolate. Flush toilets. Electric lights.

"Huh." Jacob turned and quickly scanned the forest behind them. "That's a tough one. Since I have friends and food and a place to stay... I guess I'd wish to have my family with me."

Willow swallowed. She had that, and it wasn't too great at the moment.

"What about you?" He pushed a branch out of their way.

"I'd love to have a box of books. You know, for this winter?" Her eyes met his. "We'll be holed up in the cabin after the snow gets deep, and I'd love to have books. There were some at the last house we scavenged, but they weren't a priority because there was so much food."

"Escapism," he said. "To stave off cabin fever."

"Exactly!" She fell silent, watching the group ahead of her on their southward march. The snow came down heavier now, in larger flakes. She turned to Jacob.

"Have you ever heard that saying, 'Little snow, big snow. Big snow, little snow?'"

"Uh... no." He gave her a funny look.

"It means, if the snow storm begins slowly, with little snowflakes, you're in for a big, snowy storm. But if it starts with big snowflakes, you'll only end up with a little snowfall from that storm."

"Is it true?"

"Usually." The clouds overhead looked heavy and foreboding. "Today we started with scattered, little flakes. So we might really be in for it."

～

RAVEN SHIVERED as the road ahead of her began turning white. She should be at John and Jeannie's place within an hour. If this storm didn't let up, maybe she'd stay with them for a day or two before pressing on to the cabin.

She'd stopped using the pitchfork as a walking stick, because that wasn't working out so well. Maybe she should ditch it by the side of the road. Or hide it in the trees in case one of her friends needed it later.

On the other hand, the Andersons had two horses and a couple cows, so maybe they could use it. In the future, barn tools wouldn't be too easy to come by. And maybe they didn't have a pitchfork anymore, since their retreat had burned down.

So she'd take it to them as a gift.

She grinned at the thought. Never, in her previous reality, would she ever have considered gifting a pitchfork to anyone!

The air chilled as the snow persisted. Her toes were cold. She couldn't wait to get to the house and warm up!

Maybe it'd help to walk faster. She picked up her pace, hoping the increased circulation would help heat her body.

WITH THE ROOKIE a few steps behind, Marcus jogged until his breath grew ragged. Raven was the marathoner, not him. Anyway, she couldn't be that far ahead anymore.

She was just walking. He knew, because her prints were clear in the fresh snow. How lucky could he be? Thanks to that snow, he'd know exactly where to find her, even if she tried to hide.

He smiled. The universe was on his side. That snow was proof of it!

Any moment now, he'd catch sight of her around a bend in the road or on a straightaway.

And then what?

He'd catch her, of course, but then what? He hadn't given that any thought when he'd realized she'd slept in his barn. His only thought was to get her. And something about revenge.

Mostly, he wanted her to suffer for all the grief she'd caused him.

And he wanted to get her chipped.

It was the law. Who was she, to think she was above it? To think she could look down her nose at him. Like she was better than him. Like she condemned him, while she flouted the law.

No, she was going to get chipped. And she was going to be sorry.

Somehow, that might make up for it. At least a little.

To do that, he'd have to take her all the way back to the Ponderosa, to the police station. If only he had that horse, it'd be no problem. Otherwise, it was quite a hike. Especially in the snow.

But it'd be worth it.

To see her beg forgiveness, beg for mercy, beg for the chip... yes. It'd totally be worth it.

RAVEN'S TEETH were chattering when she finally approached the Andersons' driveway. Her feet felt like ice. Her legs were almost numb. She wasn't dressed for this.

When she'd gone for that fateful run, it'd been summer. The weather had been hot. The wildfires were still burning in many places.

At least she was wearing long pants. And Denis had given her a raggedy old coat for her journey. It was thin, but she pulled it tighter around herself.

Well, very soon, she'd be warm. And fed.

With snowflakes landing on her eyelashes, she plodded on, pitchfork dragging behind her.

She lowered her head to keep the snow out of her eyes. Just a few more minutes, and she'd be greeted by friends and welcomed into a warm home and offered a delicious meal. She couldn't wait to see Jeannie's happy smile and open arms. Maybe there'd be a pot of soup on the stove. And homemade bread. Was that possible? With honey and butter?

Soon, she'd find out.

Just a few more minutes.

As WILLOW and her group crested the ridge to the Andersons' original retreat, the snow came thick and fast. It didn't matter so much now. They were nearly there.

BOOM!

That was a big rifle! Willow whipped her head around, checking on her group. They were startled, but apparently unhurt.

How far away had that been?

A mile, perhaps less?

Probably just a hunter getting a deer.

BOOM!

Another shot, and this one carried a different note. From a different caliber gun!

She had to get her group off this ridge. They were exposed up here. There was no cover, and the only concealment was behind burned snags!

"Everybody! Hurry!"

Running forward, she waved her arm. "Follow me!"

A third shot rang out. Something bad was going down, and not far from here!

She ran down the slope. If she could find that old mine shaft that John had converted into a root cellar on his retreat property, they could take refuge in it. Her eyes darted left, then right, as she scurried. She remembered it was built into the hill.

It couldn't be far!

Finally, she spied the entrance. "This way!"

She yanked the door open, and everyone rushed inside. Another shot rang out. Number four?

"What if that's at the Andersons?" Jacob asked as he stepped past her.

"We will go," Clark said. "We must help them."

Willow's mind whirled. "Okay. Beth and Delia, you have to stay here with Danny and Maria."

"I want you to stay, too, Deb," Alan said. "With our daughter and granddaughters."

That decided, Willow, Jacob, Matt, Josh, Alan and Clark exited the mine and shut the door.

"Can they open this from inside?" Clark asked.

"Yes," Willow nodded. "There's a latch."

"Let's go!" Jacob checked his ammo.

Another shot rang out as they ran down the road. It definitely sounded like it was coming from John and Jeannie's new place.

Soon, they reached the driveway.

"Let's circle through the trees," Willow whispered.

She led the way, stepping quickly but carefully to avoid making too much noise. The snow helped deaden the sound of their footsteps, but only a little. It wasn't yet deep enough to prevent snapping twigs on the forest floor.

When she reached a spot where she could see the house, she stopped and hunkered down. Nothing seemed to be happening there. Smoke drifted lazily from the chimney into the cold, snowy air.

Then she noticed a rifle barrel extending from an upstairs window. Moments later, it roared.

Taking note of the direction it'd been aimed, she waved her group forward.

"I think the looters are over there!" She kept her volume down and pointed in the direction the rifle had fired.

Stealthy steps moved them forward into danger, where they could try to save their friends.

TREMBLING, Raven sidled up against a tree. Her jaw loosened, leaving her mouth gaping as she stared.

That was her brother!

Marcus was maybe forty yards away, but even with the trees and shrubs between them, she was sure it was him. He wore a beard now, which she'd never seen before. But even if his face were totally obscured, she'd know that posture, that stance, that stride, anywhere!

Why was he attacking the Andersons?

Were the police still tracking down Christians? After the EMP and everything?

Or what if he'd followed *her* here?

Maybe he was after her, and she'd led him straight to her friends.

A massive shiver shook her spine.

Along with the pitchfork, she did have her handgun. Since she'd taken a few pot shots at wolves those first nights she was lost in the forest, she only had six rounds left. Heart hammering, she drew it.

Could she kill him?

Maybe. Maybe not.

A younger man crept up beside Marcus and spoke into his ear.

She knew that guy! He'd been the one in the barn this morning!

Her chest constricted. They *had* followed her here!

How many were there? She'd seen three, perhaps four, in the trees ahead. Did he bring a whole army with him? There were five bad guys, minimum. Possibly six or more.

Her friends were outnumbered. And apparently pinned down in the house.

She'd have to take out as many as she could with her six rounds of ammo. Her handgun wasn't any good at distances. Plus, she wasn't a great shot. She'd have to get real close before she fired, or she'd waste her bullets.

She stepped forward, away from Marcus, staying low and quiet. First, she'd try to take out the bad guys ahead of her. If she ran out of ammo shooting them, she wouldn't have to kill her half-brother.

MARCUS CROUCHED beside a stump and stared into the trees ahead. Raven was up there somewhere.

"Let's get out of here!" Carlson hissed. "This is crazy!"

The rookie was right, it was crazy. Just about the time Raven turned in the driveway to this house, guns started blazing. At first, he'd thought they were shooting at her.

Her tracks indicated she thought the same – they'd veered off the road, into the forest.

Now, though, he wasn't sure. People were shooting from the house, but other people were shooting from the forest toward the house.

He had wandered into somebody else's battle!

Who were these shooters? Were they Raven's cohorts? Was she with the group attacking the residence? Had she met them here to lead an assault on this house?

After she'd entered the forest, her tracks got mingled with several other people's tracks, making hers difficult to follow.

Maybe the rookie was right.

Maybe they should get out of here.

Let these groups sort out their issues, then grab Raven later, when bullets weren't flying all over the place.

On the other hand, if he backed out now, he'd lose this opportunity to catch her. And he might not ever get another one.

FOLLOWING THE SOUND OF GUNFIRE, Willow led the way toward the bad guys. She didn't dare get too close – John and his friends in the house might see her movement in the trees and not realize it was Willow and her group.

They might take a bullet in the confusion.

Was there a way to let John know they were here?

She glanced toward the house.

Not without revealing herself and her location to the looters, too. And probably taking a bullet from them.

No, they'd have to proceed in secret. At least they had the element of surprise on their side. For whatever that was worth.

As her heart beat her ribs, she looked toward heaven and breathed a prayer. It might be her last one.

25

Through the trees ahead, <u>Willow</u> thought she saw movement. She motioned for her group to stop and get down. Those murdering looters were going to be in for a big surprise!

She dropped to her stomach, then body-crawled to the top of a little hill. Snow flurries covered her hair and body, which was great for camouflage, but unfortunately also camouflaged the looters.

Slowly, she brought her rifle around.

<u>Jacob</u> crawled up beside her on his elbows.

"See them?" he whispered.

"Not yet," she breathed.

Maybe she'd need to reposition. That'd be a shame, because this was a good vantage point. Eyes and ears on high alert, she prayed as she waited.

There!

Something moved, much farther to the right than she'd expected. She nudged Jacob and pointed him that way with her chin. His rifle barrel swung right.

She glanced back to the rest of her group, then pointed

toward where she'd seen movement. They went into nearly silent action to relocate.

She pressed her cheek against her rifle and gazed through the scope.

Raven's face filled her vision.

What?! Willow nearly dropped her gun in astonishment. Raven was alive! She was here!

With the bad guys?

No, of course not. Unless she was their prisoner?

She looked frightened but resolute, looking back over her shoulder.

Willow scoped the forest behind her friend.

And nearly fainted when she saw Marcus! He was staring at Raven, raising his handgun... and heavy snow unloaded from a tree branch directly above Willow, landing on her rifle and blurring her view through the scope!

She could barely see him. She did her best anyway, squeezing off a shot.

Had she hit him? Had she missed? She couldn't tell. All she could see was snow clumped at the front of her scope. Some of it had hit the lens.

"Come on!" She wiped the glass with her fingers, smearing the cold lens.

Jacob's rifle roared.

"Did you get him?"

"He's down."

"Marcus?"

Jacob's head spun toward her. "No! Marcus is here?"

"Yes! Who were you shooting at, Raven?"

"Some young dude. Black hair."

"Raven's over there. And Marcus is after her!"

Willow looked through her wet scope. Couldn't see anybody.

A rifle boomed at the same instant as a bullet cracked a tree limb just over her head.

"Time to move!" She and Jacob scuttled backwards down the slope. Her friends were nowhere to be seen. Their tracks indicated they were circling around behind the house, toward Raven and Marcus.

Which meant they would run into the murdering looters on their way there.

A rifle boomed from the house.

Fear and prayer gripped her at the same time.

Oh, Lord! Please don't let my friends get killed by accident! Or on purpose!

She glanced at Jacob. His cheeks flushed red with cold. Melting snow dripped over his ears.

"I think the looters are still a bit south of us, and Marcus and Raven are almost straight across," she whispered.

"Got it." He pushed himself off the snowy ground.

A gunshot ripped the silence, quickly followed by three more. Sounded like her group had found the looters. Or the looters had found them. Josh was in that mix, along with her friends.

She went into rapid fire prayer.

Jacob followed their friends' tracks, and Willow trailed him.

Several times, they plastered themselves to trees as guns boomed volleys of ammo.

Finally, she spotted Matt and Josh. They were alive. Flat on the ground against a big log.

Pinned down!

RAVEN GOT AS close as she dared, then leveled her sights on a tall, skinny guy in black pants and a brown shirt who was firing a rifle at John's house.

Pausing her breath, she squeezed the trigger.

Her gun clicked.

She was out of ammo!

The tall guy obviously heard that click, though, and swung his rifle her direction. She ran three steps, then dodged behind a tree. A bullet slammed into it, spraying her shoulder with wood chips.

Pressing against the tree trunk, she prayed. Marcus and the young guy from this morning were behind her somewhere, and there were still bad guys in front of her.

She might have taken out two of them, she thought. Or at least injured them seriously, putting them out of the fight.

How many did that leave?

Two more? She wasn't sure.

What she was sure of, was that the remaining ones were still fighting, and she'd used all six rounds taking out two guys.

The pitchfork had been a hindrance to running and shooting, so she'd ditched it in the trees. Wasn't sure where, exactly, but she wasn't going to look for it, either. Marcus was back there.

She'd done all she could do.

It was time to run for her life.

~

WILLOW RELOADED.

Josh turned his head and spotted her.

She motioned for him to stay down.

A bullet slammed the log he and Matt were lying against, splintering wood off the top.

She glanced over her shoulder. Jacob had taken off. She'd have to handle this one herself.

Pressed into a tree, she wiped the snow off her scope lens.

Then she crouched and ran left. Hopefully she could get a sight on whoever was shooting at her brother.

A shot rang out.

Her left shoulder sizzled.

Hit!

But still running.

She tucked in behind a massive cedar. The outside of her arm warmed from the blood trickling down. She looked.

A bloody mess met her eyes. She swung her arm. It screamed with pain but moved unhindered. Besides, it was her left shoulder.

She pressed the rifle into her right, and moved forward, her eyes scanning the trees ahead. The shooter had to be in there somewhere!

RAVEN SHOVED her empty pistol into the back of her waistband and turned to run. As she straightened out for her first stride, an iron fist slammed her middle.

She doubled over.

The air stalled in her lungs. She tried to inhale, but couldn't.

Darkness crowded the edges of her vision, but she managed to look up. And saw the face of her brother.

A cold evil filled his eyes.

She fought the darkness. Fell to her knees and managed to pull in half a breath.

Dear Jesus – she looked up. Maybe this was her last breath. Dear Jesus!

Marcus grabbed the front of her jacket, keeping her from toppling over.

The anger smoldering across his face was like nothing she'd ever seen. The hatred! He was like a man possessed.

Her diaphragm suddenly relaxed, and she gasped.

Sweet, cold air!

He yanked her up, and she scrambled for footing.

His eyes were a demon's eyes. She could see them, staring at her, taunting her. Ready to reach through Marcus's hands and strangle her!

His grip closed around her throat. Tightened like a python. Then his eyes darted left. Suddenly, he released her and she fell onto her back as he brought his handgun up. But not on her.

Someone else!

She kicked him as hard as she could, striking his shins because they were the only part within range.

He yelled. His gun roared.

She flipped over onto her stomach and pushed away from the ground.

Jacob!

He was twenty feet away, and falling. His rifle dropped from his hands.

WILLOW SAW him at the same moment he spotted her – a tall, skinny man. She recognized him. He'd been one of the looters they'd seen on their first scavenging trip with John. One of the three men with the woman who'd come in the driveway where Josh and Clark had been hiding.

She leveled her rifle and squeezed off a shot the instant his chest filled her sights.

Two guns roared simultaneously.

26

Willow inhaled. She was still breathing! And standing. And the only place that hurt was her left shoulder.

The other guy was down, though. For good.

Now Josh and Matt could safely get away from that log where they'd been pinned down. She could hear sporadic gunfire in the woods, but none from the house. Praying they were okay, she turned her thoughts – and feet – toward Raven.

She was alive! Or she had been, minutes ago. And she was here!

Willow's heart raced as her feet propelled her through the trees.

She couldn't get distracted. No time for emotions.

Just find her friend, and get her away from Marcus!

"Noooo!" Raven screamed, scrambling toward Jacob. He landed with a crashing thud.

A hand grabbed her ankle like a vise and yanked her back.

Turning, she looked up just in time to see Marcus's boot swinging toward her.

It crashed into her ribs.

Pain ripped through her middle. Darkness threatened her peripheral vision again. When she inhaled, she cried out. Hurt so bad!

Marcus moved toward Jacob.

"Lord Jesus!" Her gaze fell on the tines of her pitchfork. There, just beyond that bush! "Help me, Jesus!"

She scrambled toward the tines.

Grabbing the tool, she whirled toward Marcus.

He approached Jacob, stood over him with his handgun – she launched herself at him, screaming like a banshee.

As he turned, she drove the pitchfork into his chest. It was like hitting a brick wall. Was his torso made of concrete? He absorbed the blow, grabbed the handle, and wrenched it, throwing her to the ground.

Then he whirled on Jacob and pointed his handgun at his chest.

"BOOM! BOOM!"

Screaming, Raven plastered her hands over her ears, staring at the unfolding drama.

Slowly, her brother's knees buckled. Then he fell to the ground.

She scrambled forward.

"Marcus? Jacob?"

Her ribs, and every breath she took, shrieked with pain. Tears obscured everything as she rushed to the downed men.

Her brother was dead. A head shot.

"Jacob?" She crawled to him.

He dropped his gun and pulled himself to a sitting position. There were two holes in his clothes. He yanked off his jacket, then his shirt.

He was wearing a bulletproof vest! Emblazoned with "Ponderosa Police."

What?! Where did he get that?

Was he with the police?

No, couldn't be! Marcus, the police captain, had just tried to kill him.

Jacob pulled off the vest. His eyes wildly examined his upper body as his hands felt his chest and stomach.

The shots hadn't penetrated the vest! He'd have some impressive bruises and some pain, but he'd be okay!

Raven exhaled and let the darkness close in.

WILLOW SPOTTED Jacob sitting in the snow, bare-chested.

She ran toward him.

And then spotted Raven, prostrate on the ground. Very close to Marcus. And the white snow was soaked with crimson.

"RAVEN!" A sob broke from her throat as she rushed to her friend.

She dropped to her knees and skidded across the snow to Raven's side. Her face was pale and vacant. Snow fell and melted on her closed eyelids.

"Nooooo!" Willow searched Raven for injuries. She didn't seem to have any wounds. Where had all this blood come from?

"Raven!" Willow slapped her face. "Wake up!"

Her fingers flew to her friend's throat. There were marks there, like she'd been choked. Had Marcus killed his sister with his bare hands?

A weak heartbeat pulsated under her fingers. Raven took a huge breath. Her eyes fluttered open.

"Raven!" Willow flung herself over her friend, pulling her

into a hug. Her injured shoulder screamed in protest, but she ignored it. "Thank God!"

Raven moaned. "Don't. Hurts!"

Willow released her gently. Her gaze traveled to Jacob, who was putting on his shirt, then to Marcus. That was where all the blood was coming from!

She looked again at Raven.

"You're alive!" She stared into her eyes. "After all this time! Where have you been?"

"Long story," Raven whispered. She shivered, then winced. "I'm so cold."

The forest grew quiet as Willow and Jacob helped Raven to her feet. The battle must be over, finally. Willow prayed a final prayer for her friends and brother.

"Where does it hurt?" she asked.

"My ribs," Raven breathed, steadying herself against Jacob's arm. "I think they're cracked. Marcus kicked me. Felt like his boots were made of steel."

"Let's get you down to the house." Willow picked up her rifle, then spotted something else. "Huh! What's this pitchfork doing out here?"

"Your shoulder!" Raven stared at Willow. "You're shot!"

Pain burned again across the wound. It hadn't been so bad in the heat of battle, when adrenaline was blasting through her veins. Now, though, it began to throb.

Jacob's gaze swung between her and Raven. "Okay, you two! To the house, so we can get you patched up!"

Willow grabbed her friend's hand and squeezed it, a smile rushing across her face. Raven. Alive! They would get the story out of her soon enough.

As they emerged from the trees, the back door of the house swung open, and Jeannie rushed toward them.

"Oh, thank the Lord!" Her concerned look swept over Jacob, then Willow, and landed on Raven. "You're here!"

She opened her arms and reached forward, but Raven hung back.

"No hugs!" Raven held up her hand in front of her. "Cracked ribs!"

"Oh, my!" Jeannie's grandma eyes swung to Willow. "And you! Your shoulder!"

She motioned them inside. "Let's get in the house, where it's warm."

Willow didn't need a second invitation. She followed Raven up the steps and through the door. Jacob stopped there, though.

"I'm going to look for the others." He checked his handgun, slung his rifle over his shoulder, and strode back toward the forest.

Willow tried not to worry. It'd been a while since the last shot had been fired. The battle was over. Now, they needed to find out who'd survived. Jacob was the right man for that.

Inside, Jeannie brought out a book on home care, and looked up broken or bruised ribs.

"Well, we're not supposed to wrap it." Her gaze skimmed the page. "Hmmm... you can take over the counter pain meds, like ibuprofen or acetaminophen, which we do have. And you'll need to do some deep breathing exercises so you don't get pneumonia."

She handed the book to Raven, who sat at the dining table. "Look this over."

Jeannie turned her focus to Willow. "I'm afraid that shoulder will be more complicated. Let's take a look at it."

"Can I get some ibuprofen, too?"

"Sure." Jeannie brought out pain reliever and water for them both. Then she went to work on Willow's shoulder, cleaning and dressing it. "This could have been a lot worse, if the bullet had hit half an inch over."

Willow turned her focus to Raven, trying to ignore the painful poking and prodding on her shoulder.

"About that day," she started, her eyes blinking back tears. "Raven, I'm so sorry!"

"I am, too – I've wanted to tell you – I've thought about it so much, and I was so stupid!"

"No, you were right. I was the stupid one. Will you forgive me?"

"Only if you'll forgive me." A tiny, teasing smile played over Raven's face. "Of course you're forgiven!"

"It's amazing to have you back. I missed you." Now, Willow couldn't hold in her tears. "I'd almost given up hope...."

"Hold still," Jeannie said. "This might hurt."

Pain zapped through Willow's shoulder like a branding iron. She yelped.

"I'm sorry." Jeannie frowned. "That was the worst of it, I think."

Soon, she finished up and gave Willow a clean shirt to put on. Minutes later, the back door bumped open and the guys came in. Willow mentally tallied as they stepped over the threshold: Clark, Jacob, John, his friend Mike, Matt and Josh. Her gaze swept over her brother. Uninjured. Thank God!

"Where's Uncle Tony?" Raven's lip quivered as she strained to see past the men, out the door. "And Alan? And everyone else?"

Jacob held up his hand in a calming gesture. "They're all fine."

Raven's shoulders relaxed.

"Uncle Tony is coming tomorrow," Willow explained. "But where is Alan? He came with us."

"He went to get his family and the children from the mine," Jacob said. "Now that it's safe to come down here."

Willow looked from one person to the next, searching for wounds and injuries. It appeared that she and Raven had gotten the worst of it. The room filled with buzzing explanations as each person filled in part of the missing puzzle.

John had been outside on patrol duty when the looters struck. His buddy, Mike, had been in the barn and unable to escape, due to the shots directed toward the house and outbuildings. Quiet Julie was actually the one upstairs, shooting out the window. Jeannie's eyesight was too poor, so she'd been reloading for Julie.

"And praying up a storm!" Julie said, smiling at her friend, who nodded demurely.

John had exchanged fire with the looters, but wasn't able to score a good hit.

"I was walking up the driveway when it all started," Raven said. "I thought you all were shooting at *me!*"

She'd headed into the forest, and soon discovered the bad guys, then saw Marcus and his guy tailing her.

"That was about the time we got here," Willow said. "I fired off a shot at Marcus, but I guess it didn't hit him. A tree dumped snow on my rifle scope."

Soon, the women and children arrived with Alan, and more accounts and stories were shared. Willow sat quietly, watching her friends animatedly exchange their version of events. Her eyes turned to Raven. Her dearest friend.

Whom God had brought home. She raised her eyes and breathed her thanks.

Now, her only pain was for her mom.

And her brother. Although, watching him fill Beth's ears with his tales, he seemed to be alright.

Smiling at that, her gaze shifted to Jacob. He caught her looking, and shot her a wink. She lifted her chin in response.

After an hour of chatter and enjoying the soup that had been on the stove before the shooting began, John cleared his throat.

"I hate to break up the party, but we men have some grave work to do." He frowned. "Oops. No pun intended."

"He's right," Jacob said, taking his bowl and spoon to the sink. "Between the looters and the police, there are five dead guys and one dead woman out there getting buried in the snow."

He frowned and turned to Raven. "I'm really sorry about your brother."

"You had to," she said quietly. "He was going to kill you. And me."

As the men filed out of the house to take care of the dead, Willow rose from her chair. "Let's get these dishes cleaned up."

Jeannie blocked her approach to the dishpan. "Not you, young lady! You and Raven hustle yourselves upstairs and take a nap. You'll be needing plenty of rest to recuperate."

She couldn't argue with that. Julie showed Raven to her own bedroom, and led Willow to the guest room.

Dropping onto the bed, she was almost asleep before her eyes were closed.

27

The next morning, Jeannie checked Willow's shoulder after breakfast.

"It's looking better already," she said as she dressed it.

"Clark prayed for me and Raven last night," Willow said. "I've been seeing the Lord work powerfully through his prayers for healing."

"God is good, isn't He? We have so much to be thankful for."

Willow smiled. "And today is our Thanksgiving! I hope Tony brings a turkey!"

As they washed breakfast dishes, Willow told Raven why Gilligan wasn't with them, and explained what had happened with the wolves.

"He's a hero dog," Raven said. "But he's okay, right?"

"He seems to be on the mend."

Raven nodded thoughtfully.

"I can't wait to see him." She looked at Willow. "It's good to be back. You don't know how much I've missed you all."

Julie came down the stairs, covering a yawn. She'd been on watch part of the night, and then she'd slept in.

"Where're the guys?" She asked.

"They headed out early this morning," Jeannie said. "John got one of the looters, before he died yesterday, to say where they'd been staying. John's hoping to find some gas and oil over there for the chainsaws."

"Oh." Julie glanced out the window. "And it looks like the ladies are carving pumpkins with the children."

Willow grinned. "We're gonna have pumpkin pie for our Thanksgiving dessert!"

A light knock sounded on the front door. Jeannie dried her hands, then looked at Raven.

"Do you want to get that? It should be your uncle."

Raven flew to the front door, peeked through the peephole, then flung it open.

"Uncle Tony! Gilligan!" An instant later, she protested, "No hugs! No hugs! Hurt my ribs."

"I knew you'd be alive," a gruff voice said, choking a little. "My little bird."

Willow walked to the front door. Tony's eyes shone with delight as he took in his very alive niece. He held two turkey carcasses by the legs, one in each hand. He lifted them higher.

"We brought dinner."

We? Him and Gilligan? Willow stepped left, so she could see past Tony's shoulder.

"Mom!" Willow's voice stretched as her heart reached for her mother. "I thought you weren't coming!"

"Honey!" Mom's arms opened to her. "I couldn't stay away."

Willow fell into her embrace, her eyes running over. Just like the thankful joy in her heart.

"I am sorry," Willow whispered.

"It's not your fault," Mom breathed into her hair. "I'm sorry, too."

Mom patted her shoulder, and Willow yelped and pulled back.

"What? Are you okay?" Mom studied her. "What happened?"

"Long story." Willow looked at Raven, then back at Mom, and grinned. "We'll have to tell you all about it over dinner."

"Raven! It's so wonderful to see you!" Mom reached over to hug her, but she scooted away.

"No hugging," Raven said. "You'll understand why, when you hear what happened yesterday."

She bent toward Gilligan, who wagged wildly and licked her ear. "My good boy. I hear you're a real hero!"

Gilligan nearly wagged his tail off. Then he darted around her and headed straight for the kitchen.

"Well!" Willow laughed. "Somebody's got priorities! Let's go prepare our feast."

∾

AFTER THE FOOD BEGAN COOKING, Willow drew her mom aside.

"I'm a little worried about Josh. How he's taking the Maria thing," she began, but Mom stopped her.

"Don't worry. Give it to God, and let me talk to him." She sighed. "Anyway, I think he'll be okay. He has plenty of distractions these days."

Her eyes turned aside, and Willow followed her gaze out the window. Beth and Delia were playing with Danny, Gilligan and Maria. The teenage girls cast frequent glances toward the driveway.

Waiting for Josh and Matt, no doubt. Willow smiled.

"Well, at least there's that." Her eyes turned to her mother. "Hey, what about the goats? You were afraid to leave them too long."

"Tony and I are going to walk back after lunch." She patted her stomach. "After we have some time to digest, of course."

Two hours later, Willow saw the guys coming in the driveway. John led his bay gelding, and his friend Mike led the mare. Bulging parcels were tied to their saddles. Jacob, Alan, Clark, Josh and Matt trailed behind, each carrying a backpack and a cardboard box.

Raven came up beside her. "That's a lot of stuff!"

"Those people were murdering looters," Willow said. "While you were gone, we found a house where they'd killed the homeowners and taken all their belongings. Then they were casing John and Jeannie's house. Well, you know...."

Willow descended the steps and approached John.

"So, did you find fuel for your chainsaws?"

Instead of answering, he grinned and turned his gelding so Willow could see his left side. Gas cans were strapped on.

"There's lots more," he said. "Maybe we'll get it after lunch."

"Excellent!" Willow clasped her hands together.

John looked over his shoulder at the parade of men. "Let's get this stuff unloaded, so we can eat!"

The guys trudged after him with their packs and boxes. As Jacob approached, he stopped in front of Willow, and set down his cardboard box.

"This is for you." His eyes twinkled. "Go on – open it!"

She knelt down and opened the flaps on the top.

Inside, she found books. Lots of books! Her fingers flew over the spines.

The Pilgrim's Progress by John Bunyan.

The Oath by Frank Peretti.

The Bielski Brothers.

Fugitives of the Forest.

Lots and lots of novels, and some wilderness survival books.

And a few children's books, and two Little House on the Prairie books, including *The Long Winter*.

"This is perfect!" Willow laughed and pulled it out. She looked at the cover, then at Jacob. "Today was supposed to be Thanksgiving, but you've made it Christmas!"

He winked and grinned. "You're welcome!"

As he moved to catch up with the other guys, Willow turned her eyes toward Heaven. Her hands lifted toward the skies, like Jacob's had on the day he was sealed.

"Thank you, Lord Jesus. For everything." A smile curved her lips. "For every single thing."

THE END.

Goodbye for now, Willow and Raven and our Band of Believers! Perhaps one day we will meet up again and hear more of your story. Until then, stay strong and true.

With affection,
The Author

LETTER TO READERS

Dear new friends,

Thank you for choosing this series. I hope you enjoyed it. Would you do me a favor and write a quick review on the site where you bought it? It will help me as an author, and it will help your fellow readers decide whether this book is for them. **Thank you very much!**

If you'd like to communicate with me, you can contact me at my website, JamieLeeGrey.com

May God's face shine upon you and bring you peace.

All the best,

Jamie Lee Grey

P.S. Have you already read my previous stand-alone novel, Holy War? If not, please check it out... you might enjoy it!

ACKNOWLEDGMENTS

Readers and friends – Thank you for reading, and for your support. You make it worthwhile.

Special thanks to John Rock and Deb Motley for their feedback, prayers and encouragement.

Candle Sutton – For the past decade, Candle has been my amazing critique partner, a true friend and partner in prayer. (Hey, everybody, be sure to check out Candle's books at www.CandleSutton.com .)

My husband – You are the best. Thank you for your encouragement and support of this project, and all my other crazy ideas.

Jesus Christ – My life and breath, my inspiration and the giver of all good gifts. Thank You.

BOOKS BY JAMIE LEE GREY

Holy War

~

Band of Believers series

Book 1: Dissent

Book 2: Duplicity

Book 3: Destruction

Book 4: Darkness

~

Daughter of Babylon series

Book 1: California

Book 2: New York

Book 3: America

Book 4: Oregon

~

My newsletter readers will be notified when my next novel is ready. My free newsletter goes out about once a month. It includes updates, discounts, and freebies and giveaways.

You can sign up at www.JamieLeeGrey.com

EXCERPT FROM DAUGHTER OF BABYLON, BOOK 1: "CALIFORNIA"

If he stared any harder at that phone, it'd either burst into flames or ring. Nadir Omar Salem Abdullah flexed his fingers and cracked his knuckles. What was taking so long?

The moment it lit and buzzed, he snatched it off the desk and strode out to the veranda. He couldn't risk his father over-hearing, or anyone else in the governor's mansion, either. And although it was still quite early on Saturday morning, there were always too many eyes and ears around this place.

"Well?" he demanded.

"Your line is still secure?" Kamal's anxious voice filled Nadir's ear.

"Of course! What is the status?"

"Everything is on schedule."

"You haven't had any trouble?"

"No. Before breakfast, one thousand torches will be raised."

"Allah be praised," Nadir breathed, feeling tension seep from his shoulders.

"Allahu Akbar!"

The line went dead.

Nadir slid the phone into his pocket and pulled in a long,

deep breath. His gaze swept over the Sacramento landscape. Before the day was out, California would be on its knees. Before the weekend ended, the Great Satan would fall on its face.

Something didn't smell right. Katie Nelson blinked and rolled over, rubbing her eyes. Sunlight slanted through the windows of the old motorhome.

Campfire smoke? What kind of idiot would be lighting a fire in these conditions? A burn ban had been in place along the California coast for months. Still, there was always someone who thought they were special and the rules didn't apply to them. Hopefully, the campground host or the park ranger would show up soon and deal with it.

She pushed herself up on her elbows. Zach was gone, probably taking Duke on a run. She climbed down from the bunk over the cab, admiring the way the sun highlighted Timothy's golden eyelashes. He looked like a perfect angel, lips puckered in a four-year-old cherubic pout. He sprawled across the folded-down dinette, his pillow flung to the floor and his blanket tangled around his legs.

Katie reached to straighten the blanket, but then stopped. It might waken him. Then the angel would disappear and the boy would bounce to life, all hungry and noisy and rambunctious.

No, better to enjoy the few quiet moments while she could. She picked up his pillow, dusted it off, and put it up in her and Zach's bed.

The acrid smoke smell grew stronger. She pushed back the curtains over the tiny kitchen sink and peered out. The Sonoma Coast campground was still mostly full, but she couldn't see any tendrils of smoke.

After washing her face in the cramped bathroom, she

dressed in jeans and a black tank top, smoothed on moisturizing lotion and a dab of lipstick, then combed her light brown hair into a ponytail. Good enough for camping. Time for coffee!

Just as she lit the propane burner on the stove, the door swung open and Duke bounded inside, his leash draped over his back. The Great Dane plunked his massive head on Timothy's cushions, staring into the boy's face. Little blue eyes opened, then a little hand reached out toward the dog.

Zach stepped inside and pulled the door shut.

"How was your run?" Katie glanced his way.

His jaw was set, his lips pinched straight. Deep blue eyes darted around the old RV.

"We need to get packed up." He pulled Timothy's blanket off the child. "C'mon, little man. Time to get up!"

"What? Why?" Katie turned off the burner.

Zach lifted Timothy off the dinette bed and looked his wife.

"There's a fire," he said quietly.

"Not a campfire? Where? Did you see it?"

"North of here, about a mile. I saw the smoke. Didn't you hear the sirens?"

She shook her head. "What about everyone else? What about the Coastal Cleanup?"

"At this location, it's canceled. I sent a group text to our members." He pulled out clean shorts and a red shirt for Timothy. "Isn't your phone on?"

"No. We're camping! I wanted a break from all that."

"Maybe you're not the only one." He hustled the boy to the bathroom with the clothes. "Get dressed, buddy."

Turning back to her, he said, "The camp host said they're going to close the campground because the wind is supposed to be bad this afternoon and they don't want to risk anyone getting trapped here if they have to close the road. I'll go make sure our team knows what's going on. Would you get things ready to roll?"

She nodded. "Sure."

As Zach headed outside, Katie grabbed Duke's dog dish and poured kibble into it. He sat politely until she gave him the okay. Maneuvering around a giant dog in a tiny RV was always a trick, but she loved that dog and refused to board him. She pushed past him to open all the curtains and set up the dinette.

Through the windshield, she saw Zach making his way from one campsite to the next. Twenty members from their church had camped here for the weekend. Close to a hundred California churches were participating in the annual cleanup today, from Eureka clear down to San Diego. The state organized the event and the volunteers, but Zach had been the point man in recruiting the churches.

She sighed. Was theirs the only church that wouldn't finish the project?

"I'm hungry." Timothy emerged from the bathroom with his shirt on backwards.

"Good morning to you, too, Sunshine!" She pulled off his shirt, turned it around, and put it on right.

There was no sense in waiting for Zach to return for breakfast. He'd be in a hurry and want to hit the road. Katie handed Timothy a banana and a granola bar.

"At the table, please."

Timothy scooted onto the bench seat and peeled the banana.

"Did you ask a blessing?"

He bowed his head. "Thank you, Jesus, for my food. Amen!"

The boy took an amazingly huge bite and gave her a triumphant look. Duke finished his kibble and sniffed at Timothy's banana. The kid broke off a piece and fed it to him.

"Don't feed the dog at the table! How many times do I have to tell you?"

Although her words were meant for her son, the dog responded to her reproving tone by slinking away from the dinette, gulping his piece of fruit.

Katie rolled her eyes. Between that dog, that boy, and that man, her hands were full!

She quickly cleared the counter, putting all the food and dishes away and latching the cabinets. Then she lowered the vent cover and scanned the RV for anything that might fly or fall while they traveled down the road. She secured items in the bathroom, turned off the water pump, and double-checked in the fridge. More than once, she'd left an open can of sparkling water in there, and found it all over everything when they stopped at a rest area.

As Timothy worked on his breakfast, she went outside and rolled up the awning. Then she unplugged the solar panels. Zach could put them in their case when he returned. She grabbed the tablecloth off the picnic table.

Maybe she was imagining it, or maybe the smoke smell was getting stronger. She definitely was seeing a faint haze, but that could be fog from the ocean.

A light breeze fanned her face as she glanced over their little Minnie Winnie. It was almost twenty years old. Zach said it looked dated, but she found it charming. Plus, it'd been afford-able, and hardly gave them any trouble. They weren't hooked up to water or electric, so all they'd need to do before taking off was remove the tire chocks, drive off the leveling blocks and stow them in their bin.

Minutes later, Zach returned, his thick blond hair glowing in the sunlight.

"You ready to go?"

"Except for the solar panels and the chocks, yeah."

As soon as Timothy was buckled into his car seat on the dinette bench, they finish the final chores and pulled out of the campsite.

"I'm so bummed about the cleanup day." Katie was disappointed about their week-long camping plans, too, but didn't mention that.

"Everybody is." Zach eased the motorhome over a speed bump.

It looked like half of the campground had already emptied out. As the Nelsons drove by, other campers bustled around their sites, gathering up their things and preparing to leave. Katie rolled down her window and waved to her friend Monica, who was rolling up her tent.

As they approach the highway, Zach turned to her.

"Well, we still have the week off. Where do you want to go?"

Katie frowned. It was the middle of September, and the weather was perfect. They'd been all set to spend the whole week at the coast. Where could they possibly find a campground that wasn't booked up?

"Left or right?" Zach glanced her way as he pulled up to the stop sign.

"Uh... right." They'd be headed south, towards home. But all of the coastal campgrounds would certainly be full. Maybe they could go inland somewhere, camp along a lake or something.

Timothy was being uncharacteristically quiet. Katie glanced over her shoulder to check on him. He was letting the dog lick granola crumbs off his fingers.

"Ugh, gross, Tim!" She unbuckled and climbed out of her seat, grabbed the container of hand wipes, and went back to clean his hands.

"Curve!" Zach called from the driver's seat.

Katie steadied herself as the RV rounded the bend. Then she returned to the co-pilot seat and buckled in.

"I'm going to text the newspaper," she said. "Just in case anything comes of that fire."

"It's just a little brush fire on the beach. Miles from Almonte. They're not going to care." Zach applied the brakes as a car whipped onto the highway in front of him. "Sheesh!"

"You never know. Sometimes those little fires turn into infernos that kill people and destroy communities." She fired a text off to her editor, then turned to her husband. "Besides, they were planning to do a piece on the Coastal Cleanup Day. Now it will be more interesting."

"Uh huh." Zach turned on the radio to catch the top of the hour news. National news came first, with nothing unexpected – some old rock star Katie had never heard of had died during the night, the President was golfing over the weekend, authorities in Boston had picked up a suspected terrorist, and the stock market was heading into another shaky week.

Then the local news came on... the big fires near Yreka and Crescent City were still less than fifty percent contained, and the highways remained closed south of each town, restricting the primary access points to Oregon.

"I'll bet that makes the Oregonians happy," Katie groused. "They hate us."

"They love taking our money, though," Zach said.

"Not when we drive up their real estate prices."

"Depends on whether they're trying to buy or sell." He grinned at her.

"Hold on!" She turned up the radio. The announcer was saying something about a coastal fire, but she'd missed part of it.

"...and a third fire reported this morning south of Santa Cruz, which is predicted to grow rapidly in high winds this afternoon," the announcer concluded.

A commercial came on, and Katie turned down the dial. "There were three new fires this morning?"

"Sounded like it." Zach pulled into a gas station. "We're getting a little low. And we need to decide what we're going to do with our week."

"I know." Katie took off her seatbelt. "I think we should head east, maybe the National Forest? But let's stop at home and pick up a few things first. I only packed beach gear."

"Home isn't exactly on the way there, Katie."

"It's not that far out of the way." She flashed him a smile. "Besides, it's our anniversary, so you're supposed to make me happy."

The Daughter of Babylon series is available on Amazon.com.

Made in United States
Orlando, FL
26 September 2024

51988673R00147